GUARDIAN

About the Author

Jen Lawrence was born and raised in the picturesque winelands of Cape Town, South Africa. She grew up with a fascination for interpersonal relationships and the human psyche, which led to the pursuit of a master's degree in Psychology she now nefariously uses in a successful Sales & Marketing career. As a first-time novelist and author of the fantasy romance book *Guardian*, her love of the sci-fi and fantasy genres stemmed from far too many hours spent in MMORPGs and single player role-playing video games. Experiencing the unique and fantastical worlds, races, and magic systems of these games inspired her to develop the Darke Universe, which features a variety of romance stories between magical beings, many drawn from familiar myths and legends, to complement the original world and race of elf-like warrior women she created in *Guardian*.

GUARDIAN

Jen Lawrence

BELLA
BOOKS
2021

Bella Books, Inc.
P.O. Box 10543
Tallahassee, FL 32302

Printed in the United States of America on acid-free paper.

First Edition - 2021

Editor: Ann Roberts
Cover Designer: Heather Honeywell

ISBN: 978-1-64247-235-6

Acknowledgments

Naming conventions play an important role in this story and the broader Darke universe. A Spanish friend of mine reviewed my Basque language translations and while agonizing over the grammar, we both decided that when it comes to names, some creative freedom was permissible. So thank you Sonja, for your time and your support of my writing over the years.

Finding someone who'll listen not only to plot ideas and characterisations, but also the middle-of-the-night venting and ranting of a frustrated writer, is rare. Which is why I treasure my friend Melinda who has been with me from way at the beginning, enjoying my writing and characters before I took either seriously and always providing feedback and encouragement when I most need to hear it.

I would like to thank my editor, Ann Roberts, for her mentorship and kindness throughout the daunting task of getting this book ready for publishing. As well as Linda Hill and Jessica Hill at Bella Books, for taking a chance on a novice with so much still to learn. *Guardian* holds a special place in my heart and it means the world to me that you saw enough potential in this story to give it a platform.

CHAPTER ONE

A dull clattering sounded as another piece of pitch-black armour fell onto the mahogany floor. Dirtied sabatons were pulled off, followed by a chest plate splattered with dark red. Exhausted, muscles stiff and sore, Luna pressed a hand over the torn silver skin on her upper arm, gold blood seeping through slender fingers while she applied pressure. Dressed in a black doublet and a matching pair of tights, she lightly limped down the hall and into her spacious bathroom.

The white marble tiles were soothingly cool on her bare feet and she headed for the medicine cabinet, removing a glass vial of healing potion. Popping the cork with her thumb, she quickly downed the thick liquid and ran her tongue across her teeth in an attempt to rid herself of the saccharine taste.

Discarding the flask in the waste bin, Luna opened the golden faucet on the side of the claw-foot porcelain tub, a strong stream of crystal-clear water running out. After depositing a few drops of bath oil, she finished undressing and turned to the full-length mirror, examining her willowy frame for further injury.

She tentatively ran her fingers over her silver skin, gently tracing the dark yellow bruises that had bloomed on her side and thigh. Three raw gashes crossed her upper arm but would disappear entirely within the following three days. She gathered her mass of wavy obsidian hair, tying it into a messy bun, and tilted her face to the side to get a better view of the red blood smears that covered her cheek and neck, right below a long pointy ear.

Her eyelids narrowed over inky black irises.

Chimeras had the head of a lion, a goat torso growing from their side, and a tail embodying a venomous snake, with a head able to strike just as fast. There had been two of them in the earlier battle. An enthralled mother whose juvenile offspring had joined the altercation later. Luna had just managed to save the mother when the juvenile pounced, wild and reckless, impaling itself on her sword.

She shuddered and inhaled the soothing floral scent emanating from the bathtub, loosening her tight shoulders. Another deep breath, and she walked over to the glass encased shower in the corner, opened the doors, and quickly washed the dirt and grime from her hair and body. Once done, she twisted the gold-plated taps shut, exited the stall, and gracefully climbed into the filled tub.

Nearly nine feet tall, Luna submerged into the warm water with a contented sigh and absently traced the cool faucet with the pads of her fingertips, blunt obsidian nails occasionally tapping against the metal. Her wound dully ached but, thanks to the potion, it had become more of a light irritation. She closed her eyes and attempted to clear her mind to help her battered body rest and recover.

The chimera mother's mournful cry echoed in her mind and Luna swallowed the thick lump in her throat, squeezing her eyes tightly shut. One heart and three heads. The lion's maw had been ready to sever her head. It had been instinct on her part to move into a defensive stance, a century of training turned to effortless precision.

The worst part was that the chimeras hadn't meant to attack her. The mother couldn't help it and the juvenile had been trying to protect his mother. Pushing back the image of the chimera desperately nudging the unmoving body of her child, Luna inhaled a steadying breath and purposely relaxed the muscles in her face. Another deep breath and she focused on the buzz of magic in her veins to help heal her faster.

Inhale and exhale... Inhale and exhale...until her mind cleared and her body unspooled.

Not long into her deep meditation, a soft familiar tug in her chest had her eyes fly open.

In fear of losing the feeling, she remained as still as a statue, only her heart frantically thumped against her ribs when the tug gradually grew stronger and her tight grip on the edge of the tub increased with it.

She hadn't ever felt the Call that clearly before.

Over two hours later, neck stiff with tension, water cold and silver skin wrinkly, the feeling had grown so intense, Luna threw herself out of the tub, water splashing everywhere. She grabbed a white fluffy towel, drying off while she walked down the hall and entered her bedroom.

The large bed was covered in handmade black and white bedding and flanked by two black side tables that mimicked the colour scheme of the entire space. Across from it, an intricately carved wardrobe stood near the door. On the other side of the room a menagerie of white pillows decorated a window seat next to the corner where her armour display stand stood mounted atop a chest of drawers.

She pulled on a silky black dress that flowed down her body to her ankles, starkly contrasting against her skin. Thin straps covered her shoulders, revealing prominent collarbones and a long elegant neck. Loosening her hair, Luna glanced in the mirror on her dresser, at the damp obsidian waves that fell all the way to the centre of her back. She shakily tucked some behind the pointy tip of an ear, making sure she'd washed off all the blood, and for the first time in her life, second-guessed her appearance.

The uncertainty couldn't keep the wide smile from her face, though, and her dark eyes sparkled in anticipation. Her heart hadn't ceased its frantic rhythm and the Call had settled in her chest, warm and buzzing, making her feel slightly dizzy. There was hardly time for deliberation on looks, though, and Luna's heart excitedly skipped a beat. Barefoot, she padded down the hall, past the black marble floors and dark granite countertops of her white kitchen, and the wooden floors, soft cream carpets and warm brown leather of her living room.

She exited the front door, went down the three wooden steps that led up her wraparound porch, crossing a lush green lawn, but stopped in the centre of it. The colourful flowers that lined the edges of the grass and sat in pots on the porch, some ranking up the thin white pillars, trellises and railings, went unnoticed. Instead, Luna's attention was drawn toward the edge of the forest that cupped the back and sides of her cottage.

Each species of tree and shrubbery varied in a stunning array of pastel-coloured leaves. Light pinks, blues, and lilacs mixed in with whites were thickly cropped together. And in the shadows they cast, an unfamiliar white pegasus stomped its hoof and shook its head. Its long mane whipped across its muscular neck and flickered the same light pink flames that tipped its wings, made up its tail, and licked at its hooves.

Luna's toes curled into the grass in delight and she had to remind herself to breathe. The pegasus was exquisite, because of course it would be. Even from that distance Luna could sense familiarity in the magic it emanated. Its appearance only solidified the realness of what she was feeling.

The pegasus nickered, shook its fiery mane and impatiently trotted in place.

Luna looked up into the pale orange sky, the late afternoon sun shining bright red on its way to set behind a magenta ocean. It looked like an ordinary day, almost too ordinary for such a life-altering event.

She closed her eyes and listened to the tug on her frantically beating heart and frowned when the location of the Call became clearer. Every Guardian she knew only went to that awful world when absolutely necessary.

Opening her eyes, she inhaled a deep breath and focused until the air in front of her grew thick, rippling like the surface of a puddle of water, before the particles seemed to separate, creating a vertical tear, edges burning with cerulean blue flames and revealing a dark murky void.

Luna stepped into it on trembling legs and the air curled like thick liquid around her, swallowing her up. When she walked out on the other side of the portal, she squinted at the sharpness of a yellow sun set against a light blue sky.

It was second nature to cloak herself the moment her feet touched the grass in front of a suburban home in Lur Tristea. A loud crash had her gaze snap to the spilt contents of a cardboard box. Broken pieces of ceramic plates littered the paved pathway that led from a moving truck in the street to a quaint two-story home. A Human-looking woman stood beside the carnage. She had golden brown skin, and long dark braids decorated with pretty silver pieces cascaded down her shoulders. The cloak rendered Luna invisible and yet wide hazel eyes stared directly at her, a trembling fist pressed to the woman's heaving chest.

"*Ree, are you okay out there?*" a deep voice called from the house in that Tristean language that grated in Luna's ears.

"*Yes!*" Ree cleared her throat, eyes trained on where Luna stood. "*Tell Vanessa I said hi!*"

"*Wait for me to help you unload! Mom wants to talk to you too!*"

"*Be right there!*" she called, but instead of going inside the house, she walked past Luna, both gasping when they nearly touched, and rounded the corner of the house.

Luna wordlessly trailed after her, completely confused.

Ree only stopped when they both stood hidden in the tight space between the brick wall and a concrete slab fence. "You can't be here," she whispered.

Their language fell from Ree's lips in a stilted foreign way. Dumbstruck, Luna took in the garish green sundress she wore and scanned the Human face. Reaching out, she stopped herself inches from a pink-tinted cheek.

Ree shuddered and pushed her face closer to the invisible touch. "Show yourself..." she shakily said, her head level to Luna's chest.

Luna immediately dropped the cloaking spell, her back straightening when Ree gasped, neck craning and gaze lingering on the wound on her arm, then dragging up to Luna's face where it seemed to get stuck.

"I want to see you too," Luna rasped, heart furiously pumping and ears burning hot.

"You need to leave."

Bending at the waist, she searched those eyes that weren't quite right, took in the oddness of the silver pieces of jewellery that decorated the side of Ree's button nose and pierced her eyebrow. "Let me see you."

"You know what I must look like."

"I need to see."

"I can't. You need to leave."

"What a strange thing to tell me." Luna straightened again and tilted her head, utterly baffled. "Have you been in Tristea all this time?"

"Yes. Please, go…"

"Tell me your name."

"Rhianna Black."

"Tell me your real name."

A pink tongue licked over a full bottom lip, before a delicate jaw jutted out. "Argia Erretzea."

"Argia Erretzea…" Luna murmured, smiling at how right the name sounded from her mouth. Guardians had existed for millennia, names were passed on like precious heirlooms. Argias were almost always either a Gia or an Ari. "Gia?"

Gia nodded, pressed up against the wall of the house despite them not being nearly as close as Luna would have liked.

"May I call you by that name?"

Another shaky nod and Luna grinned in pure happiness.

"My name is Gerlari Iluna," she breathlessly offered, "though my Arima may call me Luna."

CHAPTER TWO

Luna's silver skin glinted in the afternoon sun and Gia fidgeted with the crescent moon charm hanging on one of her braids to keep from touching her. The Call in her chest was stronger and more insistent than it had ever been, and the visage of Luna left her slightly dazed. It didn't help that those obsidian eyes intently searched her face when Luna bent over, hovering far too close and still not close enough. She smelled like the fresh ozone of a raging thunderstorm. Resisting the urge to fall into her arms took every ounce of Gia's self-control. Not outwardly reacting to being called *Gia* again had taken so much already.

Luna was beautiful, more beautiful than Gia could have ever anticipated. Her sharp features, the pointed ears, long thin nose and narrow face made her look intimidating. But a pair of charcoal-coloured lips were glossy and parted in awe. Dark eyes beneath long, lush lashes, tenderly travelled over her body and touched Gia in ways she ached for silver fingers to do.

"You've made yourself so small…" Luna husked, continuing her intense perusal. "Why are you wearing this ugly glamour?"

she absently wondered, seemingly as affected by their proximity as Gia was.

"Humans find this glamour attractive. Don't be racist," Gia mumbled in an attempt to break the spell between them.

"I can accept Humans as a valid people without needing to find them attractive, Gia." Luna stepped closer and Gia's body arched toward her, stopping herself in the nick of time before they could touch. She instead twirled the end of a braid around her finger, flicking the thin metal moon, content to listen to the warm melodic cadence of Luna's voice forever.

"Do you know a lot about Tristean politics and society?" she asked for the sake of saying something.

"Most of my life, something has drawn me beyond the Veil and now I know why," Luna softly said, and Gia's ears and cheeks grew hotter, braid forgotten and arms falling helplessly to her sides. "I couldn't leave the Rift for too long to explore Tristea like my heart was telling me to, but you've finally come to me. What has taken you so long?"

Reality slapped some sense into Gia and she hung her head, reaching for her braid again. "You need to leave."

Luna's jet-black brows knitted together. "Why?"

"*Ree?*"

When Luna straightened at Sean's voice, Gia instinctively reached out to keep her away from him, though as soon as her fingers touched Luna's unbelievably smooth shoulder, they both groaned and fell into each other. Foreheads touching, a large hand clasped her own and the surge of magic that rushed between them had Gia's knees buckling.

She felt full. Her chest expanded. Luna's magic blended with her own and surged through her veins, leaving her breathless. Tears pooled in her eyes, overcome by how perfect and right it felt to be touched by Luna.

"*Babe, where are you?*"

With a pained whimper, Gia tore herself out of the bubble of contentment and stared up into a dark, caring gaze, hating herself for what she would say next.

"I'm happy here," she shakily forced out. "I'm going to bond with a wonderful Human. I won't ever be returning to

Lur Ederra." As the meaning of her words hit, the confusion in Luna's perfect face turned to panic and pain. "Please, leave me alone."

"*Ree?*" Sean's worried voice called again.

Luna straightened to her full height, features darkening. She stalked around the corner, floating like a spectre in broad daylight, her black dress and hair billowing theatrically. Silver skin shimmered ethereally in the sun, and Gia had to run to match her long strides, placing herself between a gawking Sean and a fuming Luna.

"*Oh…*" Sean breathed, green eyes glittering beneath a shortly-cropped, faded haircut. "*She's from there? She looks like an Elf from that game—*"

"*Later, Sean.*"

"You're choosing to bond with *him*?" Luna seethed, her entire body erupting in blue magic, surging like the flame of a blowtorch, blue fire gathering in each of her palms. Barely managing to recover from the magnificent sight, Gia brought up a transparent pink shield.

It was as simple as that for Luna's fury to dissipate. Her magic fizzled out as easily as it had erupted and she stared at the shimmering pink separating them and hovered her silver fingers over the crackling magic.

Gia's chest ached and tightened when pained inky black eyes shifted to her and a lone tear, shiny with golden glitter, slid over Luna's sharp cheekbone.

"You would use your magic against your Arima?" Luna whispered, her voice cracking and her other hand pressed tightly below her bellybutton. Though her flames had been snuffed out, her entire essence burned with utter devastation Gia felt as though it were her own. "You shield him, instead of me?"

"Luna—I—this is my life," Gia croaked. The words tasted acrid and wrong. "I'm not ever going back to Ederra. Please accept that."

Luna stared at the ground, looking equally hurt and confused, before the Veil tore apart behind her and she seemed to be swallowed up into the void.

The air stilled its electric crackling and Gia's chest ached with sorrow and abrupt longing when the Call dulled as the Veil separated them once again.

"It's really real," Sean whispered, brown cheeks dimpling deeply with excitement. "Are you okay?" At six feet, he used to seem so tall as she fit snugly beneath his chin.

"You didn't believe me?" Gia thickly joked and walked into the house to buy herself some time to recover from the encounter, worrying whether anyone had seen the magic being performed in their front yard. Hopefully Luna would've had enough sense to cloak them, because the thought hadn't even occurred to Gia at the time.

Sean chuckled, following her into the kitchen that was cluttered with boxes. "Of course I believed you, but seeing her was a whole other experience. Who was she? Don't take this the wrong way, and I know you warned me, but I think I was bedazzled by her anyway."

That was what happened when Guardians showed themselves in Tristea. People had reported that they couldn't bear to look at them, and yet all they could do was stare in rapture. She'd been told that much when she received instruction on how and why to use the invisibility cloak.

Still, the wonder of the Tristeans wouldn't ever come close to what Gia had experienced sharing magic with Luna for the first time. It took every last bit of her dwindling emotional energy not to follow her through the Veil. She should never have touched her. Their connection was so much stronger now and nearly impossible to ignore.

Gia had felt the Call growing stronger on the drive to their new home and even when she'd anticipated and dreaded the Meeting for hours, she'd been grossly unprepared for the encounter. For how ready she'd been to simply drown herself in everything Luna.

Luna. The name had irrevocably branded itself across Gia's heart. Already as familiar as though she'd known it forever.

"Could you give me a moment, please?" she softly asked, absently rubbing the hand Luna had touched. It continued to warmly buzz with their shared magic.

Sean's excitement dissolved into concern. He never crowded her and was as patient as Gia had always needed him to be. She loved him as much as she possibly could.

He walked up beside her but kept an arm's length away. "Why don't you go lie down and I'll finish unloading the truck?"

"Sorry to leave you doing all the heavy lifting."

He gently kissed her temple, making sure not to pull her into a hug like she knew he wanted to, and still Gia had to stop herself from flinching.

"I've got it covered. Go rest, you didn't look that great during the drive, either."

"Thank you, Sean."

"No worries," he said with a caring smile and once he exited the kitchen, Gia lowered her elbows onto the counter, dropped her face into her hands, and softly sobbed.

CHAPTER THREE

Luna couldn't believe she had finally met her Arima, and in Tristea of all places. What was Gia doing there? And with a Human no less, in some farcical imitation of a bond. It was all too surreal, like yet another dream to taunt her with what she didn't have.

It was supposed to be the happiest day of her life. She'd been waiting nearly a century for the Meeting. Gia not becoming a Novitiate at the Sanctum had been unprecedented. Nothing made sense, yet they were undoubtedly bonded. The shared magic now pulsing in Luna's veins was proof of that.

Luna cradled the teacup in her palms, the liquid having grown cold a while ago, and gently rocked on the porch swing she had painstakingly crafted with her bare hands. The bench was just big enough for two, like many of the items in her home. The home they were supposed to have built together. But, as the years passed by, Luna thought she would keep busy while she waited and present her efforts as a gift. They could still have expanded together in preparation of their first daughter or renovated whatever features her Arima wanted to change or add.

She'd chosen that particular plot of land because it was close to their assigned Rift and also stood at the edge of the forest, a quarter mile from the top of the cliffs overlooking the most beautifully purple-pink ocean in the Western Lands. That evening, the cerulean moon hung above it, casting the night in a soothing blue glow and appearing larger than it ever would in Tristea. Everything in Ederra was bigger and better. Every colour more vivid, the world more vibrant and brimming over with life and magic.

Luna had taken it all for granted as a child, until she'd come of age and was finally permitted to open portals. She'd followed the strange pull beyond the Veil and into Tristea, discovering a dull world, air thick with toxins, a cloud of which hung over everything like a heavy cloak. Living things seemed in a state of perpetual decay with fleeting lifespans. Humans were plagued by a menagerie of illnesses ready to eliminate them at random if they didn't strike each other down first. The senselessness of their destruction had been horrific to witness.

Luna couldn't fathom why Gia would choose to live there. How she could choose someone else. How it was possible for her to make that choice in the first place.

The Meeting couldn't have been real. The chimera had clawed her shoulder and she'd been careful to stay far out of reach of its venomous snakehead, though a fever-induced hallucination on a sickbed would be preferable to her current reality.

Her Arima had rejected her, had chosen to shield and bond with another. Hurt and betrayal stuck in her throat and tears streamed wet and warm down her face. The Meeting was supposed to signify a new beginning, setting her on a path to unbridled happiness.

Lost in sorrow and listening to the distant waves crashing against the rocks at the foot of the cliff, it came as no surprise when a worried voice called out from inside her house.

"*Lulu?*"

Releasing a breath, she stood from the swing and went inside, making no effort to wipe the glittering tear tracks from her face. She walked into her cosy living room, placed the teacup on the coffee table, and went to stand in front of the freestanding full-length mirror decorated with patterned brass. A spark of white magic left her fingertips when she lightly touched the frame and the surface distorted.

The mirror had been a gift from the Guardian whose visage appeared in the reflection, whose skin shone golden beneath a set of brown robes. Her copper hair was tied atop her head, the same colour as the eyes that swept over Luna's face.

"Darling, what's the matter?" Saso asked from the mirror's surface.

Luna pressed a hand against her aching stomach, her attempt to be strong dissipating entirely. "I'm hurting, Mama."

Years of waiting, the bouts of longing and despair were natural and expected. Her family and friends couldn't begin to fathom what it was like to wait that long for the Meeting, but they had helped where they could, though nothing they did could ever fill the emptiness reserved for her Arima. Having found Gia only made the ache for her that much stronger.

"Please allow us to come see you," Saso said. "Your mom's going mad with worry. We're unable to ignore your distress any longer."

She'd barely finished nodding her acquiescence when the mirror surface rippled and her other mother, Uda, rushed through, golden hair fluttering back and golden eyes scanning Luna's person. Before Luna could say anything, copper arms wrapped her in a hug and she melted into Uda, wracking with uncontrollable sobs.

Saso embraced them both a moment later, only making Luna cry harder.

With ageless faces, they seemed more like three sisters huddled together. Their magic calmed Luna, but she knew the persistent ache in her chest wouldn't leave her now that she'd met Argia Erretzea.

"Did something happen?" Uda asked, earnest golden brows squished together. It was difficult to lie to them, especially to Saso whose copper gaze rested heavily on Luna, as though she could tell that her world had been flipped upside down. Luna could tell them anything and they would love and support her through it. But how was she supposed to tell them that her Arima had rejected her? Never in the history of their people had something like that happened. A Guardian's entire adolescence and early adulthood was spent in anticipation of the Meeting. In finding that missing piece to their souls that only an Arima could complete.

Tristea must have tainted Gia somehow...

"Uda, she's injured," Saso said and Luna scowled at the small smirk directed at her when Uda immediately began to fuss.

"It's only a scratch," Luna mumbled, gently squeezing her mom's shoulder who futilely attempted to heal her.

From a young age, Guardian Shields are able to heal other Guardians to assist in their training, but after completing the Binding Ceremony with her Arima, a Shield's main purpose was to protect her Sword. She was only able to heal her daughter until that daughter's Initiation Ceremony.

Uda scowled at Saso, who smirked amusedly.

"I took a healing potion," Luna said. "I'll be fine, Mom."

"Chimera?" Saso asked.

"Two."

"She'll be fine, Uda. Perhaps stop squeezing her."

Luna hid her smile when her mom immediately released her tight grip. "What potion did you take?" Uda asked. "One from the Faeries or one from the Halfling apothecary in Erdiko?"

"The Ama Gorria brewed it for me," Luna said and the tension immediately left Uda's shoulders.

"We can start looking again," Uda offered. "We know she's out there, no doubt as eager as you are to be united."

Luna shook her head, chest painfully constricting. The Guardians were needed to protect the Rifts. There already too few of them for even that. She'd asked them to stop looking before, guilty at the neglect of their duties while they empathised with her lament. She certainly wouldn't allow them to go looking for someone she had already found.

"Then come live with us at the Sanctum," Uda said. "The Circle of the Western Lands will understand. You can monitor your Rift from home, help us guide the Novitiates and have them assist you here too. When your Arima comes, she will most likely go to the Sanctum for Initiation."

It wasn't the first time they'd made the offer. Luna had never agreed to it because her Calling had been to join her Arima and protect the Rift in the field north of her house. She hadn't taken the offer before because she'd been waiting. She'd been hopeful.

"I'll think about it," she softly whispered and Uda audibly released a breath. Luna inadvertently met the sage, copper eyes of her other mother, still carefully studying her.

They thankfully spoke no more of her sadness, nor her move home, but they stayed and tucked her into bed as though she was a child again, soothing her with their magic until she fell asleep.

* * *

"Is that what you look like, too? Who was she? It seemed like you knew each other," Sean asked, eyes still shining with awe when Gia tiredly climbed into bed beside him that night. She'd thrown herself into unpacking and had successfully avoided and distracted him with tasks for the remainder of the day.

"We haven't met before."

"Really? Was she about to attack us?"

"No, it was only a misunderstanding."

"Yeah? About what? And what's that language called you two spoke in? Does everyone there speak it or only your people?"

"Sean, please," she tiredly pleaded, massaging her temples and fighting down tears. Luna's sorrow echoed in her chest, confusingly mixing with her own feelings until she wasn't entirely sure which of them was feeling what.

Like learning to walk and talk for Humans, young Guardians learned what it meant to be either a Sword or a Shield. And with those lessons came the inherent understanding of the Arima bond, of what that foreign presence was in your chest and how it tethered you to the missing part of your soul. Gia had been told that the Meeting would be intense and yet she had still been utterly overwhelmed by how familiar Luna had felt.

"I've told you that I won't go back," Gia said. "I want to stay here. I want"—her breath hitched—"I want to marry you and continue building our life together."

"You don't have to convince me of that. But don't you want to visit the place where you were born, maybe take me with you to see it?" He charmingly grinned and comically lifted his eyebrows. "Whatever you decide, I'll support it, okay? Maybe you can invite your…angelic acquaintance to the wedding? I know we have the same friends and you're already part of the family, but it would be nice to have someone from your side there too."

None of the Guardians of Lur Ederra would ever support their marriage, least of all her Arima.

"Maybe," she said and ached at his beaming smile.

"She can glamour herself too, so your secret will stay safe."

Gia highly doubted Luna would glamour herself given her obvious aversion to Gia wearing one, and she would definitely not attend their wedding, but Sean's excitement was pleasant to watch and slightly soothed the hollowness in her chest since Luna had left.

She listened to him talk about the wedding, enthusiastic enough for both of them. It wasn't as though the thought of spending her life with him was something she dreaded. What did fill her with apprehension was the entire concept of a wedding, a gathering where she would be the centre of attention.

When they'd discussed marriage, Sean had suggested they go sign the license at the clerk's office and then have a small party for everyone they knew. It sounded like heaven and Gia would've said yes, had she not known how such a dreary affair would've killed him a little inside.

He was open and sociable in ways that left her in awe. The colours he used in his wardrobe and in decorating their home and the natural vibrancy of his personality made Tristea bearable. *He* made every day easier. Gia had smiled more on that first day of meeting Sean than she had in the previous decade of her life. She would agree to any wedding he wanted—walk and stand where he needed her to, even learn a wedding dance if he felt like adding that to the list. And she would smile throughout it all, if only to keep the happiness on his handsome face.

They'd moved clear across the country when he got the position of deputy sheriff in Bluewater Bay and had both instantly fallen in love with the ocean views and mountain backdrop. It was a tourist town, teeming with visitors over the summer holiday season. Violent crimes were almost nonexistent and Gia had found some peace of mind because she didn't need to worry as much as when Sean had been a patrol officer in Ridge City.

She listened to him go through colour schemes and place settings, because his mom, Vanessa, had been asking about them, eager to get started planning, and that eventually came full circle to head count and a certain special possible guest of honour.

"Luna was…disappointed when I explained I won't be returning to Ederra. Ever. I doubt we'll see her again," Gia guiltily lied.

She had lived with the Soulbond tugging her toward Luna long before she was taught what it meant or could form the words to ask. She had spent a century yearning for someone she had never met, craving the Meeting like a constant hunger left unsatiated. And now she and Luna had touched. Had shared magic that existed solely to complement the other. The tether that bound them had strengthened exponentially.

She turned her back to Sean and switched off the lamp on her nightstand.

Getting the message, he did the same, and when she stiffened at the strong arm that wrapped around her a moment later, he moved back and softly wished her goodnight.

* * *

The instant her mothers left for home, Luna woke and couldn't fall back asleep. Her mind and heart continued to race while her stomach painfully knotted until she eventually got out of bed and went to retrieve the armour her mothers had gathered and neatly placed on her coffee table.

The couter that covered her elbow had been destroyed by the chimera and Luna sat on the window seat in her bedroom, checking whether any of the other pieces required repairs. She wore no rerebraces, attempting to keep the armour as light and easy to move in as possible. The couter and pauldron over her shoulder covered most of her upper arm anyway, and both had been mangled severely enough to require a professional to fix them.

It was simple dumb luck that the strike from the chimera mother's massive clawed paw had landed at the only vulnerable area on her arm. Luna had been distracted by the juvenile who lay dying at her feet, pained grunts gargling from the blood that poured from the lion head's mouth.

Releasing a heavy sigh, she packed the leg pieces into the middle drawer of the cabinet where her freshly polished chest plate was mounted. The arm parts went in the top drawer, each tucked into the moulded slots like puzzle pieces. The ones in need of repair were individually wrapped in velvet cloth she retrieved from the bigger bottom drawer that contained her cleaning materials and extra gear pieces, and were then placed in a leather satchel she propped up against the display stand.

The process of cleaning and polishing her armour set was immensely soothing. She was tempted to restart the entire process again but paused when the Call in her chest grew stronger. After years of only a vague awareness of each other, it was unsettling to feel their intense connection now. She recognised the exact moment Gia stepped through the Veil and into her front yard.

Was she dreaming again?

Pulling the short black robe tighter across her chest, she carefully padded down the hall to the front door where the doorknob was frantically being turned. Gia's magic gently hummed on the other side, warm and inviting. And almost afraid as to what she would find, or what Gia had come to tell her, Luna shakily unlocked the door and pulled it open.

That ridiculous Human glamour still cloaked her and her hazel eyes were trained straight ahead. She was dressed in a gaudy orange T-shirt and Luna could barely make out the hem of a pair of light-blue sleep shorts above her knees. The colours gave her a headache and irked her beyond reason.

Gia entered with no acknowledgment and Luna confusedly followed her down the hall to her bedroom, where Gia climbed onto the bed with the fumbling effort of a toddler, pulled a pillow to her chest that she smelled with gusto, before snuggling it with a contented sigh.

Well, then.

Her Arima was in their home, in the bed Luna had chosen for them. As the bathroom had been built with two basins, matching mirrors and a very large tub, the wardrobe too had ample space left that Luna's clothes would never fill. Everything in her home had been crafted in hopes of sharing it. And there Gia lay. In their bed. In their house. Where she belonged. Her subconscious seeming to have pulled her there.

Luna wasn't sure whether her own desperate Call was the reason Gia had shown up at her door, and despite wanting to get into bed and hold her all night long, Luna turned and dragged her feet toward the living room where she laid down on the couch with a miserable groan.

With Gia in Ederra and so close, the Call was amplified and infinitely harder to resist. But thankfully Luna was still recovering from her injuries and the excitement of the day, and soon her eyes fluttered closed where she lay sprawled on her back. She shifted restlessly in and out of sleep, fighting the desire to go to her bedroom each time she woke in a haze, until a small warm body stretched out on top of her.

Gasping in surprise, Luna instinctively hugged Gia to her chest to prevent her rolling off the couch. She nearly sobbed for the second time that day when Gia tucked her head beneath Luna's chin and wrapped her arms tightly around her.

Despite the glamour, it was as perfect a moment as Luna had ever felt in her life. Their mingling magic was more effective than any potion the Faeries could make. A wave of contentment washed over Luna along with a glimmer of hope, because while Gia softly breathed into Luna's neck, her magic reached out and easily healed what remained of Luna's injuries.

There was no way Luna would be able to sleep after that, and she lay unmoving. Her back ached to shift position, but she could've cared less as she held Gia throughout the night, absently fingering the tips of her braids and soothingly rubbing circles in the centre of her back.

Before the sun could rise, Luna carefully gathered Gia in her arms and stood, cradling her like a child, disconcerted by how small she was in that form, and carried her back through the Veil, opening the portal directly into Gia's home, and placed her on the living room couch.

She stared down into the odd face Gia wore, knowing it didn't matter what she looked like, and yet she still ached to see her. Reaching out a hand, needing to feel Gia's magic again, Luna stopped at the sound of footsteps coming down the stairs. The Human Gia wanted to bond with walked into the room and Luna cloaked herself in the nick of time.

Her stomach burned when he peeked over the top of the couch and lovingly smiled at Gia. When he reached down to tenderly touch her cheek, something Gia had most likely permitted, the fire in Luna's belly flared hot and magic blazed from her pores. She wanted to strike him down, remove him from existence. It would be as easy as a twitch of her wrist and his fragile body would be incinerated.

Instead of succumbing to the impulse, she marched to the front door and roughly flung it open, ripping the lock clear through the frame, the door hitting the wall with a deafening crack.

Gia startled awake, grabbing at her chest as though pained, and even as Luna craved to remain near her, she stalked through the Veil before Gia could sense her presence.

CHAPTER FOUR

The best thing about small-town living was all the extra space. Yards were bigger and streets wider with ample room for parking without the risk of being clipped by a passing car or needing to find a spot miles from your destination. Things were less expensive too, yet somehow nicer and fresher. People were seemingly friendlier and more helpful, which Gia supposed was something to be liked.

The highlight of her new home, though, was definitely the quaint flower shop with its massive greenhouse at the back. She'd fallen in love with it at first sight when they'd flown down for Sean's final interview and looked at available property for sale. Luna must not have been home during that time, because Gia hadn't felt her Call as strongly back then. If she had, they would likely still be living in Ridge City.

Perhaps they could move again. But would it be fair to Sean to run? Could Gia even escape Luna now with the Call so much stronger? Was it fair to *Luna* to run now that they had shared magic?

She would need to stay firm. She would make Luna understand that she didn't choose that life.

When Sean got the job as deputy sheriff, it felt like their lives were finally falling into place. His mom wasn't happy about the distance, but no one who saw pictures of Bluewater Bay could fault their decision to relocate. Their friends were supportive and would no doubt visit once they'd settled. But despite what they all thought, they were Sean's friends, not hers.

How could you truly be close to anyone when hiding so much of yourself and your past? When so much of who you were with them, felt like pretend?

Out in her greenhouse, Gia gently touched the petals of a Black Beauty Pansy.

She'd always loved watching things grow and bloom. The irrigation system that ran down the aisles was automated and adjusted for each species, but what Gia enjoyed most was tending to her plants and she preferred to do everything in the outside garden manually. There was nothing she found more relaxing than walking around with a watering can and watching the gentle spray cover the plants and soil.

A feeling of warmth flooded her chest and Gia halted, the hair at the back of her neck pleasantly prickling.

Her eyes fluttered shut and she softly released a breath.

That morning, after a 'freak wind' slammed the front door wide open, she and Sean exited their home to the sight of a tree in the front yard on fire. Eerie blue flames drew their neighbours' attention to the oddity. Not the best way to meet everyone, but the town certainly knew about them now. Talk of the fire was all over the local radio station and people spoke about it in line at the grocery store, contemplating what could've caused the fire's colour. A possible gas leak had everyone in a panic and poor Sean was at home dealing with it all. He'd mercifully sent her off to get groceries in anticipation of town officials and onlookers invading their yard that Saturday morning.

That was the bad thing about small-town living: everyone knew everyone else and their business as soon as that business happened.

How long would it be until someone saw Luna in all her magnificent, blue-blazing glory?

"What are you doing here?" Gia whispered, opening her eyes and shivering at the light magical breeze that blew through her braids and caressed the back of her neck. The previous night she'd had the best sleep in as long as she could remember, which was strange, considering the absolute mess she was when she'd gone to bed and the second she woke up that morning. Emotional exhaustion had never acted as a sleep remedy for her before.

She hopelessly pretended to continue her inspection of the pansy without taking in any of its details. The remainder of her senses were focused entirely on where she could feel Luna's presence behind her.

No answer was given but the breeze blew a little stronger. Magic poured over her skin like liquid silk, leaving her breathless and pleasantly warm. The plants around her grew and bloomed into vibrant colours—big, robust and beautiful in ways that nothing in Tristea could ever match. Even those species found on both sides of the Veil paled in comparison to their Ederran counterparts.

"You cast spells?" Gia softly asked, enraptured by the colours and scents invading the greenhouse.

"It's only a simple glamour spell. I have permission."

Swallowing dryly, Gia leaned into the warmth at her back, wishing for long silver arms to embrace her, and took comfort in the strong presence in her heart.

"You smell like Sweet Alyssum," Luna murmured over her shoulder, breath tickling her ear, making Gia's whole body quiver. "They grew in the gardens at home and whenever I was upset, I would lay on the grass and soak up the sun and their scent until I calmed."

Breathless, Gia considered turning around. She craved seeing Luna again but she was terrified, already dazed by only her voice and the insinuation of what Luna had just admitted.

"*Oh, these are lovely!*" a high-pitched voice exclaimed and Gia startled, her gaze snapping toward an elderly lady, thankfully engrossed in all the Ederran flora around her. "I don't think I've ever seen these species before. Are you cross-breeding them?"

"Yes, I am."

At least Luna had kept the flower glamour simple. In addition to wielding their innate magic, Guardians were taught to cast only two spells: the human glamour and the invisibility cloak. It allowed them to smoothly move amongst the Tristeans should duty require it. To her knowledge, there had been no Guardian sightings in Tristea in modern history. It would no doubt have been all over the Internet had that been the case.

Gia was therefore confident that Luna would remain hidden, but one thing she'd learned as a florist was that random elderly people could know as much about gardening and plants as any professional.

The lady went to touch a petal on an Ederran flower and when it immediately wilted and died, she turned to Gia in shock, who feared she would have a stroke at the improbability of what she'd just seen.

Gia elbowed nothing but air behind her, though she felt the warm puffs of Luna's silent laughter against her cheek, making goose bumps spread up her arms.

"I flew them in from South America. They've unfortunately been dying all morning," Gia explained and hurried toward the shocked woman, ushering her toward the front of the shop. "I'm actually not trading yet, but I hope to see you at our opening next Saturday."

The lady's mouth was still agape, eyes wide while Gia guided her out the front door. "Come say hi and I'll get you something on the house," she promised with a strained smile as she closed the door in the lady's face and locked it. The poor woman stood bewildered on the sidewalk and Gia watched her through the signage on the front window where she had a menagerie of potted plants on display. Slowly the lady waddled down the boardwalk and out of sight.

Bracing herself, she took hold of her braid and turned, unsurprised to see Luna standing there, yet it still knocked the breath right out of her lungs. She wore the standard robes all

Guardians did and Gia could only compare them to choir robes, without all the extra frills and attachments. They opened over her neckline in a V-shape, and hidden buttons went all the way to the knee. Luna's were predictably a silky black and accentuated her frame, complementing her dark eyes and hair. She stood with her hands casually clasped behind her back, head slightly tilted to the right. Wild windswept hair gorgeously framed her face and tumbled over her shoulders and down her back in the most enchanting way.

Nothing in any world would ever compare to how striking she was.

"So your plan is to haunt me now?" Gia remarked, despite the burning need in her heart.

"I don't have a plan."

"Can your non-plan please include not scaring Humans to death? That woman could've had a heart attack, or a stroke, or something equally fatal."

"Forgive me for not responding to your entirely absurd actions in a manner that pleases you, Gia."

The way her name rolled off Luna's tongue made her stomach flutter. "Call it what you want, but this is my life and I will live it the way I please. You should do the same."

"You know it's not that simple." Luna looked at her as though she were insane and Gia felt like it in that moment.

"I'm managing just fine."

"Are you?" Again, that slight curious tilt of her head. "You just so happened to move to the exact place where I'd be on the other side of the Veil? My front yard practically mirrors yours."

"No, it's—"

"Coincidence?" Luna laughed beautifully and Gia's breath hitched, her body aching with longing. "There's no such thing for us, Gia. There's no me and no you. There's only us. *Our* magic." She shook her head. "You have clearly become as much of a fool as these Tristeans if you believe it can be any other way."

"I don't want us," Gia's mouth proudly stated while her stomach twisted with nausea. "I want only me. And I want you to leave me alone."

Hurt and anger flashed in Luna's eyes and before Gia could apologise and take it back, blue magic tore open the Veil behind her and she disappeared back to Ederra.

It took a while to recover enough to move again, but when Gia shakily walked back into the greenhouse, wiping the tears from her cheeks, all the flowers had returned to the way they were supposed to be. And the only thing that had brought her a modicum of joy when she'd first come to Tristea seemed suddenly dull and inadequate.

CHAPTER FIVE

Lake Beltza was as picturesque as it was ominous, yet whenever she was home, Luna was inexplicably drawn to it. Tearing her gaze away from the dark, placid water ebbing and flowing onto a white-pebbled beach, she continued further into the green forest and away from the large castle looming behind her. The structure was old, situated against the cliffs on the very top of Mount Bularreko. Some of its walls were built into the rocks, blending into the natural scenery. Rolling green lawns and flowerbeds stretched half a mile on either side of a set of rocky steps that stopped at the edge of the thick forest surrounding the lake. On the opposite shoreline, twenty-one homes were cosily nestled between the scenic foliage, each yard stretching at least half a mile apart.

Mount Bularreko was the highest peak in Ederra and only Guardians had easy access to the lake and castle atop it.

Closing her eyes, Luna let her magic guide her way, blindly lifting her feet and sidestepping obstacles. It used to be difficult to move confidently without her eyesight, and with the initial assistance of a blindfold, it took years of practice to suppress the instinct to take a peek and check where she was going. Now, though, she walked without stumbling or hesitation and soon found her way, smiling when her shoulder was excitedly nudged.

She was petting the white fur on a unicorn's neck before her eyes had opened to take in her surroundings.

"It has been a while," the Ama Gorria's familiar voice said from the herd of twelve grazing in front of her. They were the size of pegasuses, a long golden horn growing from their foreheads.

"I have a duty, Sua Orro," Luna answered when the Red Mother stepped out from between the unicorns. Her hair, eyes, and robes were red like rubies and her skin smooth and pale, nearly as white as the creatures she tended.

"You only seek me out when you falter, little warrior. I've come to dread seeing you."

Luna averted her gaze and Sua came to stand in front of her, over two feet shorter.

"What's the matter, child?"

Her stomach twisted into knots and hurt stuck in her throat like a rock. "I found her."

"Your face shows a rather unexpected response to that news."

"She has unexpectedly decided not to want me."

"Impossible."

The pointy tips of Luna's ears heated and she ducked her head. "She defies expectation, Sua. I'm as heartbroken as I'm proud."

"How long since you've met?"

"Two days."

"Perhaps she needs time to adjust. You're both a rather unique circumstance."

"It hurts more than ever being without her."

"Undoubtedly." Sua nodded sagely. "I have no advice to give you."

"You always have advice to give me. More often than not it's not the advice I sought."

"Then why do you come?"

"You understand because you're as alone as I am."

"How am I alone if I have you always seeking me out?"

Luna smiled, and Sua Orro's fingers slipped behind her neck and she rested their foreheads together. "Stay strong, dear one. Only a fool won't love you after she has known you."

Instead of using one of the many mirrors located around the Sanctum, Luna walked past the numerous courtyards along the stone-paved pathways designated by neatly-trimmed box hedges. Her feet mechanically carried her through the castle corridors, atria, and foyers, up sets of ornate staircases perfectly lined with long red carpets, trimmed with gold and flanked by grey marble balustrades.

After she'd finished her cottage in the woods, the Sanctum had seemed cold and barren in comparison. Now it once again offered the comfort of home, perhaps because her mothers lived there, rather than the actual structure and décor that housed the young Novitiates. It was there where Guardians trained until their Initiation Ceremony and subsequent assignment to a Rift, or to a life with their Arima in the charming cabins on the other side of Lake Beltza.

"How long have you been here?" Saso asked when Luna entered the Viewing Room.

One hundred mirrors stood on the floor and lined the walls of the rectangular space and served to swiftly transport the Sanctum Guardians to where they were needed. The hall held no windows and was dark, save for where they stood at the front of the mostly undecorated space. It was easier to see when a mirror lit up in the darkness to indicate trouble in any town, city, and unguarded Rift across Ederra.

"A while," Luna answered and sat down in the matching chair beside her mom, whose gold irises flickered unseeing and unaware of her presence. A coffee table stood in front of them, laid with snacks and a few card and board games to occupy whichever pair was on Viewing duty.

"You went to see the Ama Gorria?" Saso asked.

"I did."

"Did she call for you?"

"No."

"Is she well? It's been a while since she's allowed anyone else see her."

"She's well."

"What's the matter, Lulu?"

"Nothing, Mama."

"You could never lie to me."

"Perhaps then you can accept that I have my reasons for lying now."

"I will try if that's what you need."

"Please."

Saso nodded reluctantly and turned to Uda who blinked rapidly and smiled when she saw Luna. "No Darke detected," Uda said and planted a kiss on Luna's cheek. She then wrapped her fingers around the back of Luna's neck and briefly pressed their foreheads together in greeting.

"That's good to hear," Saso replied, walking closer and placing a hand on her Arima's shoulder.

They had the type of relationship Luna had always admired and wanted for herself, but recently, she was overcome with envy and pain at their closeness instead of aspiration. Bitter in ways she knew she shouldn't be and that left her guilt-ridden and morose.

"Will you be staying?" Uda hopefully asked.

"For a few days, unless I'm called away."

"We're always happy to have you here."

Luna nodded distractedly and both of them waited on her, Uda's hand gently covering her own.

"Is it possible not to have an Arima?"

"Every Sword has her Shield," Uda easily replied, while Saso's copper eyes burned into Luna's face. "You would feel it if she wasn't there. You do still feel her, don't you?" she asked, voice slightly raising in concern.

"I feel her all the time…"

"Good. Everything happens when it's supposed to happen," Uda said. "We need to trust in the Soulbond's magic that will guide you to each other when the time is right. And once you experience the Meeting, you'll be so happy, Lulu, that all this despair will be nothing but a distant memory because everything will have finally fallen into place."

Saso softly smiled down at Uda, and Luna's chest ached.

"What if I decided to move on? Find another Shield?"

Uda laughed lightly. "That's impossible, darling. You know that," she said, entwining their fingers.

"Are you sure it's impossible to choose someone else? To be with someone who isn't your Arima? To be with someone who isn't a Guardian?"

Uda tilted her head. "Where is this coming from?"

"What if my Arima has found someone else and that's why she's staying away?"

Uda squeezed Luna's fingers, and stood with their hands still clasped. "I can't imagine how difficult it must be for you, Lulu. But I promise that you will find your Arima. As long as she lives, she lives only for you and you for her. Whatever the reason that's keeping you apart, I'm certain it's not her choice to stay away. And certainly not because she's chosen someone else."

Luna swallowed thickly and gave a jerky nod.

"Now come. Mama made oatmeal cookies earlier. Perhaps they'll tempt you into extending your visit."

Saso said nothing and Luna couldn't bear to look at her.

CHAPTER SIX

Sean laid back on his elbows and Gia stretched on her stomach across the blanket they'd spread beneath the oak tree in their small backyard. They were still getting used to having a space like that to themselves, and both were determined to spend as much time outside as they could. The garden had been well kept by the estate agency, but they would need to buy a lawnmower soon. Once the flower shop was turning a profit, they would start landscaping. For now, though, they simply enjoyed the fresh air and planned their vision.

"When are you going to see your friend again?" Sean asked out of nowhere.

Gia's jaw clenched and she picked at the stitching on the blanket. The Call from Luna was weak and all Gia did was worry and wonder whether she would ever see her again, while simultaneously dreading the possibility. "Wow, you really fell in love with her, didn't you?" she teased and swallowed thickly.

He laughed, carefree and light, unaware of the tension that had slowly been brewing inside her for days. "I want you to make friends here. Is that so hard to believe?"

"You're my friend."

"And you're mine, but she understands you in ways I never will. I want you to have that."

"I want you to please stop talking about her," Gia mumbled and sat up.

He straightened into a seated position too. "Did you guys fight?"

She laughed wryly. "You don't want me to be her friend."

"I don't?"

"Nope."

"Is she like a villain, or something?"

"No, she's a Guardian."

"What do guardians do?" Gia opened her mouth but Sean pointed and said, "Don't say guard things." He flashed her a cheeky grin and she laughed genuinely for the first time since Luna had appeared in their front yard.

"They guard the Rifts against the Darke."

"Ooh, ominous. What are rifts and the dark?"

"A Rift is a weakness in the Veil separating our worlds. The Darke are creatures trying to escape Ederra and come here to spread across Tristea."

"Oh, she's a soldier, protecting us and not even her own world...wow."

"I was supposed to help her and I chose to run away. So things aren't that great between us right now."

Sean nodded, understanding filling his features and then frowned. "But you were a child when you left your world. They draft kids into these guardian armies?"

"I wasn't expected to take on any duties until I was an adult. When Guardians are born, though, magic determines our future and we all share the same purpose: to protect the Veil from the Darke."

He studied her face and she ducked her head, fiddling with the crescent moon on her braid. Even when he didn't understand where she came from, Sean had always understood her.

"You did a brave thing walking away from that," he said.

"Doesn't feel like it now with her right there, continuing with her duty despite my absence."

"Is she making you feel guilty?"

"Not on purpose…It's mostly me."

"And you're not regretting your decision? You don't want to go back?"

She shook her head.

"Then you're doing what's right because you're doing what's best for you. That's always something I've admired about you, Ree. You're brave enough not to fold under the expectations and pressures of other people."

Gia sent him a weak smile, unable to tell him how many doubts she was having about what was right and best for her.

CHAPTER SEVEN

Five days.

Five days of wondering whether Luna would ever be closer again, of restless nights plagued by dreams of silver skin glittering beneath a cerulean moon. Stunning and soothing, only for the images to incessantly haunt her in her waking hours.

Sequestered in her shop, Gia was halfway through completing an arrangement of Black Forest Calla Lilies, when Luna's Call hit her like a freight train and a cold chill crept up her spine. Then her heart dropped into the pit of her stomach. Despite being overwhelmed by the intensity of the sudden onslaught of sensations, instinct took control of her body.

She'd never allowed herself to try it before, yet it was second nature to tear apart the fabric of the Veil, pink magic licking at the edges of the portal as it expanded to accommodate her size. When she stepped into Ederra, the rich landscape was almost too much to process. The colourful trees were massive, even the blades of golden grass stood thick and unusually long beneath her feet. The world dwarfed her in her glamour, and Gia stood momentarily stunned by the warmth and familiarity. By the red sun and orange sky. Ederra glowed in its beauty and splendour.

Another dreadful twist in a gut dragged her out of her stupor and Gia pushed her disorientation aside and ran toward Luna's desperate Call. There was a prickling at the back of her neck, a sinister awareness that she couldn't explain. Simply understanding the wrongness of its presence and needing to rid herself of it.

Usually the Darke's approach would be sensed well in advance, giving Guardians time to prepare and either get to the Rift or intercept it. But Luna was broadcasting so strongly, it could only mean that she was already engaging.

The last time Gia had been anywhere near the Darke flashed through her mind and terror made her insides burn and tumble. She clenched her jaw and sprinted through the forest, arms and legs speedily pumping with the aid of her magic, across a wide-open field at the top of a cliff where she was in time to see the Darke Husk screeching, pulsing with violet lightning that surged like electricity currents through its form.

It was the size of a Guardian, with no discernible limbs, and shaped like the silhouette of a cloaked and hooded figure that floated in the air like a thick plume of black smoke. An almost deafening cry tore from the hooded part of its body when a powerful current of blue magic burned it into nothingness.

The wrongness in Gia's belly dissipated with the disintegrating shadow.

Luna turned, beautiful black armour glinting in the sunlight, the pieces perfectly fitted to her frame. Her chest plate cinched at the waist, ridged across her flat abdomen, and hanging faulds accentuated her hips. She still glowed brilliantly blue, her magic reflecting in her eyes as the air between them remained thick and electric.

Gaping at the sight of her, Gia attempted to snuff out the pink magic licking up her own arms, embarrassed to be seen with her magic responding so flagrantly to Luna's own.

"What are you doing here?" Luna asked. Her cold gaze trailed over Gia's glamour with unmasked distaste.

Gia straightened invisible wrinkles on her lime-green T-shirt. "I-I came to help."

"I don't need your help."

"You were Calling."

"I could hardly control that under the circumstances."

"Look, I get why you're angry—"

"You know nothing about me!"

"I know that you're hurt because I chose my own destiny."

"Hurt? I wish I was only hurt by you."

Gia's brows furrowed, fingers mechanically twisting her braid.

"I wish I'd never met you. I wish you had remained only a dream. At least then I would still have hope of an Arima I could respect."

Gia flinched. "You know nothing about me either."

"I know that you ran from your duty like a coward."

"I chose not to be a slave to a predetermined destiny."

"You chose to turn your back on your people. You chose to be with someone you'll never be able to love. I may care little for him, but at least I have the decency to know he deserves more than your lies. Both he and I deserve better than *you*, Argia Erretzea."

Luna lifted her chin and ripped the Veil apart behind Gia. Watching the tears pool in Luna's eyes, Gia's chest clenched with guilt and shame, and she took a wobbly step back through the Veil before she was told to.

CHAPTER EIGHT

Gia's stricken face haunted Luna's every thought for the following days. Years of longing gave her the strength to resist going to Tristea and taking her words back. Anger helped to smother the pain, but it was difficult to maintain her ire when each night since their argument Gia had shown up at the cottage in her sleep. She would enter like that first time and lay down on the couch if Luna was there, or she would follow her to the bedroom when Luna attempted to escape her. It was as bothersome as it was endearing. Remaining angry with her felt impossible.

On the fourth morning, with Gia carefully cradled in her arms, Luna exited her front door at the same time her mothers landed on their griffins for an unannounced visit. The connection she had with them wasn't anywhere near as intense as with Gia. The maternal bond only allowed them to sense extreme distress that grew fainter as daughters aged.

She should have gone through the Veil inside her home, but part of her had wanted to prolong the contact with Gia. Perhaps this was her punishment then, for taking such liberties while Gia was unaware.

Twin looks of shock crossed her mothers' faces and they unabashedly gawked at Gia peacefully asleep in her arms. No one moved for a long moment until Luna bit her lip and fled through the Veil.

She laid Gia on the couch, refusing to go find the bedroom Gia shared with someone else, and paced in front of her. Her distress must have been notable because Gia began to stir and Luna had no choice but to go back home.

Uda still sat on her griffin, her golden hair shining in the morning sun, apparently in shock, but Saso waited on the swing, gently rocking it back and forth.

Luna sat down beside her and the three of them nearly suffocated in the silence.

"You've broken your mom," Saso said, the hint of amusement enough to ease some of the tension.

"It's not what you think."

Uda dismounted in a flutter of golden robes and marched up to the house. "Lulu, you know that we love you very much, darling, but this is no life for a Human. It's dangerous here and you will only break her heart in the end."

"She's not Human."

Luna didn't want to tell them. She knew what would happen once she did, but the idea of them thinking she was having some impossible and illicit affair with a Human caused a wave of panic to settle in her stomach.

"She's—her name is Argia Erretzea, and she's my Arima."

* * *

Gia hid in her shop. She had flipped the sign on the door to CLOSED and spent the morning tending her flowers and plants. Most of her sales came from deliveries ordered through the store's website, and she wouldn't suffer too much of a loss in profit. The town was too small to solely rely on walk-ins for income and she'd secured contracts with a few businesses as well as the local and neighbouring funeral homes.

Luna's words still rang loudly in her head. They'd stung, not only because of their meaning, but because of who was saying them. Gia had convinced herself that if Sean was happy, how could she be hurting him? If he felt that what she gave him was enough, did it matter how closed her heart was? She may not have told him that she was tethered to someone else, but he accepted her as she was. Shouldn't that be all that mattered? Telling him the truth about her connection to Luna would change nothing and only hurt him and make him doubt her commitment.

She felt the tear in the Veil inside her shop as though it was ripping through her gut.

Luna's anger had faded over the past few days but the hurt remained. Gia had calmed when she did, but her heart rate picked up in anticipation of another confrontation. But when she cautiously entered the front of her shop, two unfamiliar Guardians stood there instead of Luna, whose Call still came from beyond the Veil.

"Argia Erretzea?" the Guardian with copper hair and eyes asked. Her gaze was stern, yet the one with golden hair and eyes looked as though she was seconds away from running forward and pulling Gia into a hug.

"Who wants to know?"

"I'm Itsaso Amorratua, and this is my Arima, Uda Akastuna."

"You may call us Uda and Saso," Uda said.

Gia slowly nodded, carefully moving to place the counter between her and them. "You may call me Gia."

Uda smiled widely. "It's a pleasure to finally meet you, Gia."

"Forgive me, but why are you here?"

The Veil tore open again and Luna stepped out, looking wildly between all of them.

"My apologies," she said to Gia, then turned to the Guardians. "Mothers, please. Leave this. You said you would go home!"

Gia's stomach painfully flipped then dropped and a hot wave of panic rippled through her body.

"No," Saso said, her cold gaze trained on Gia. "I want to know how she can do this to you."

"This is why I didn't tell you, Mama."

Uda stepped forward. Kind golden eyes close to tears attempted to strip Gia of her defences. "Why are you doing this?" she softly asked.

"I'm making a choice," Gia mumbled at the counter, unable to hold her solemn gaze.

"You're making a choice that influences you both!"

"Saso..." Uda chastised, her gaze not leaving Gia.

"No, Uda! How many years has Luna been waiting and for what? For *this*? For someone who denies her people and her Calling? When have you ever heard of any Guardian doing such a thing?" Saso turned on Gia and she shrunk into herself. "Who are your mothers? They can't possibly condone this! What Circle would allow this behaviour?"

Gia's chest tightened and tears sprung in her eyes.

Uda stepped in between them. "Enough, Saso," she said, and the Guardian took a step back but kept her glare on Gia.

"Do they know what you're doing?" Saso desperately asked. "Do they know how you're hurting my daughter?"

"Mama, please..."

Gia wished she could say that she hadn't thought about them in years, but she had thought of her mothers almost every time Luna's Call had tugged at her heart. And not fragments of memories that lost detail with time. That wasn't how Guardians captured memories with their loved ones. A daughter's bond with her mothers during childhood was nearly as intense and significant as the one she would someday share with her Arima. Gia recalled every moment. Every hug. Every laugh. She remembered their scents that had clung to her clothes only to be washed away during those first scary nights in a Tristean orphanage.

"My mothers are dead," she whispered, staring at her hands gripped on the counter's edge.

Out of the corner of her eye she could see Uda's golden robes rounding the counter, stopping a few feet away, tilting forward as though she was forcing herself to keep some distance between them. "What were their names?"

"Ur Zurrunbiloak and Ibaia Lasaitzea."

Uda gasped but it was Saso who asked, "From the Southern Lands?"

"Yes," Gia said, and clenched her fists at her sides. The room fell silent and she impulsively leaned into Luna's desperate attempt at comfort through their bond.

"We thought—" Uda whispered. "We thought the Darke got all of you."

Gia shook her head, tears falling freely. "Only my mom, Ibaia. My mama knew what would happen to her after. That she wouldn't survive the Mourning. She was…I watched her waste away…She said she never wanted me to know that pain." Gia swallowed thickly, growing angry, and locked eyes with Uda standing beside her. "I lost them both because of this—this *curse*. How is that fair? Neither of them had a choice. Mama showed me how to do the Human glamour and took me through the Veil. She gave me a choice. She allowed me to decide my own path. This was what she wanted for me."

"We would have taken care of you," Uda said, taking a careful step closer.

"I wanted my mothers!" Her voice cracked, chest squeezing tight and she struggled to breathe. "You want that for your daughter? To have her bound to me in such a way that the only thing she can do if she loses me is *die*? That not even her own daughter would be enough to make her life worth living?"

Copper arms wrapped around her and Gia hated the immediate comfort she took in them. She sobbed like she hadn't since that day the Darke had attacked her mothers, and laid her head below Uda's breasts, feeling like a child again because of her glamoured size and the memories flooding her mind.

Uda quietly held her for so long that Gia only noticed Luna and Saso leaving when the Call in her chest weakened. She'd allowed herself the comfort for long enough, though, and should never have accepted it. Sniffing, she wiped her face and quickly placed some distance between them.

"Do you know how to use mirror portals?" Uda asked.

Gia shook her head. "I wasn't old enough to travel by myself when I left Ederra."

"I'll show you how. Can you consciously travel through the Veil?"

She nodded.

"I'll be there when you need me."

"Luna needs you."

"I'll be there for you both."

"I'm hurting her."

"You're hurting too. And I understand much better now, and I'm here for you, Gia, like I couldn't be then."

"I'm not your responsibility."

Uda slowly stepped forward, seeming to offer Gia the opportunity to move away. When she didn't, Uda carefully placed a hand around the back of Gia's neck and lightly pressed their foreheads together. "We are your family too, and if you let me, I will love and protect you as though you were born of my blood."

Gia let out another sob and Uda's arms wrapped tightly around her again.

* * *

Saso held her hand while they waited for Uda to return and gently rocked them on the porch swing. Silent tears ran down Luna's face and her heart ached to go back and offer comfort to Gia, but Saso had ushered her away. Had she the slightest inkling that Gia would accept her embrace, she would've fought her. But Uda was there. Her mom would know what to do better than she would. Mom always knew.

"Why would her mother send her there?" Luna wondered. "All alone in a new world."

"You're young, Lulu. Fortunate to have only been witness to it once, but the Mourning makes Guardians do strange things. We're no longer ourselves. Every pair is different, but it's a universal truth that once you lose your Arima, it's like losing your heart. It's impossible to survive without her. Some go mad with grief while others are suffocated by sorrow. It's not uncommon to experience both the craze and melancholy as seems to have been the case with Ur."

"If you had lost Mom, would you have taken me to another world and away from my people?" Luna asked, failing to smother her growing anger.

"I can't say what I would have done in Ur's place. Though we shouldn't judge the actions of someone who had lost herself in grief. Ur had ceased to be Ur the moment she lost her Arima."

Luna sighed and hung her head. "Did you know them?"

"Living at the Sanctum, we tend to meet all of the Guardians. I remember them because of their deaths. We knew of Gia's existence too. We had honestly thought the Darke had gotten all three of them. Members of the Southern Circle found Ur's body beside the two memorials she had built," Saso gravely said.

Luna nodded. Ederra was large, the lands spread far apart. The Guardians lived at their assigned Rifts in practical isolation and tended to only mingle with the Circles responsible for their respective lands.

"How old was she? She remembers a lot and couldn't have been too young. There isn't usually much of an age difference between Arimas."

Saso let go of her hand and rested her elbows on her knees, stopping the swing, then ran a golden hand through her hair. "We should've known that a decade was too big an age gap. I'd never seen it before, but when no other fatalities were reported during that awful time, we could only assume that whomever was meant to be her Arima hadn't been born yet, and with her loss, wouldn't be."

"You couldn't have known she was in Tristea, Mama."

Saso shook her head. "You were ten years old when you told us your chest hurt and that you couldn't stop crying. Your mom and I were so worried…We thought you were sick. You cried for hours on end, so badly that we gave you a sleeping potion when your mom couldn't find anything physically wrong. You continued to cry even in your sleep."

Luna stared at Saso fidgeting and picking at her copper-tinted nails.

"We learned of their deaths a few weeks after. You'd woken one morning, long before then, and said you felt better. I can only assume it was because she'd gone through the Veil at that point, smothering the strength of your connection. That year, though, you would have bouts of sadness and we thought perhaps you had a unique mind and tried our best to support you through it."

"I remember. I didn't understand. One moment I would be playing and the next I would go lay down in my room and feel sad for no reason."

"It never occurred to us that the two were linked. Children don't share emotions with their Arimas to that extent," Saso said and turned to her. "We never saw Argia, and didn't know of her colours or role as a Shield. At the time of her Naming Ceremony, your mom hadn't Ascended to Apaiz Nagusia yet. I swear to you, Lulu, had we known Argia was still out there, we wouldn't have stopped looking until we brought her home, no matter who she was bonded to."

Luna nodded her acceptance through her disappointment. Being a Guardian wasn't safe. Guardians died. They died in pairs. Daughters were often orphaned and taken in by extended family or lived at the Sanctum.

"She'd been so scared and heartbroken."

"I can't even imagine," Saso murmured. "She's only a few months older than you. A child, and she survived in that awful world. She kept her secret and built a life for herself. She's... impressive."

Luna smiled. "She is. And tenacious."

"Which explains why your mom has taken to her so quickly."

Luna laughed softly. She wanted to go back to being angry. It had helped before, simply calling Gia a coward.

"What do I do now, Mama?"

Saso's arms wrapped around Luna and she laid her temple against her mother's warm golden cheek.

"I can't tell you that, darling. But fighting the Soulbond will only continue to hurt you both."

CHAPTER NINE

Like they did most nights, Sean and Gia sat eating dinner in the living room in front of the TV. Well, Sean ate while Gia moved her spaghetti across the surface of the plate on her lap. Almost a week had passed since she'd met Luna's mothers, without a word from Luna herself. Gia could still feel her, but Luna had miraculously figured out how to effectively hide most of her emotions, leaving Gia with only a faint sense of hurt, sorrow and disappointment, that might still have only been her own feelings.

"Mom called," Sean said and Gia hummed in acknowledgment, blankly staring at the marinara sauce streaked across her plate. "She said she hasn't heard from you since we moved in."

He sat on the couch, his plate of food on the foldout table in front of him, staring intently at her.

"I'll call her tomorrow."

"You said that three days ago."

Gia sighed and set her plate on the corner table beside her. "I'll go call her now."

"Ree, what's going on with you?"

"Nothing."

"Don't be dismissive."

"Don't push."

"So I'm supposed to leave it even though you've barely spoken to me in a week?"

"What do you want to talk about, Sean?"

"I want to know what's wrong."

"I don't know what's wrong." She honestly didn't. Yes, it was Luna, her mothers, her duty, but Gia had no idea what she wanted to do about any of it. Luna was leaving her alone. She'd thought she wanted that.

"I thought it was about that guardian woman. I can understand why meeting her would stress you out, but I don't understand why you've been withdrawing from me?"

"I just need some time to work through this. It's definitely not you, I promise."

"Then why are you flinching again when I touch you? Why are you getting up in the middle of the night to sleep on the couch?"

"I told you, I must be sleepwalking because I don't remember doing that."

"You've never sleepwalked before, and now you're sleepwalking seemingly only to get away from me?"

"I swear, Sean, this isn't about you."

"Then who's it about? I headed out on a call last night and you weren't anywhere in the house and you didn't have your phone on you. I went out on the call, not too worried because you're practically indestructible here, but then I remembered that the Darke was a thing apparently, so I searched for you on the streets. And when I got home to check if you were back, there you were, fast asleep on the couch again."

"What?"

"Please, don't."

"Sean, I have no idea what you're talking about."

"Are you having an affair?"

"*What*? No! Who would I be seeing? Where would I find someone to have an affair with? We only moved here a couple of weeks ago and you know I have issues with Hu—people."

He stood, frustration all over his features—jaw tight, fists clenched, but took a calming breath, relaxed his hands and sat back down, running a hand over his face. "You usually talk to me when things are getting hard, then I know how to act around you. Ree, I can't just leave you when you're clearly in distress, and I don't want to crowd you, so you need to help me out here. What's happening? Are you regretting moving here? Do you want to go back?"

Gia sighed. "I honestly don't know."

"What do you know?"

"Nothing anymore."

She got up and walked out the door, knowing she was being dramatic and unfair, but unable to look at his genuinely hurt and confused expression any longer.

It wasn't a conscious decision to go through the Veil. Perhaps it felt like the only way to escape Sean while she had no answers to give him. There was nowhere for her to go and yet Ederra called to her nearly as loudly as Luna's heart. The only conscious choice she made while fleeing from her fiancé was to avidly avoid Luna's home.

The picturesque cottage stood cupped by the forest. Large white flowers prettily bloomed in the garden and ranked up the walls. Gia wasn't sure what they were called, but she had named them moonflowers, years later, during the brief moments she had allowed herself to think of Ederra. They bloomed under the moonlight and softly illuminated the colourful buds and plants around the rest of the cottage.

She was dying to see them up close—touch and smell the other flowers when they bloomed beneath the sun—but quickly walked in the opposite direction, out toward the cliff, along the edge, until she was out of sight of the cottage that was so damn perfect she could've dreamed it up herself.

Sitting down on a rock, she stared out over the calm dark water. The magic buzzing in the air settled on her skin, as crisp and light as the scent of salt from the ocean. Gia had grown up near a beach and was struck by a memory of her toes digging into wet sand as cool foamy water rushed her ankles. Her small hands clasped by a mother on either side of her, periodically lifting her into the air to shrieks of laughter pealing from her mouth.

Waves of nostalgia wracked her body and bitterly lumped in her throat.

Surrounded by millions of glittering stars, a thin crescent moon hung low over the ocean like a massive smile in the sky. It shone a soft cerulean, casting the world in a soothing blue glow. Gia impulsively reached for the trinket that hung on her braid, mesmerised by the multicoloured luminescence of the barrier reef sparkling beneath the ocean over a mile away, lighting the water around it in a pretty pink reminiscent of her magic.

A familiar roar drew her attention to the left, toward the mountains in the distance where a lone wyvern streaked across the sky and toward the cliffs where it was no doubt nesting.

Gia's chest ached and her shoulders hunched and gently shook.

Her mothers had ridden wyverns. They looked like smaller dragons with large webbed wings for arms and long, spindly bird-like legs. Gia had flown on their backs, safely cradled in one of her mothers' arms, laughing into the wind while she gripped the smooth scales that ran down the wyvern's neck.

The day her mom died, they'd roared and screamed in their grief. Sometimes in her nightmares Gia could still hear their heart-wrenching lament. It was difficult to understand how being back in Ederra could provide such comfort and yet hurt so much at the same time.

She startled at the long nose that pressed over her shoulder and jumped to her feet, taking in the black horse with the cerulean flames on its mane and licking up its hooves, the same colour as the moon. Like all things Ederran, it was massive. Its chin easily clearing the top of her head.

"Hey," Gia softly greeted and smiled when she was playfully nudged again. "Are you an aethon?" she wondered, then noticed the large black wings curled against its sides, smooth and shiny like a raven's.

Tilting her head at the mesmerising blue flames, Gia ran her fingers through them and down a muscular neck. The earthy scent of a thunderstorm hit her out of nowhere and she quickly stepped back.

"*No,*" she told the black pegasus walking toward her, clearly wanting to be petted. "No, no, no, *no.* You need to leave me alone!"

Gia ripped open the Veil behind her and fell back through it.

* * *

"Who decided it was bad parenting to use magic on a baby?" Haize Bolada asked while she sat on Luna's living room carpet, a long glass bong resting in her lap. "I haven't slept in days. I would tell you how many, was I at all able to recall the concept of time."

"Surely it can't be that bad," Luna wondered, stretched out along the length of her couch.

"It is. It really is, Lulu," Bo mumbled, a blue finger lighting up with an orange flame she placed over the bowl and took another long hit. Smoke left her nostrils and she brushed pink bangs from her eyes, extending the bong to Luna who declined with a lazy wave of her hand.

"Any more of that and I'll fall asleep."

"I want to fall asleep."

"You came to my house to sleep?"

"Yes. For sleep and quiet. At least you're not constantly leaking foul-smelling excretions from various orifices on your body. My home has been invaded by something straight out of a hallucinogenic nightmare."

"And Ukitu is fine with you abandoning her and your daughter?"

"Her mothers are there helping out. She would've come too, but I think she's far too attached to the little monster."

"At least one of you is."

Bo hurled a ball of light at Luna, who deflected it with another lazy wave, laughing lightly. "It's good to see you."

"I've missed you," Bo said, growing earnest. "I'm here for an actual reason, though."

"Sounds very serious."

"It is very serious."

Frowning, Luna sat up. Her mind was blissfully empty, but her previously calm heart beat a little faster. "Are you all right?"

"Yes, everything's fine, Luna. Please calm yourself."

"Why are you here?"

"You're so intense and perfect for this."

"For what?"

"You are my oldest and dearest friend."

"I was there when we met and I'm an active participant in this friendship, so I'm well aware, yes."

Laughing, Luna ducked out of the way of another ball of light that dissipated harmlessly behind her head.

"As you know, our daughter's Naming Ceremony is coming up. Kitu and I were hoping you would agree to stand as zaindaria for her should anything happen to us."

Luna's heart soared, swelling with pride, but then painfully clenched. "Me? Alone?"

"Yes. We're already so fortunate that our daughter will grow up with you in her life as someone to look up to. If you'd rather not, though, we understand."

"No, no. It would be an honour, Bo."

Bo grinned brightly and lit up her finger again. "We should sleep to celebrate."

"What in the name of the Mad Mother!" Bo exclaimed.

A scream followed and Luna reared up in bed, a blue flame cupped in her palm, ready to be hurled at whatever threat there was as she blinked the sleep from her eyes.

Gia stood gawking from beside the bed and Bo launched an orange fireball at her, a pink shield seemingly instinctively went up while Gia dumbly stared between them. Their eyes locked and Luna was almost too late to stop the second ball of fire about to be launched at a distracted Gia's head.

"Bo, stop!"

Her friend thankfully listened and sent her an incredulous look. "You know this Tristean?"

"I do."

"Why is there a Human in your house?" Bo said and glared at Gia, who seemed to have recovered from her shock.

"The question is, what are *you* doing in my Arima's bed?"

"Your what?"

"You literally saw me put up a shield. How many Tristeans do you know who wield magic that way?"

"Why would I know *any* Tristeans? And I have heard that some of you can."

"They're casters. Their magic isn't the same as ours."

Luna blinked, staring between them.

"Why are you in Luna's bed?"

"Why are you in Luna's house?"

The question seemed to almost knock Gia over and her shoulders sagged, staring around the room and then helplessly looked at Luna. "I don't know how I got here. You have to believe me."

"Bo, can you give us a moment, please?"

"No, I cannot. What's going on here? She said she was your Arima."

Luna swallowed thickly. "She's nothing of mine," she quietly whispered, and refused to wonder why that made Gia flinch when that was what she'd wanted and asked for.

"We'll go talk in the living room then. Grant us some privacy, please?" She climbed out of bed, feeling Gia's gaze on her small nightdress.

Bo confusedly looked between them. "If you're certain you're all right?"

"I will be, and I'll tell you what's going on once she's gone back to Tristea."

Bo relented with a nod, her gaze returning to Gia who was staring at the floor.

Luna padded across the room and slipped on a silky black robe. It was a warm evening, but she felt the sudden urge to cover up. "I won't be long," she said and was surprised and relieved when Gia quietly followed when she exited the room.

Following after Luna's very long silver legs, Gia's brain had pushed aside exactly how she'd gotten to the cottage and instead she tried to decipher who, or rather how, Luna had someone in her bed. Her mind absently catalogued every detail of the cosy space, wanting to linger and maybe grab one of the passion fruits in the bowl on the kitchen table, but they passed the small living room and exited onto the front porch.

She mechanically sat down on the swing beside Luna, who jumped up as though burned, and stood in front of her, awkwardly crossing her arms, causing her robe to rise up her thighs.

"You're seeing someone," Gia said, unable to comprehend it as nausea steadily built in her gut. "How?"

"You know that I will not—cannot—be with anyone else. You're the one defying everything we are."

Gia frowned. "Did I imagine the Guardian in your bed? And do you know how I got here? I don't remember…"

"You've been coming here almost every night."

Her lips parted to deny it, until she remembered her argument with Sean about where she'd disappeared to the other night. "What do I do when I'm here?"

"You sleep."

"And then I leave?"

"I take you home."

"Why didn't you tell me?"

"Talking to you isn't something I enjoy very much."

"So your plan was to go out of your way and take me home every night?"

"Yes, I doubt you can help the sleepwalking and I saw no point in making you aware of it only for you to shout at me for something neither of us have any control over."

"I wouldn't have shouted at you."

Luna didn't respond and Gia hung her head, tracing the intricate patterns carved into the swing set. She felt like a child seated on it, her feet barely touching the wooden porch floor. "This is beautiful. Your home is beautiful."

"Thank you," Luna rasped.

"Your friend must like it here too."

"She prefers being at home with her Arima and daughter." Gia couldn't hide her relieved smile and Luna's face darkened. "You have no right."

"I know," she admitted, not bothering to even pretend she didn't know why Luna was angry.

"Do I come into your home and berate the Human you chose to have in your bed?"

"I'm not having sex with him."

"You're waiting for your Binding Ceremony?"

"Sean isn't interested in sex."

Luna seemed to process her words. Her arms dropped to her sides and she leaned against the nearest wooden pillar, half seated on the porch railing as though she needed assistance to keep upright. "He doesn't want to touch you?"

"Not touch like what you mean, no. We have intimacy in our relationship, just not like that. That's not all that matters, you know."

"I'm aware."

"That doesn't change anything. Neither of us are attracted to each other like that. We work."

"We've touched," Luna carefully stated. "You do understand what that means?"

"I know."

"And you're willing to ignore that?"

"I am."

"And when he dies of old age, you'll find another Tristean with no sexual desire to be with because you're lonely?"

"Don't make it sound so vapid. I'm marrying Sean because he's my best friend."

"Then why isn't he *only* your best friend? Why marry him?"

"Because I want to."

"You're pretending you have control when you don't."

"Luna, please…"

Luna fell silent and stared off to the side where Sweet Alyssums grew in their own little nook. "What do you need from me, Gia?"

Unprepared for the question, she sat there, searching Luna's face glimmering in the moonlight. "Could we be friends?" She wasn't sure what made her ask that, but realised how much she actually wanted it. "Staying away from you seems impossible. And with me this close, I could help guard the Rift. Maybe if we spent time together, things wouldn't feel so intense all the time and maybe I'll stop invading your home on a nightly basis."

"What if I like you invading my home?"

It was teasing and flirty and made Gia's stomach swoop in an unfamiliar, terrifying and exciting way. "I could visit you consciously. Knock on your door and wait for you to answer it and everything."

A stunning smile spread across Luna's face.

Goodness.

Gia stared at her, open-mouthed, and waited for an answer in anticipation.

"I suppose we could try that for a while."

She grinned widely. More so, when Luna shyly ducked her head.

CHAPTER TEN

Gia walked from the kitchen into the living room with a six-pack of beer hanging from her fingers, a seafood pizza balanced in her other hand, and some paper plates and napkins balanced on top of the box. She smiled at Sean when he looked up from where he was watching TV on the couch.

"Hey," he said, and rose to help her place their dinner on the coffee table. "You're in a good mood."

"It's been a good day."

"Did Luna finally let you help?"

Shaking her head, Gia sat next to him and handed him a beer. "Not yet, and I don't blame her. I never went for Practicum so I doubt I'll be able to help." She hung her head, her magic swirling inside of her.

She'd been practicing every free moment she had in the greenhouse. The thought of Luna out there on her own filled her with constant dread. Yes, Gia's duty was to protect the Rift, but more than that, she'd been born to protect Luna. She hadn't thought they would allow her Sword to protect a Rift on her own. Luna's been placing herself in danger for decades.

"The only way you'll get better is if you keep practising," Sean said. "Don't be so hard on yourself, I know you'll get there."

Gia smiled. "Uda's been helping me a lot and Luna's so powerful. I wish you could've seen her today, Sean. If the Husks could reason, that one might've flown with its tail between its legs all the way back to Lake Beltza."

"Maybe I could come with you one day?"

Gia stilled. "It's too dangerous," she said, which had unfortunately been her second thought. Her first had been that she didn't want to share her time with Luna. Her third was that Luna might tell her to go away if she showed up with her fiancé in tow. Luna barely tolerated Gia's presence, remaining aloof and closed off, yet always answered all of her many questions.

"But it's safe for you, right? I know she hasn't asked you to help and you hate that, but it's at least giving me some peace of mind that you're not out there hunting down demons."

"We don't hunt them down," she said, softly smiling at him. "They're attracted to weaknesses in the Veil. The Rift is where they try to get through to Tristea. They can't help but come to us."

"And you're sure the Darke can't make portals like you guys?"

"I'm not aware of any other being in Ederra or Tristea who have the ability to open portals and traverse the Veil like Guardians can."

"So cool," he said, grinning widely. "And you're supposed to be her backup? She's the muscle and you're like the medic?"

"I'm more defensive magic. Healing, shields, and I amplify her power. She's more offensive, wielding her magic like a weapon."

"Oh my god," he exclaimed, eyes lighting up in delight. "You're a healer and she's a tank!"

Gia laughed at his silly grin. "Yes, you nerd. I guess that's similar to how we work together."

"It's still strange that they don't just let the Darke through to our world. Why would they make it their problem?"

"I actually asked Luna about that and she said that each time the Darke forces their way through weaknesses in the Veil, they risk creating another Rift. And each time they go through a Rift, or create one, it weakens the entire Veil. So Guardians are literally protecting the structural integrity of the Veil itself."

"And I'm guessing if the Veil comes down it won't be good?"

"She explained it as the worlds existing on different planes, parallel universes, and the Veil keeps them separate, but as soon as it collapses, there would be double of everything attempting to occupy the same space, and the merger would cause both worlds to effectively crush each other."

He quietly processed the information for a moment, the same way Gia had done when she had heard it.

Before she'd started spending time with Luna and bombarding her with questions, she had grossly underestimated the importance of the role Guardians played in protecting both Ederra and Tristea.

"So like an Extinction Level Event?" Sean asked and Gia nodded. "Well, at least Luna looked very capable of protecting the Veil."

"Still in love?"

"I'm surprised you aren't," he said, and thankfully grabbed a piece of pizza, allowing Gia time to recover from the punch to the gut that was that throwaway statement. "Are you going to invite her over sometime?"

"She doesn't like it here."

"A bit snobbish, yeah?"

"No, not that…She has her reasons. I'll ask her, but she's very busy."

He easily accepted the flimsy excuse with a nod. "I'm going out with some of the guys at the station for drinks on Friday. Are you up to meeting a few new people?"

She bit the inside of her lip to stop herself from immediately saying no. "Is this important to you?"

"No. I'll be fine on my own. Thought I'd start working on filling those seats at our wedding."

"You want it to be bigger?"

"Well, with the move, our initial guest list has more than halved. Not everyone will be able to travel out here."

Gia nodded and they both pretended she wasn't relieved by that. "Maybe after Friday when you have an idea of who you click with, you could invite them over for a barbecue or something, and I'll meet them then?"

He grinned. "I'll separate the cream of the crop?"

"Exactly," she said and gave him a quick peck on the cheek.

She grabbed a napkin and a slice of pizza, but paused when she felt him staring at her. "What?"

"You're different."

"What do you mean?"

"I can't remember you ever showing affection so comfortably."

"Must be all this small-town air getting me to loosen up."

"I think it's this friendship with Luna."

Straining through a smile, she opted to take a long sip of icy cold beer to avoid answering.

"I'm happy you're working on a friendship with her." He patted her knee and she barely thought about the touch.

He was right; it was easier being around him. Even dealing with customers who entered her shop wasn't as stifling as it usually was. No, now all of her awkwardness seemed to be reserved for when she was around Luna, and it took all of her mental effort to close her mouth and avoid simply staring at her in awe and longing.

CHAPTER ELEVEN

"Put your back into it!" Gia cheerily called to Luna, who struck at the Darke Husk with her magical sword. The blade consisted entirely of blue magic made solid and serrated at the tip. Her hair flew back from her face as she struck out and parried, and gleamed as brilliantly as her armour in the sunlight.

Luna was magnificent, even when she clenched her jaw and sent a glare Gia's way, refusing to ask for help.

Unperturbed, Gia spread out her jean-clad legs and lay back on her elbows in the tall golden grass that grew atop the cliff overlooking the ocean and soaked up the red sun through her thin yellow tank top. The fight was happening well out of her way and she'd watched Luna easily dispose of Husks over the past few weeks. This one was on its last leg, too. Husk sightings were sporadic and they'd had four in eight weeks, though Luna said that at times she only saw one a month if at all. Gia was only grateful that the exposure had allowed her to somewhat relax during Husk attacks and not stand there, frozen in terror, as she'd done those first couple of times.

When the Husk retreated into the air, Luna holstered the sword handle at her hip, the magical blade disappearing the second her fingers left the hilt. The Husk screamed at her, dark purple lightning shooting down. She blocked the assault with a five-foot rectangular shield that magically grew from her jet-black armour.

Luna gathered her magic and Gia could feel a reciprocal coiling in her own belly even from that distance. When the lightning attack stopped, Luna lowered her shield and hurled a flaming blue streak that caused the Husk to shriek before it dissipated into nothingness.

Gia got to her feet and brushed herself off, heart fluttering and a grin spread on her face. Before she could attempt a conversation, though, an icy chill went up her spine. She realised the feeling of wrongness hadn't left with the Husk an instant before a dark shadow swooped down. The red dragon landed so close that the force of its massive flapping wings knocked her off her feet. It was as big as a house, and dark inky eyes had her quietly swearing as she scrambled backward, her knees too weak from fear to make a run for it.

Unable to entirely turn away from the deadly creature, its steaming breath added to the perspiration on her brow. Its jaws unhinged, red flames gathering in its throat, and Gia froze when a ball of fire came rushing at her. She choked on a scream when black armour blocked her view, taking the brunt of the fiery assault. The large shield had come up just in time, but was too narrow to fully protect them both from the rushing flames and Luna angled it to cover Gia's prone form.

She was struck dumb by the image protectively looming over her and the obsidian stare burning into her own.

"*Run!*" Luna commanded, jaw tightly clenched. She turned to the dragon, hurling a streak of blue magic at it. It roared and reared back, the flap of its wings blowing dirt into Gia's eyes. She watched in teary-eyed horror as white light blasted from Luna's hands.

Oh no.

"It'll take too long! You need to kill it!" Gia shouted over the thunderous growls of the dragon and shakily got to her feet.

Luna ignored her and Gia instinctively stepped forward, laying a hand at the centre of her back, healing her fingertips as they burned against the hot metal. Arching at the touch, Luna's white light grew in intensity and Gia let out a relieved breath and licked her dry lips. Closing her eyes, she focused on amplifying Luna's power. She'd learned about it mostly in theory and in brief practises with her mothers, but it came naturally then. With more practise, she wouldn't even need to touch Luna for it to work.

Soon the dragon's roar turned into a screeching cry as the Darke Husk tore from its large mouth and swooped down toward them.

A pink shield went up and the Husk glanced off its surface before a ball of blue blasted through its centre. Gia took hold of Luna's hand and her magic surged so powerfully that there was nothing left of the Husk once it hit.

Luna turned to her, smile wide and amazed. Gia's own cheeks hurt from grinning back, breathless as she squeezed the gauntlet-covered hand she still held, despite it being flaming hot to touch.

The dragon lifted into the air with a powerful flap of its massive wings that caused a gust of wind that made them cover their eyes, hair whipping around their heads. It roared once in farewell, or perhaps gratitude, and flew off over the forest.

The area around the Rift fell quiet and Luna dreamily stared at her until Gia felt as though her neck, cheeks, and ears were on fire.

"Thank you, Gia," Luna drunkenly mumbled, then glazed eyes rolled into the back of her head and she collapsed to the ground.

Gia's heart jumped into her throat and she fell onto her knees beside Luna, blasting her with a bolt of healing magic that had Luna's eyes flying open, groaning in pain. Wincing, Gia knew she would definitely need to practice a little bit of finesse too.

"Where does it hurt?" she asked, taking in the singed hair, scorched armour, and nasty blisters covering Luna's neck.

"Everywhere?" Luna grimaced.

"I'm taking your armour off."

Luna offered no protest. Gia's fingers shook and burned against the too-hot metal, which meant the reason Luna had fainted was possibly a result of the extreme heat. The soft material on the gloved parts of her gauntlets had melted away, and the metal that covered the top of her hand was hot above scorched fingers.

Gia struggled to find the clasps for the armour pieces and eventually realised that the armour's enchantments were holding it together with magic. On a hunch, she sent a pulse of white magic between a gauntlet and vambrace and the pieces easily slipped apart. She diligently worked on the others while devotedly ignoring why her magic worked on Luna's armour.

Smiling tremulously, she gently pushed Luna's burned fingers away when Luna clumsily tried to help, seemingly unable to move her fingers. Panic rose in Gia's chest. Sniffing, she swallowed the lump in her throat and inhaled a shaky breath when she finally tossed the last piece to the side until Luna lay in the grass in a pair of ruined black tights and a thin doublet. The right side of her upper body was marred with raw burns and welts.

Tears pooled in Gia's eyes at the sight, blurring her vision. Trembling fingers undid the front laces of the doublet, revealing a white chest band, and Gia gently placed her hands on a patch of unaffected flesh on Luna's stomach. She was taking much longer than she should've, and tentatively sent a stream of cooling magic across Luna's silver skin.

Luna moaned deeply and arched her back off the ground and Gia hated herself for her body's reaction, her stomach pleasantly and inappropriately tightening in response to the sound.

"What do you usually do when you get injured like this?" she roughly asked, hoping for a distraction from the novelty and intensity of her salacious thoughts. There was no doubt that Luna got injured often. Gia had only seen her fight one Husk at a time before, but a Dragon or a Griffin Thrall on your own would be a great challenge even for a Guardian. And if Luna was apparently adamant on saving each magical creature…

She should have shielded herself and Luna before the dragonfire had hit. It was all her fault for not being able to even run away properly.

"I have potions," Luna mumbled and it took a moment for Gia to remember why she was saying that.

"I doubt a potion would've helped with *this*, Luna!" she spat, angry at herself more than the stubborn Guardian softly staring at her with glittering eyes.

"I have a friend who I can call on."

Gia nodded, focusing hard on knitting together the scalded tissue. It shouldn't have taken so much concentration, but eventually she got the hang of it once she stopped looking up to check whether Luna was okay, each time finding only a reassuring smile, despite the pain Luna must surely have been in.

Focusing on her task, Luna's pained groans grew muffled and her taut body relaxed beneath Gia's touch. It didn't take long before there was nothing but gorgeous, flawless skin spread out across the grass.

Licking her lips, Gia chanced another glance at Luna's face, knowing she'd been staring far too long and grew hot when she found Luna intensely staring back.

"Please let me see you?"

It had been decades since Gia was without the glamour, and yet without further thought or contemplation, she removed her shoes, kneeling in the grass while she unbuttoned and unzipped her jeans, settling into her natural skin with a deep exhale.

Luna rose into a seated position as though an invisible force had pulled her upright. She took in the way Gia's tank top had shrunk to look almost like a sports bra on her taller frame. Seemingly in a trance, Luna reached toward Gia's face with parted lips, but halted uncertainly. Gia leaned her cheek into the open palm, covering Luna's hand with her own, their magic sparking at the connection.

Both had tears in their eyes and Luna tenderly cupped Gia's cheeks. "I've been dreaming of you all my life."

Gia touched Luna's face too, awed by the perfect contrast of her obsidian fingers against Luna's silver skin. "I still dream about you," she mindlessly confessed.

It was all a logical thought process, the way she understood their undeniable attraction and how using their magic together only strengthened their bond. That it came from a place of utter relief that Luna had survived the dragon attack. Gia knew it was the reason her stomach anxiously fluttered while she caressed her fingers over Luna's pretty face. She knew it was why she was overwhelmed by the urge to kiss Luna, even as she leaned forward and softly pressed their mouths together.

Magic crackled like static between them and Gia's heart wildly thudded. Luna's fingers threaded through her hair and her lips clumsily skidded across Gia's mouth, as uncertain as she was eager.

Realisation hit her like a stab to the heart and Gia gently broke the kiss to press their foreheads together, tears burning down her cheeks as she continued to hold Luna's face close.

"I'm so sorry," she murmured and immediately kissed Luna again, needing to be good for her. Hating that even when she'd had no interest and had felt nothing, she'd forced herself to kiss two Humans in defiance, simply to prove that she could. Guilt overwhelmed her and she gently shook while she cried over the fact that Luna had been patiently waiting for her all this time.

It was Luna who pulled back, only to tenderly kiss her face, her eyelids, and the tip of her nose before she pressed their temples together and loosely held Gia in her arms.

"I could always feel you," Luna murmured, stroking Gia's hair. "I knew you were alive and I wasn't sure what kept you from me." She released Gia then and shifted away, smoothly getting to her feet.

When Luna started dressing, Gia quickly scanned her body to make sure she'd healed properly, before she averted her gaze to give Luna some privacy, her lips tingling while she remained seated on the ground.

"You were born to be with me, Gia," Luna eventually stated, adjusting a vambrace and picking up her ruined gauntlets, the only pieces of armour she hadn't placed back on. "And though I understand now why that scares you so much, knowing that my future was with you had only ever brought me comfort and hope."

When she could only sit there on her haunches, feeling the tears warmly slide over her cheeks, silver strands of hair fluttering in and out of her vision in the breeze, Luna sadly smiled and walked in the direction of her cottage. The sound of neighing and hooves thumping across the ground was heard long before the black pegasus came into view and fell into step beside Luna, who blindly reached out and threaded her fingers through the blue flames of its mane.

Gia didn't bother looking back at the shuffling behind her and leaned her temple against the hairy white cheek that appeared over her shoulder.

* * *

Luna's world hadn't tilted on its axis. On the contrary, everything had steadied and come into a sharp, clear focus. Her existence had righted itself the instant Gia's lips had covered her own. Those plump silver lips had tasted like inevitability and sated a need Luna hadn't realised had been brewing inside her for decades. The first kiss had been a cure for her ennui and the second had ripped her apart entirely.

She wanted to be angry that Gia had kissed her, but her fluttering heart refused to obey her wary mind. Her lips still tickled in remembrance and she was incessantly flooded with images of Gia's perfect face.

It had been worth it.

Luna knew what it meant that Gia had let her walk away. To her, the kiss had likely been a mistake rather than any sort of declaration. Of course it hurt, but her Arima had shielded her and healed her injuries. Nearly getting burned alive was an afterthought considering that she'd finally *seen* Gia, who was more beautiful than Luna could have ever imagined. The image of her smooth obsidian skin and those enigmatic silver eyes was scalded into Luna's brain forever.

In a bid to keep herself from going through the Veil in a foolish hope that Gia might kiss her again, Luna decided to build a shelter for the pegasuses who had followed her home. Flying on the black one to the nearest village, it took a while to gather all the materials and borrow a cart to take them back to the cottage.

The pegasuses were self-sufficient but wouldn't stray far from the cottage now. She wanted them to be comfortable, though, and decided to build a canopy to protect them against the weather and enclosed it with wooden planks. She enjoyed spreading out the wood pellets and shavings, laying out fresh straw with a smile, and stacked the rest of the hay bales beneath the awning she'd constructed at the back of the structure.

A few steps from the stable, she shovelled deep down into the earth until she hit the underwater stream she used for her home's plumbing. Using a hollowed stick of bamboo for the water to flow through, she built a small pond to gather the water and pushed a spigot she'd whittled into the bamboo stick, smiling when a light stream slowly trickled out and over the smooth, flat rocks she'd creatively packed around the bamboo.

She'd always found the sound of flowing water soothing and stood there in the dark, petting the pegasuses' flanks, her mind still reeling with thoughts of Gia's kisses, of her hands cupping dark cheeks, and the way her own skin perfectly matched Gia's silver eyes, hair and lips. Those lips... They'd been so soft and the mere thought of them made Luna's stomach flip and tighten.

Though nothing would come of it, at least Gia had kissed her willingly.

Her mood fell.

Had it been out of pity? The memory soured considerably at the thought. Had Gia come back sooner to tell her she didn't want her, perhaps it would've been easier to let her go. Perhaps if she wasn't now living almost in Luna's front yard, her longing wouldn't constantly threaten to engulf her. But whatever comforting lies she told herself, Luna couldn't deny that the more time they spent together, the stronger their bond grew.

CHAPTER TWELVE

Eyes closed and drowning in waves upon waves of wistfulness, Gia pressed her nose to the smooth bark of the Passion Fruit tree, pitch black fingers reverently tracing over the trunk.

"Passion fruits are my favourite," she murmured, eyes fluttering open and turning to Luna. Her chest clenched at the awed smile and dark gaze skidding over her face.

"I know," Luna rasped and gently cleared her throat. "I planted this tree as close to our—my house as I could."

They were on a golden grassy hill, surrounded by the colourful trees indigenous to the Western Lands, save for the top where the singular Passion Fruit tree had been planted. It stood tall and proud, dark purple leaves casting a wide shadow around its trunk.

Gia looked in the direction a silver finger pointed and spotted the cottage's black tiled roof peeking out through the forest. Luna's vegetable garden and small orchard at the back made her squared plot of land more visible.

"It needs so much sun to grow," Luna explained, drawing Gia's attention back to her stunning face.

"How did you know they were my favourite?"

Luna plucked a passion fruit hanging low and ripe and polished it on the silky black dress she wore. She ran a thumb across the large fruit and offered it to Gia, who carefully took it in both hands, her mouth already watering. It was the shape of a giant pear but the colour of an eggplant. The skin was thin and the flesh similar to a plum.

"They're too sweet for me," Luna softly said, seemingly unable to keep her eyes off Gia and the fruit. "Yet every once in a while, I would crave them so strongly that I would devour them until my stomach hurt."

She grinned and Gia smiled back, before she bit into the fruit, her eyes fluttering closed again at the burst of flavour and juice on her tongue. Unlike the tangy, seedy passion fruits in Tristea, it was sweet, with one smooth pip in the centre. Biting into it was almost like drinking from a glass of juice.

Humming in pleasure, Gia's eyes opened to Luna's rapturous stare. She swallowed thickly, licked her lips, and her spine straightened when Luna's eyes flicked to her tongue.

"Of course, I'm dreaming," Luna said.

"You are?"

With a slow nod, she took a step closer, causing Gia to retreat until her back was pressed against the tree. "You're without your glamour. That's how I know."

Gia looked down at the silver dress she wore that perfectly matched Luna's and then studied their surroundings. "It doesn't look or feel like a dream," she said, though she couldn't remember how they got there or when she'd changed her clothes.

"This place is real. The tree is real. But I know you aren't here," Luna replied and placed a hand over her own heart. "It still feels as though you're on the other side of the Veil."

Gia slowly nodded her agreement but paused when Luna stepped closer. She held her breath when a hand cupped her cheek and sharply gasped when Luna's lips pressed against the corner of her mouth, a soft tongue lightly licking a drop of passion fruit juice.

The half-eaten and entirely forgotten fruit slipped from Gia's fingers and fell to the ground. "What are you doing?" she breathlessly asked, staring into hooded eyes.

"I'm going to kiss you," Luna stated. "At least I may have you here."

She looked so sad that Gia was the one who pressed their lips together, cleaning her wet hands on her own dress before she wrapped her arms around Luna's neck. Heart wildly hammering, Gia held her close and groaned when Luna's tongue licked into her mouth, curious and emboldened.

Nothing had ever tasted as good as Luna's kisses. No feeling compared to their bodies pressed together.

Luna's knee shifted between her legs, keeping her upright and Gia groaned at the teasing pressure, breaking the kiss and feeling dizzy when Luna's relentless mouth travelled to her neck. "What's happening?" she dazedly mumbled, tilting her head to give Luna better access.

Luna pulled back to search her face. "Is this all right? Does it feel good for you too?"

Gia nodded shakily, unable to speak, because Luna was caressing the thin fabric at her waist. Her warm hands felt like pure magic buzzing across her skin. Breathless, she fisted the fabric of Luna's dress and pulled her in for another heated kiss. Mind blank and body on fire, all Gia could do was experimentally slide her tongue against Luna's, who softly whimpered into her mouth.

It was too hot and yet Gia curled her fingers into Luna's hair, trying to bring her closer, scrambling to lift the hem of Luna's dress so their legs could entwine. Luna did the same, bunching Gia's dress onto her hips and they both moaned when Luna ground down against Gia's bare thigh.

"Ree?"

Gia's stomach ached and felt tight in an absurdly pleasant way.

"May I touch you more?" Luna breathlessly asked, her body trembling even as she continued canting her hips across Gia's thigh, bravely settling her fingers beneath Gia's breasts.

Unsure what to make of her body's reactions, or form the words to say what she wanted, Gia grasped Luna's hands and placed them over her breasts. They both whimpered and Gia's back arched when Luna experimentally cupped and squeezed them.

"You feel so good, Gia," Luna mumbled while they lazily rocked together.

Gia needed their dresses gone. It was far too hot, and the material was bunched up on their bellies, keeping them apart. She wanted to see Luna and touch her and she frantically pulled at the black dress, uncoordinated and clumsily unsuccessful. She gave up when Luna licked the roof of her mouth and slid a hand down her stomach around to her lower back. Her hands cupped Gia's ass cheeks, squeezing as she pressed her thigh firmly between her legs.

Gia cried out in pleasure, confused as to how she could ache so much that it hurt and yet be aroused by it. Her hips rocked and she pushed her thigh against Luna, drowning blissfully in the heady sounds that left the Guardian's throat. Sucking on the straining tendons in Luna's neck, she grew bolder when Luna fell against her in surrender.

Would she give Luna an orgasm?

The thought alone had Gia's hips jerk forward and she moaned at the wet throbbing between her legs, tightly clinging onto the strong body slowly driving her to the brink of glorious madness.

"*Ree!*"

Crying out in pleasure, Gia reared up in bed, panting heavily as drops of sweat ran down her back and temples. Rubbing at her eyes, she tried to catch her breath and decipher the pleasant oddness in her body. She bit her lip and had to tamp down the urge to touch herself where Luna's thigh had been and she remained painfully pulsing and wet.

It took far too long to notice Sean sitting up in bed beside her, eyes wide in shock. He snapped his mouth shut when their gazes met and the pleasant knotting in Gia's stomach made her feel sick.

"Good dream?" he carefully asked.

She groaned, pulled her shaky knees to her chest, and buried her face in them. "I have no idea what that was."

"Want to talk about it?"

She shook her head.

"You know," Sean said, "sometimes aces have dreams about sex. It's everywhere we look and doesn't need to mean anything. It's also not unheard of for some to experience—"

"Who says I had a sex dream?"

"You were moaning and grinding into the bed...I-I wasn't sure whether I should wake you up or not. You were sweating and I thought maybe you were having a nightmare. When you started glowing pink, I panicked."

He wanted her to say she was having a nightmare, wanted her to confirm that she hadn't been turned on, that she and Luna didn't nearly have sex—no, she needed to accept that there was no way for her to justify what had happened. That she shouldn't. Who knew what would've happened had he not woken her?

Gia was flushed. Her heart still raced and her stomach clenched again at the thought of Luna's body pressed against her. Of Luna's hands—

She needed to tell him. It wasn't fair to keep it a secret. It was cheating. But she wasn't making a choice to cheat, it was only a dream. That kiss, though... It was that kiss that had unlocked all of these new sensations happening in her body. That kiss was definitely cheating. Unlike the dream, it had been a choice. Gia had come home and had avoided Sean, laid in the bathtub while she touched her tingling lips, her heart full at the way Luna had looked at her without the glamour on. As though Gia was something beautiful and precious.

She turned to Sean and he stiffened, like he was bracing himself for whatever would come out of her mouth.

Biting the inside of her cheek, Gia drew in a sharp breath. "I kissed Luna."

It was cruel to blurt it out like that and her chest tightened when it looked as though she'd punched him in the gut.

"When?"

"When we saved the dragon."

Sean frowned and stared at their sheets. "Do you want to be with her?"

"I want to marry you."

"Do you want to explore—"

Gia grabbed his clenched fists, and he stared at her with a pained expression.

"Have I ever, in the five years you've known me, shown any sexual interest in anyone?"

"No, which only makes this hit harder."

"Guardians are born in pairs. Most meet during their training at the Sanctum. Those who don't, meet after they're assigned to the same Rift during their Initiation Ceremony. We then build a house. We have a daughter. She grows up, goes for her Practicum at the Sanctum, and is assigned to a Rift of her own, where she meets her Arima and they build a home together. That's how it's been for millennia."

"She's your soulmate," he gruffly whispered.

Gia let go of his hands and sat back. "Luna's a good person. When I told her that I don't want that life, she backed off. She agreed to a friendship because I asked, and I admire that despite what she's been taught all her life and believes in, she respected me enough not to push this. Because if she wanted to, I wouldn't be able to resist her, Sean. I would have no choice. It's not some great romance. We're all locked in this cycle. Caged in by it. I don't want it. I don't choose it."

"But you can't resist her…"

"If you need me to never cross the Veil again, I won't."

"You've been excited to help fight the Darke."

"None of that matters. I know it'll look badly on your record, but we can move again, as soon as it's possible."

If Gia remained in Tristea and moved to the other side of the country, Luna's Call wouldn't be as strong. It would be infinitely harder to ignore now that they'd shared magic, but Gia could make it work. She'd been fighting against it most of her life.

"You can't run away from this. You've been running all your life and you still found each other."

"What do you need me to do, Sean? I'll do anything you need me to."

"Do you need to get it out of your system?"

Something inside her shattered and she carefully placed a hand on his knee. "I know you've had to make compromises in the past that you weren't entirely comfortable with, but when we met, we found common ground in the fact that we both had no sex drive. I know this isn't fair to you, and I swear, Sean, up until Luna and I accidentally touched, I had none. I never lied to you about that. The way I'm built, I can only ever be sexually attracted to her."

"And if you continue guarding the Rift together, what are the chances that you'll kiss her again?"

Gia averted her gaze and her hand slid from his knee when he got out of bed. She released a breath when he only stood beside it and didn't leave.

"I don't know what to do," he said, running a hand over his head. "I want to say let's leave if this is something you can't control and you don't want, but that's your world, Ree. You should be able to go there whenever you feel like it. What do you want?"

"I don't want to lose you."

His shoulders loosened and he smiled sadly. "It feels wrong to agree to run away with you."

"Why don't you think about it? I put a lot on you tonight and I'm really sorry about that. We can talk more tomorrow and maybe you'll have more questions and have an idea of what you need to happen going forward?"

He nodded and Gia's body unspooled when he got back into bed. "Wait," he paused and tilted his head at her, frowning. "Have you been sneaking out at night to go see her?"

"No! Well, not consciously. I-I can feel her," she said, touching her chest, "and sometimes it feels as though she's Calling to me and I can't help but go to her in my sleep. I wasn't aware I was doing it. But she's been bringing me back each time. She's been…She hasn't been inappropriate. This is all on me. I'm the one who's hurting both of you."

Gia hung her head and tears spilled from her eyes when Sean got back out of bed.

"Uh, I'm gonna go sleep in the guest room," he said, looking almost apologetic about it, and Gia wished he would shout at her and be angry instead of hurt.

She only nodded, a knot stuck in her throat, and sadly watched him take his pillow and walk out the door without even trying to kiss her head.

* * *

In a blissed-out stupor, Luna sat on her porch swing, absently rocking back and forth, a cup of tea nestled in her palms. Unbidden, another giddy grin spread across her face. She didn't know what had woken her the night before, but it was probably for the best. She doubted she could've handled much more of what was happening beneath the Passion Fruit tree.

And was it supposed to feel that intense? Like she couldn't breathe and yet didn't care whether she ever would again? It was only a dream, though. What would it be like if she could actually feel Gia's magic surging into her body?

"Whose legs have been wrapped around your neck?"

Luna startled, tea spilling all over her hands and lap, thankfully cooled as she'd been daydreaming for a while. She glared at the Ama Gorria who sat down beside her, a prominent mischievous twinkle in her ruby eyes.

"Don't be crass, Sua."

"Was it good?"

Her ears heated and she looked over to where the pegasuses grazed in the golden field, side by side.

"It was only a dream."

Sua hummed. "The pegasus suits you. It's very rare of them to volunteer as Companions."

Luna had been pleasantly surprised too. "I'm happy they chose us."

"When will I meet her?"

"She doesn't wish to be met."

"She still hasn't come to her senses?"

"She kissed me."

"Did you enjoy it?"

"Very much."

"That's good," Sua said and removed the half-full cup of tea from Luna's hands. Her magic gently thrummed before steam rose from the cup as she brought it to her lips and took a sip. "You make the best tea."

"Thank you?"

"You could stand to work on your manners, though, and offer your guests some when they arrive at your home."

"You have long since ceased to be a guest in my home."

Sua smiled and leaned back into the seat. Luna relaxed her leg when she felt Sua pick up her own gentle pace.

"You should try touching yourself. It will clear your mind and hopefully prevent you falling into another catatonic state. It really isn't safe for you to go into a trance out here on your own."

Luna tilted her head. "My home is shielded, as you very well know, but is that what you do?"

"I used to. I think with time my body has lost interest in such things entirely."

"And when you think of your Arima?"

"I feel nothing but love and longing."

Luna nodded. It had been an extremely long time for Sua. "Will the dreams become more frequent? Will they remain so vivid?"

"Perhaps, if they remain only dreams. One never knows with these things. The Arima bond is ancient and mysterious."

"How do I touch myself?"

"Your mothers haven't spoken to you?"

"Bo has told me some. I think my mothers didn't want to make me feel bad because Argia hadn't showed for her Practicum and no Novitiate matched me in colours."

Sua nodded sagely. "You will know what to do once you try."

Luna laughed, unsurprised by the answer.

"Do you know a fun Tristean word I learned the last time I was over there?" Sua hid her smirk behind a sip of tea.

"What?"

"*Pussy.*"

"*Pussy?*"

"Yes. *Pussy.* You should work it into conversation next time."

"How do I use it in a sentence?"

"Tell her you look forward to worshipping her *pussy* for the rest of your lives."

Luna grinned. "It's a dirty word, isn't it?"

"You're no fun anymore."

"Not so gullible anymore, you mean?"

"You grew up far too fast."

Luna smiled softly. "What brings you here, Sua?"

"I can't simply want to see you?"

"Anytime you wish."

"After you left I was concerned about this Arima of yours that sounded as obstinate as she was intriguing."

"I thought you were confident that she could do nothing but love me?"

Sua Orro stared at nothing for so long that Luna's stomach anxiously knotted and the smile dropped from her face entirely.

"And I stand firm in that sentiment, but love isn't always enough, little warrior. Sometimes we do what we must, rather than what we want."

CHAPTER THIRTEEN

Sean got into the passenger seat of her car with a terse smile that Gia warily returned before wordlessly driving them to Sandy's Cove, "The Best Seafood Restaurant in Town." They hadn't been there before but it came highly recommended, a fact that was only proven correct by the ten-plus cars parked outside the building on a weekday during off-peak season.

She always felt awkward walking into a crowded room and making her way through the people already there. Everyone's eyes seemed to be on her despite Gia knowing full well that no one would possibly care enough to look. Still the urge to draw up her invisibility cloak persisted.

A large hand settled on her lower back and Sean's bulk expertly shielded her from view. She released a breath and was much more at ease during their walk to the outside patio at the back, on the beach, where they were seated with a friendly smile from their server.

They each ordered a beer from the young blond man and studied their menus far too intently for it to feel natural.

"I'll go to the butchery tomorrow to pick up some meat for Friday." Gia broke the tense silence and Sean nodded without tearing his gaze away from the Tuesday Specials. "Anything in particular you want?"

"Anything's fine," he mumbled.

It was the wrong time to ask him what he'd decided, especially when another couple chose to sit at the table directly behind them. And why did people do that? Why not move further down the patio? Sure it was less crowded and they had a better view of the ocean, but didn't personal space trump the view?

Noticing her agitation and knowing the source of it, Sean chuckled softly and the mood lightened a little, but Luna hung over them like a guillotine. Gia wasn't sure what else to talk about when she still wasn't sure whether he would leave her or not. Besides, she already knew which cuts of steak he preferred. Perhaps she would get some burger patty meat too, if she wasn't homeless come Friday.

She opted for a piece of pan-fried salmon and Sean got a T-Bone steak. Service was fast at least, so the period waiting for their food was spent staring out over the ocean and watching people walking or jogging up and down the beach.

They ate quietly, making small talk over the quality of the food, offering each other tastes and deciding unanimously that the food was indeed very good, especially at the prices offered.

When they finished, she paid the bill. That was their rule: whomever invited the other out paid, which meant they usually alternated.

She carefully took Sean's hand, settling a little when he didn't pull away. They made their way down the beach as the sun set over the ocean. It was romantic. Everything Gia had learned throughout her lifetime told her as much, but they still needed to discuss her betrayal.

"I want you to be happy," Sean softly said.

"I'm happy with you."

"You've been happier since you've been going over there. I don't think it's only her. I think it's you seeing your home, too. Maybe I'm being stupid, but knowing that it's something you can't help makes your attraction to her more palatable somehow." He tilted his head. "It should worry me more, I know. But I told you I've been in open relationships before. Granted, they all ended when my partners found people who could offer them sexual intimacy in addition to emotional intimacy, and the chances of that happening here is even greater considering what I know now. But if we were to leave, who knows, maybe in a few years something happens and you see her again and we're right back to this place...I could either step aside—"

"No."

Smiling down at her, he placed an arm around her shoulders and she wrapped her own around his waist, holding him tight. "I could either step aside, or we can see if it's possible for you to be friends with her. I trust that you'll talk to me first if anything between you and her changes."

"I will, but you don't need to do this. I don't need to go there ever again. I managed it just fine for a century, Sean."

"But you weren't very happy during that time," he said and rubbed the back of his neck.

She hadn't been. The period between losing her mothers and finding Sean had been awful. Gia had been lonely and had isolated herself. Yearning for something that terrified her and reminded her of how different she was. Of how she didn't fit in the world she lived in. Though she had met a few good Humans, they remained foreign to her to that day.

Her mother had left her at a fairly good orphanage considering the times. Human children though, grew physically older rapidly and her mother hadn't taught her how to, or when to, age the glamour in accordance to that. She drew attention as a child seemingly frozen in time.

At first, she was treated like a medical curiosity, which came with a certain degree of kindness to put her at ease until the needles couldn't pierce her skin and fear filled their features. One physician had attempted to stab her with a scalpel—a fatal strike, had the blade been able to cut her. Gia hadn't understood at first and continued to believe they were trying to help. That they were afraid *for* her, not of her, until anger and suspicion accompanied their fear. And then the clergy got involved.

She had allowed them to restrain her, lock her in a shed, and had to use her healing magic when the shed was lit on fire. The only reason she survived in Tristea was because she could cloak herself. For over a decade she remained invisible, living on the streets, stealing food, and squatting in abandoned buildings. She watched the Humans and how they lived their daily lives and practiced how to age the glamour. Once she was confident in the glamour and her act, she got a job as a shop clerk, rented a room at a boarding house, and finally had a space to call her own.

The lesson she had quickly learned was to never trust Humans. To not let them close enough to find out her secret. They didn't understand and they wouldn't even try. The magic users and magical beings of Tristea all remained hidden for that very reason. So Gia had kept her head down and hadn't gotten close to anyone, until Sean had entered her life.

"Ree?"

"Hm?"

"I love seeing you like this."

Gia stared up at him in confusion.

"I love coming home to your stories of pegasuses and dragons, of how you used your magic to protect yourself and our worlds. Maybe it's selfish, too, but the guilt of allowing you to give that up would be a dark cloud hanging over our marriage."

She stared out over the ocean, the one that made her miss the stunning view from the cliffs in Ederra. If she was honest with herself, she wasn't sure she could give it up again either.

"What do you need me to do to make this easier?"

Sean didn't think long. He'd most likely been considering it since they spoke the other night. "I want to get to know her too." Gia stopped walking and they faced each other. "If she knew me, she'd be more inclined to respect our relationship."

"She does."

"I'd like to meet her properly to see her intentions."

Gia reached for the crescent moon on her braid. "She really doesn't like it here and she won't wear a glamour if I somehow do convince her to come."

"We'll stay in the house."

"You can barely speak around her."

He grinned sheepishly. "I just need to look her in the eye, okay? Maybe I'm a bit starstruck around her but she certainly isn't around me. Once she leaves, I'll be fine and I'll know more about her."

Gia didn't know how she would handle both Sean and Luna in the same room, but if that was what he needed... "I'll try my best to get her to come over."

He flashed a grin, took her hand again and they continued down the beach, waving at a few locals who greeted Sean by name. Gia looked at the side of his face, and smiled.

He was much happier in Bluewater Bay, too. She owed it to him to at least try and make this work.

* * *

It was very difficult to look Gia in the eye when next they saw each other, almost as difficult as it was not to kiss her again. A big part of Luna felt guilty and she considered confessing the dreams she'd been having and the daydreams that would invade her mind at random. Gia didn't come to her on the nights Luna dreamt, and a small part of her was brave enough to wonder what that meant. Was Gia dreaming about her too and finding enough comfort in that to appease the Call?

"You did a great job on the stable," Gia said, shyly smiling where she stood admiring the structure, and Luna's back straightened with pride.

They hadn't seen each other in a week, but when another Darke Husk had descended on the Rift, Gia was there to shield her, and all the walls Luna had carefully constructed around herself had effortlessly crumbled when they fought together again.

It was painfully apparent now how much Gia looked like herself with the Human glamour. Her facial features were nearly identical, minus the sharp cheekbones inherent to their race. Luna couldn't help but long to touch her and hold her close.

"Thank you," she remembered to respond, grateful when the white pegasus walked between them, distracting Gia into petting her nose.

"I would've helped you, you know."

"I didn't think it would be appropriate to ask."

Gia bit her lip and nodded. "You can ask me for help, Luna." Soft and pretty hazel eyes shifted to her, and Luna hated how the glamour had ceased to be a barrier between them. Gia was simply beautiful in whatever form she took. "I can't imagine what it must've been like for you fighting the Darke on your own all these years. How dangerous it must've been."

"I've managed."

"How many times have you been injured?"

"Injuries happen. It's a part of Guardian life." Gia searched her face and Luna awkwardly touched the white pegasus, too. "You should name her."

"Have you named yours?"

She shook her head. "I've been unable to think of anything." She sighed, a little frustrated at how difficult it was, knowing the reason to be the disconnect between her and Gia. "He'll show me in time."

Gia grew quiet and Luna wasn't sure what to do with herself as her stomach anxiously knotted and she had to resist moving closer to Gia. She petted the pegasus's neck, running her fingers along the pink flames. Gia followed on the other side until they stood watching each other over a broad white back, Gia needing to tilt her chin up to maintain eye contact.

"I know things aren't the way you imagined they'd be between us," she earnestly said and Luna's shoulders tensed.

Gia rose onto the tip of her toes and a small brown hand slid over the pegasus's back to shakily grasp Luna's own. Her heart stuttered at the touch and she looked back to Gia's face.

"But I need you to know that I'm your Shield, Luna. For as long as you'll have me."

She swallowed thickly and averted her gaze, even when she clung to the tiny hand nestled in her palm. "You don't need to feel obligated—"

"I don't. I want to do this. Seeing you out there fighting to keep Ederra and Tristea safe reminded me of how important our task is. You inspired me to accept that part of myself, to make peace with something I've unfairly detested for a very long time."

Luna sheepishly ducked her head and her body lightly glowed blue as pride swelled in her chest. Gia grinned brightly, looking as though she wanted to kiss her and Luna gave her hand a light squeeze, pulling away before she flung herself at Gia's tiny body.

"Bo's daughter has her Naming Ceremony tomorrow at the Sanctum," she mumbled. "Would you like to come?"

Gia's gaze shifted from Luna's lips to her eyes. "Uda already invited me."

Luna frowned.

"I said I would ask you if you wanted me there."

"Why wouldn't I?"

"It's your home, your friends, your mom who's been talking to me, obviously behind your back."

"She told me she would reach out to you. I wasn't sure whether you would accept her, and I didn't feel it my place to ask her details about what you two discussed."

"I really appreciate that, Lu."

They softly smiled at each other until Luna remembered she'd asked a question. "Will you come then?"

"Yes."

Luna's chest lightened, expanding even more when Gia grinned back, a soft pink glow surrounding her body.

CHAPTER FOURTEEN

Gia bit her lip and leaned against the kitchen counter, staring at Sean scowling at the raw meat in front of him. She'd messed up so badly—and only a couple of days into their arrangement—this after Sean had placed his own feelings aside to accommodate her.

"Sean, I forgot, okay?"

"People are going to think I made you up," he muttered, continuing to aggressively marinade the meat for the barbecue they'd planned. The kitchen was a mess and Gia pushed herself away from the counter and cleaned around him so as not to stand there drowning in guilt.

"Don't be ridiculous. Everyone in this town already knows us."

"Are you really bailing because you need to go to this Sanctum place or are you bailing because you don't want to be here?"

"I'm not bailing. I just forgot we had plans tonight."

"You don't forget things, especially things you don't like."

"You know I would tell you when I won't—or can't—do something."

"I used to be able to count on that," he mumbled.

It hurt. It really did. Because it was true. "I deserved that."

Sean sighed. "No, you didn't. I'm sorry. I'm trying to be what you need me to be here, but it's hard."

"It's okay not to like this situation. You're allowed to be angry about this."

"Yeah, but I shouldn't keep throwing it in your face."

"You did it once, hardly a pattern of abuse."

"Don't even joke about that."

She flashed him a smile that grew when he rolled his eyes at her. Gia drew in a breath. "The reason I'm not canceling is because Uda found some family of mine."

Sean stopped spicing and grabbed a kitchen towel to wipe his hands. "What? Why didn't you tell me? Do you need me to go with you?"

"I don't know whether I'm going to meet them, yet, or whether I want to meet them. I'm really conflicted about it and she said I could decide once I got there, but they're part of the Circle of the Northern Lands and the Circle of the Sanctum, and will be there for the Naming Ceremony."

"Sounds fancy."

Gia laughed lightly, the tension easing from her shoulders. "I wouldn't know. I haven't been to a Naming Ceremony before."

"Okay. I'm sorry I freaked out on you, but you can tell me these things, okay? Then I won't add to your stress."

"I know. I'm sorry," she said and snuggled into his side for a hug. "I'll stay and meet your new friends, talk for a while, and then we can fake a call from a friend I need to go help? How about that?"

He grinned and kissed her cheek. "Deal."

Gia stood in the kitchen, leaning against the sink and sipped on a glass of wine while she watched Deputy Sarah Jones knead dough to make bread for the barbecue. She was a short blond woman, with kind green eyes mixed with hazel that reminded Gia of peppermint chocolate.

"Sean is hopelessly in love," Sarah said. "I wish Jim spoke about me with half the enthusiasm Sean speaks about you. Sometimes I doubt he remembers my name."

Gia laughed with Sarah. Jim was outside with Sean and a few others, gathered around the fire. His eyes were as kind as his wife's but he did seem like he could get distracted easily by the way he insisted on fixing the sprinkler system in the garden after an offhanded comment from Sean. Gia could've fixed it herself but had been grateful to scratch it off her to-do list.

"How did you guys meet?" Sarah asked. "Sean said he walked into your flower shop?"

She was trying very hard to make conversation and Gia took pity on her. Since Sean had insisted she go and help Sarah, he clearly thought the two of them would hit it off best.

"He did." Gia smiled. "He came in to buy flowers for his girlfriend."

"No!" Sarah looked scandalised. "He doesn't seem like the type to pick someone up while in a relationship."

"He definitely isn't. He came in every Sunday morning to get her flowers before taking her to brunch if he had the day off."

"He's a sweet guy. Was it the uniform that got you?"

"I actually hate the uniform," Gia said and went to refill Sarah's wineglass as well as her own. "I prefer how expressive he is when he dresses in casual wear."

Sarah shrugged. "I haven't really seen him out of uniform much. Tonight's the first time."

"Well, he has a great sense in fashion and flowers. I was very impressed."

"And then you stole him from his girlfriend?"

Gia laughed but soon sobered, taking a sip of her wine and sadly shook her head, leaning back against the counter. "About six months into our routine, he stopped coming in on Sundays. I was worried because Ridge City isn't safe, especially when you were a police officer with a genuine want to protect civilians and make a difference."

"Yeah, I've heard. Ridge City's notorious for its high crime rate."

"A few weeks later, he showed up on a Friday, sheepishly slinked up to the counter and asked whether I would make a Mother's Day arrangement for that Sunday."

"He broke up with her?"

Gia shook her head. "She cheated on him," she said and downed her wine. "I never met her, but I never could understand how she could hurt someone like him like that."

"So you comforted him and he realised that you were the one?"

"I got his mother's flowers ready and he started coming in on Fridays."

"Another girlfriend?"

"He would buy arrangements, bouquets. Sometimes while he was on duty he would rush in and buy a single flower. My shop was on his patrol route, so he would stop by and we would discuss the neighbourhood and how the shop was doing. We would speak about his family and friends, and I even had a few Williamses stop by the shop acting as though they knew me."

"Aw, he was crushing."

"I didn't—One Friday night I was finishing up an order for a wedding. He came in and started helping, like he always did when he had time. We ordered food and ate in the shop and when he left, he invited me to dinner and I accepted, because I missed him whenever he wasn't there."

"So cute."

"We went out together a lot. For walks on the beach, lunches at the park, movie nights at home and dinners with his mother...I didn't realise..."

"Didn't realise what?"

Gia's cheeks heated. "I didn't realise we were dating."

Sarah burst out laughing. "What? How did you not know?"

Sean had discussed his sexuality with her early on. She'd found commonality in his words and they had bonded over similar shared experiences. Still naïve and ignorant back then, Gia had foolishly equated romance solely to kissing and sexual desire. She'd thought that she had finally met a friend she could trust, not realising that she was being charmingly courted.

"It had never been as easy as it is with Sean."

Sarah tilted her head. "What?"

"Human relationships."

"Ah."

"He fell into my life as though he always belonged there. Loving him has been the easiest thing in this world."

CHAPTER FIFTEEN

When she entered Luna's cottage, Gia was unsurprised to find it empty and dark since she was really late. Sarah liked to talk, but she was funny and pleasant and Gia was glad that Sean had someone like her to call a friend at work. Ridge City police officers were often burnt-out, cynical drunks and Gia had hated the ones Sean had been forced to have in his life. They constantly taunted him for daring to take his job seriously and caring about the neighbourhood he'd been tasked to protect.

Pressing her hand against the pad beside the front door of the cottage, she sparked a little magic into it and soft light flooded the room. Four robes were neatly hung over the back of the couch—silver, black, red, and blue respectively. Despite knowing what it would look like, she chose the silver set and quickly changed.

It was her first time using a mirror, but Uda had helped her practice, and it was as natural as traversing the Veil, stepping through and emerging outside the Eastern Courtyard at the Sanctum.

The space was enclosed by a turquoise box hedge as tall as she stood without her Human glamour. Inside, cherry blossom trees bloomed year round, shedding petals that covered the ground in a pretty pink carpet. It looked like something out of a dream with the light blue moon shining down on the scene. No matter how detailed Uda had described it, it still knocked the breath out of Gia's lungs, or perhaps it was the bright grin she received from Luna, who stood up on the stage near the far hedge, in between Uda and Bo.

The ceremony was already underway and about a hundred Guardians gathered around the semicircular stage. Everyone noticed Gia enter through the metal gates when Uda, too, smiled her way with the baby in her arms, wrapped in a golden blanket.

"On this night, we gather beneath the full moon to bless this daughter who has become a part of our world," Uda said and thankfully drew everyone's attention back to her. "On this momentous occasion, we welcome her into our hearts and lives and gift her with a name of her own."

Bo's chin jutted proudly and her Arima placed a pink hand on her back. Luna had called her Ukitu when she'd shared the details of the Naming Ceremony with Gia.

"We ask the Mother of Light to bless this daughter with health, love, acceptance, and happiness. May she possess knowledge, bravery, skill, and strength."

Gia tried not to look at Luna, who seemed to be the only one still stuck on her presence. Belatedly, she realised it was her choice of robe colour that Luna found so distracting. All around them Guardian pairs stood in matching colours. That day, no one else wore obsidian and silver. Her choice was significant and she wondered whether she'd made a mistake in highlighting their connection so blatantly, though she had to admit it would still have been obvious, no matter what colours she wore.

"We ask that the Great Mother show us the destiny of this daughter so her mothers may guide her on her path to becoming a warrior."

Uda closed her eyes, the baby still cradled in her arms. A tiny green arm reached out and grabbed a fistful of golden hair. Gia nearly melted into a puddle of goo at Luna's awed smile and the baby's mothers grabbed each other's hands when the small green limb glowed yellow.

Uda's eyes fluttered open and she smiled. "From this night onward, this daughter will be raised a Shield. She will bring pride to her mothers, fight beside her Arima, and protect our world against Darkeness." She handed the baby to Bo. "Haize Bolada, what will we call this great warrior of Ederra?"

Bo shared a look with Ukitu, before sending a wobbly smile at her daughter. "You are known to your mothers and the Guardians of the Veil, as Brisa Leuna."

Ukitu added, "This is your name and it is powerful."

Uda turned to Luna. "You stand beside us because of your love for this daughter. Tell us your name."

"I am Gerlari Iluna, Sword of Lur Ederra, and chosen zaindaria of this daughter."

"Do you know what it means to be zaindaria to a daughter of Lur Ederra?"

"It means to love, nurture, and show her guidance through example. It is to counsel should she need assistance and be another mother should I be called upon."

"And what name have you chosen for this daughter to live by?"

Luna looked to Bo who beamed back at her.

"Bree," Luna said, standing taller when the mothers cooed their delight at the nickname.

Uda glowed in a golden light and in the front of the crowd, Gia spotted the matching copper glow from Saso.

"May Brisa Leuna always share in our divine connection and may she never cease to wonder at the magic in the world around her. May the Mother of Light bless her on this night and every night."

When her magic surged within her, Gia looked up directly at the blue glow from Luna, who stared right back. The connection grew less obvious when all the other Guardians' magic surged too, until finally in the bundle nestled in Bo's arms, a bright yellow glow spread out and Ukitu's eyes shot full of tears.

"We honour you, Brisa Leuna, Shield of Lur Ederra," the Guardians chorused as one.

The ceremony concluded and most waited for Bo to walk down the steps of the stage with little Bree kicking in excitement and glowing like a firefly. Luna got to hold her first, though, and even though the crowd had shifted, she somehow instantly found Gia amongst the moving bodies. The attention on anyone other than Bree had the Guardians looking her way too, and she was awkwardly aware of how, despite the distance between them, their unbound magic seemed to wildly reach for each other.

Gia's face grew hot and it felt almost scandalous when the bonded pairs around them immediately noticed, as they were all connected in that moment. Thankfully, they only looked, some smirked, and no one approached her. Gia soon realised it was because of the stern visage of Itsaso Amorratua having come to stand vanguard at her side. She couldn't help but stare at the strong set of her jaw and the defiant tilt of her golden chin.

Luna was fearless and brave and fought with a natural ease that seemed reckless but was most impressively calculated. The skill she demonstrated took decades of careful practice and commitment. Gia feared she would never be able to match her as a Shield. She'd seen that same firm look of authority and fortitude that Saso radiated in that moment on Luna a few times before.

"The way you look at me is inappropriate."

Gia jumped in her skin at Saso's deadpan accusation. "Ah, sorry, I didn't mean—"

"Here in Ederra, we respect the sanctity of the Arima bond."

"I didn't—you—Luna looks so much like you."

Copper eyes continued to glare until Saso's face softened into a smile at Uda who joined them.

"Ur's mothers are here, as is Ibaia's sister and her sister's Arima, who stood as zaindaria for you. I didn't want to overwhelm you, but I know that more will come if I told them why."

Gia looked around, various coloured eyes were still glancing their way. Uda had already informed her that her other grandmothers had passed, and she'd been saddened to hear that, which made her entirely unprepared for how many direct family members had still shown up.

Luna stood on the other side of a roaring bonfire and Gia wished she was closer but turned to Uda instead. "Soon, maybe. Thank you for finding them."

"You're welcome, darling. I haven't told them anything, but…" Gia followed her gaze to the four Guardians staring at her with wide, watery eyes. "I think they might suspect."

"Gigi?" a guardian with blue hair and orange skin exclaimed. She immediately recognised her as Aunt Zerua and leaned into the firm hand Saso placed at the centre of her back, thankfully keeping her upright.

"Would you like to see them again?" Uda gently asked.

Gia nodded, chest squeezing tightly and tears freely falling over her cheeks.

"We'll go wait in the atrium nearest to the library," Saso said and Uda smiled her gratitude before walking over to Gia's family.

A gentle press of Saso's hand and Gia mechanically began walking, looking up only once to see the concerned look on Luna's face. She smiled at her then, because she wasn't sad, only overwhelmed, and her heart lightened at the excited grin that Luna flashed in return.

Saso ushered her into the castle, removing her protective hand, and Gia felt like she would float away. She barely took in the tall ceilings, colourful landscape paintings, and beautiful armour sets that decorated the castle before they entered an atrium filled with an abundance of scents and colours she would've immensely enjoyed exploring had she not been overcome with nerves.

"Do you remember them?" Saso softly asked and Gia lightly startled at the attempt at small talk. Only Uda ever came to see her.

"Vaguely. They visited a few times but I remember them mostly from photographs in our house and stories my mothers told."

"Some of us have lived for so long that the passing of time is different than for our young daughters. We often feel that there's time and then ten years have passed before we know it."

Gia jerkily nodded, uncertain how to react to Saso actually talking to her.

"They love you. The only reason they didn't search for you was because they believed they'd lost you, too."

Gia was uncertain how to respond but Saso's intense gaze was drawn to Uda walking into the atrium with Gia's family, who were much more subdued in their excitement, no doubt because of Uda's thoughtful instruction.

Family.

What an absurd notion.

Uda made introductions, more for Gia's benefit, and Gia was thankful when she only retreated a few feet away from the crying group. The way they tentatively embraced her was awkward and sweet. They were strangers, though, and knew it. Extended family bonds weren't as strong here as they were in Tristea. She'd watched Humans grow old and frail, their children and grandchildren grieving their loss. Now she was surrounded by Guardians hundreds of years her senior, looking the exact same age as her.

And was it fair to Sean for her to plant roots deeper in this world he couldn't access? In a world that would never accept him because they wouldn't be able to fathom his existence in her life?

Yet Gia agreed to visit them, something inside of her burning to know more, to speak to those who had known her mothers. Who had known her before grief had changed her life forever. They asked when exactly they could see her again and probably noticed the look of sheer panic on her face, because they didn't push for a response. Uda—the absolute goddess— swooped in and ushered them out with an array of diplomatic excuses and they left with warm goodbyes that made Gia's heart grow tenfold.

When they were left alone in the atrium, she hesitantly met Saso's gaze. "Thank you for doing this for me."

"You're welcome, Argia Erretzea, though my Arima is the one deserving of your gratitude."

She glanced around, uncertain if she'd be able to find her way out of the castle again, but didn't want to inconvenience Saso any further by requesting a guide out, especially when she couldn't even bear to call her Gia.

"Luna will be up in her room if you'd like to see her."

Gia's heart gave an excited thump and she nodded, perhaps too quickly. "She's not with her friends?"

Saso shook her head, her expression tight. "She tends to avoid gatherings like these. Ukitu and Bo know this." Her tone was soft and the accusation solely in her eyes. "Go to the other side of the atrium. Upon your exit, walk down the Hall of Remembrance toward the stairs at the end of the corridor next to the red library doors. They will lead you up to her bedroom. She's at the very top."

"Thank you, Itsaso Amorratua."

"Don't upset her," Saso said and marched out the door.

After staring after her for a moment, Gia made her way through the atrium, attempting to distract herself with the flowers and plants around her, but her feet quickly carried her through the tiny paradise toward the double doors on the other side of the room and she halted the instant she stepped onto the burgundy carpet in the Hall of Remembrance.

The corridor was long and lined by ancient sets of chainmail and leather cuirasses displayed on armour stands. Above them, against mahogany panelling, hundreds of gold plaques lined the walls. Each contained the engraved sigil and names of bonded pairs throughout their history.

Gia scanned the names and once she realised she was searching for her mothers', her gaze snapped away and she hurried toward the red doors at the end of the corridor and peeked into the library.

Bookshelves lined the walls from the floor to the ceiling of the circular tower. Wooden steps connected rows upon rows of cylindrical walkways that went all the way to the top. Long windows separated the shelving, allowing for natural light to flood in. A variety of tables and chairs were set up in the centre of the floor, presumably for those who wanted a quiet place to read and study during their Practicum years. Gia wanted to explore but what she wanted even more was to follow the Call in her chest.

She made the climb past five floors before the staircase narrowed and wrapped around the tower, spiralling to the top where it levelled into an elegant foyer. There was a couch, a dark red carpet, a full-length mirror, and a rocky water feature that peacefully trickled away.

Gia paused there, unsure how she would be received. Aside from Uda, Luna was the only one in the Sanctum that Gia was on friendly terms with. It was only natural to seek her out.

The door opposite her opened and a redheaded Guardian exited. Well, she was playfully being pushed out by a laughing Luna who sobered, her gaze turning soft when she noticed Gia standing there.

Gia dragged her eyes away from Luna's face, shaking off the effects of that dazzling smile she'd seen and looked into the ruby eyes carefully studying her. The Guardian exuded the same protectiveness as Saso, though nowhere near as cold.

"So this is Argia Erretzea," she said. Gia wasn't sure what it was, but there was something different about her. Her ears were noticeably shorter, as was her height in comparison to the average Guardian, and though her skin was pale, it could be mistaken for Human. "She's as beautiful as you said, little warrior."

Luna spluttered, wide eyes seeming to plead with Gia before glaring at the redhead. "I never said that!"

"So you don't think she's beautiful?"

"I—she is, of course she is."

The redhead laughed and Luna scowled. Gia beamed at how adorable she was.

"And what about you?" the redhead asked, dragging Gia's attention away from Luna. "Don't you think your Luna is beautiful?"

"Sua Orro!" Luna exclaimed, saving Gia from responding "yes" out loud. But a cold shock thrummed through her body and she fell to her knees when the given name of the Red Mother registered.

"My apologies, Ama Gorria," she muttered to the carpet.

"And what exactly are you apologising for, child?"

Gia frowned, not sure either. She'd been taught about the Ama Gorria, that she was to be shown respect and bowed to. No other etiquette lessons had followed, though.

"I meant no disrespect."

"Rise, Argia Erretzea. Save your knees for pleasing your Arima."

Gia's ears burned and she glanced at Luna, who had her brows attractively knitted together, head tilted in confusion, before her eyes widened and her lips parted in shock, gaping a few times like a fish out of water.

"Sua!" she eventually screeched in outrage and the Ama Gorria cackled, regally waving to them both before she disappeared in a swirl of red flaming magic.

Feeling hot all over, embarrassed at her awkwardness and the implications of what the Red Mother had said, Gia rose to her feet and met the gaze of a sheepish Luna still in the doorway.

"It went well with your family?"

Gia nodded, happy they were going to ignore all of that. "Uda has been…She's an incredible mother."

Luna softly smiled. "She is. I've been immensely blessed. Would you like to come in?"

Gia was walking forward before she had even nodded her head in acceptance of the shy invitation.

Luna led Gia out onto the balcony, her ears still burning hot from Sua Orro's words. She was in dire need of the refreshment the crisp night air extended. It was difficult, though, not to stare at Gia with her silver brows and hair that shimmered in the moonlight. And how was it possible to find someone so beautiful that it became a hardship to form coherent thoughts around her?

Defiantly, she decided to speak. "I thought you might've decided not to come after all." She leaned her elbows on the stone wall that cupped the balcony and slowly dragged her gaze from silver eyes toward the faint white lights coming from the city at the foot of the mountain. A quick glance back showed Gia transfixed by the starry night sky. The moon was full and illuminated everything for miles, shimmering off the surface of the broad river that ran from the mountain, down the falls, through the valley, and toward the ocean over ten thousand miles away.

"I had some obligations to take care of at home."

Luna had no desire to know what they were, so she didn't ask. Gia was there. It was all that mattered.

Gia was *there*.

She peeked over her shoulder to her childhood bedroom, which looked fairly similar to the one at her cottage, perhaps slightly bigger. Thankfully the room was clean. When she'd felt Gia approach, all her energy had gone into getting Sua out of there, who of course stubbornly stayed simply to tease her.

"What's that place called?" Gia asked, pointing to the white lights.

"Erdiko Village. We have all our armour made there."

"Do you ever wonder why Ederra isn't more evolved with all this magic everywhere?"

"What do you mean?"

"With access to magic, you could easily build greater societies."

"Greater bigger, or greater better?" Luna asked and looked back over the vast landscape beautifully illuminated in a soft blue glow.

"If you look out over the Central Lands," Gia said, "you see only forests and mountain ranges and very few lights indicating people living there. I'm just surprised that there isn't more… growth."

Luna looked back into those eyes that brightly shone against the smooth dark canopy of Gia's gorgeous face. "The people of Ederra are happy. They have everything they need."

"But shouldn't they be striving for more? Humans are always trying to better themselves."

"Humans are a blight on any world they occupy."

"That seems very harsh, especially since I doubt you've met many Humans."

"Were you ever taught the story of the Darke?"

"Only that it's always been here. And served as a way to balance worlds until the Humans of Tristea expelled their Darke to Ederra."

"Sua Orro told me that the magical beings in Tristea were able to keep the Darke under control until it began to specifically target Humans. Do you know why they spread so easily amongst them? Why the Humans of Tristea felt the Darke was such a threat that they had no qualms in dooming our world by sending it here?"

Gia shook her head.

"Because Humans, with their inherent drive to have more— to be greater—were the most easily corrupted. The Darke took to them like fire to paper."

"What's so wrong with wanting more?"

"Everything, when it comes at the expense of others."

Gia nodded. "There's still magic in Tristea."

"And some Darkness too, though the magic isn't enough to bring balance. They're spiralling like a dragon with its wing cut off mid-flight."

"Sean isn't like that."

"Too many of them are."

"Is that why you hate it there?"

"I didn't used to care enough about Tristea to hate it."

"But you hate it now?"

Luna sent her a meaningful look.

"Oh," Gia said and shyly ducked her head.

Luna looked back to the lights at the foot of the mountain. "The Dwarves of Erdiko build the most intricate infrastructure.

Their innovative enchantments continue to make our lives easier and better. The Halfling alchemists keep everyone healthy and strong. Goblins weave the finest fabrics and craft the most extravagant jewellery. The Faeries, or as they refer to themselves, the Tuatha Dé Danann, are known to offer wards and protection spells to those who are trustworthy. Not everything needs to be big and shiny to be considered progressive, Gigi."

"Says the princess up in her tower, in the castle she grew up in," Gia teased with a cheeky grin that made Luna's face heat.

"I'm not a princess."

"You're close enough. This place is beautiful. I never realised how close it was to Lake Beltza. I mean, I knew both the castle and the lake were up here, saw some pictures, but I never realised it was practically in your backyard."

"Well, we're here to protect it."

"And the Veil."

Luna nodded. "Ogres roam the forests, vile and deadly. Dragons rule the skies, strong and temperamental. Our world is rife with danger, but we maintain the balance. Nothing in abundance, especially the dogged pursuit of it, can be good. The people of Ederra have learned that. Our Humans paid the price for it. Tristeans seem not to care for the warnings of the past."

"Is that what the Ama Gorria taught you?"

"Yes. And I have my own eyes to see it. Tristea is a cautionary tale. Without the clear threat of the Darke, Humans have risen to become that threat. After nearly a century in that place, you must've seen it for yourself."

"I have," Gia agreed. "When I arrived in Tristea, it was in the glamour of a Human boy who grew into a Human man."

Luna's brows slightly rose at that, thankful she hadn't needed to deal with that particular glamour, or perhaps it would've made Gia easier to resist. It had reached a point where thoughts of Gia occupied the majority of her day.

"My mother said it would make my life easier," Gia explained. "It had. I was allowed more and better opportunities. So a few decades ago, I joined the military and was deployed for warfare as a medic."

"Sua Orro has told me about recent Human wars."

Gia nodded. "I knew I was meant to be a warrior, to fight and protect. It felt like fulfilling a calling at the time. I thought that perhaps if I couldn't guard a Rift, at least I could do that much."

"But?"

"As a medic, you bear witness to the true cost of war. I soon learned that Humans don't simply fight a common evil. More often than not, the lines are considerably blurred when it came to who the enemy was or why they were even considered the enemy. Fighting their wars brought no sense of accomplishment, only guilt and uncertainty. Terror and nightmares."

Luna sadly shook her head.

"It seems to be only a handful with all the power, while the rest suffer the repercussions of their choices," Gia concluded.

They fell into silence, Luna sneaking looks at Gia, who stood so close their elbows nearly touched. Luna had never thought that simply talking to her this way would bring her such contentment. Learning more about her—her past and opinions—felt like the most precious gift.

"It's strange not seeing the ocean," Gia eventually said.

"You grew up on the coast?"

"I did. But when my mama sent me through the Veil, circumstances took me inland. It took a while to understand Tristea had been torn apart into separate continents."

"Side effects of the spell they'd used to vanquish the Darke."

"I never realised how big Ederra actually was until I travelled across Tristea. So, though I spent most of my life without it, whenever I thought of home, I thought of the ocean, like Ederra was some beautiful little island filled with only happiness."

"It was an adjustment for me to move to our Rift and I had reached adulthood by then. I can't imagine what it must have been like for you, alone in a foreign world, trapped in a body that wasn't your own."

"It helped feeling your joy at times." Gia fully faced her for the first time since they'd stepped out onto the balcony, silver eyes prettily shining. "The Sanctum is beautiful. Your mothers love you so much. I wasn't a happy child, or a happy adult for that matter, but sometimes, before my mood could sink too low, a sudden burst of pure joy would hit me out of nowhere. I know I grew up to resent our connection, which was no fault of yours and entirely the influence of my own issues and insecurities. But as a scared child who had lost everything, stuck in a new world, having you in my heart made me feel less alone. It kept me going, and sometimes thoughts of a gangly little silver-skinned Guardian play-fighting with swords, and weirdly enough, riding unicorns, would be the only thoughts to soothe me enough to eventually fall asleep."

Perhaps if she'd thought about it more, she wouldn't have dared to, but Luna slipped her fingers behind Gia's neck and gently pressed their foreheads together. Gia's eyes fell shut and she exhaled through parted lips. Silver hair tickled Luna's nose and Gia snuggled closer, Luna wrapping her in an embrace. She made herself bigger when smooth obsidian arms encircled her waist and Gia's head rested against her shoulder. The scent of Sweet Alyssum pleasantly wafted up her nostrils.

Gia fit there perfectly, was Luna's only thought as they swayed to the gentle buzz of the magic wildly sparking between them. Her heart was so full, she feared it would burst as it undoubtedly broadcasted her feelings to Gia's cheek resting against her chest. Despite feeling extremely exposed and fearful of frightening Gia away with the intensity of her emotions, her bigger need was to offer comfort, perhaps show an acknowledgment of the life Gia had lived. One so vastly different to her own. A show of appreciation and acceptance of the person Gia had grown into despite all life had thrown at her.

No matter how much she might want to, Luna couldn't change the past for Gia, but she could hold her in that moment, and melted into the embrace, their magic softly glowing beneath the starry moonlit sky.

CHAPTER SIXTEEN

"What do you mean I can't make my barbecue ribs?" Sean confusedly stared at the meat on the counter. "They're delicious. Everyone says so."

Gia wasn't sure who was more nervous about their dinner with Luna: Sean or herself.

"They are, but she doesn't eat meat."

"And you waited until *now* to tell me?"

"It doesn't affect our dinner plans. I was going to make some flatbread paired with curried vegetables and lentils for her."

"Like Ethiopian food?"

"I...I don't exactly remember Ederran recipes, but yeah, what I do remember from the food my mothers made, was that it tasted and was presented similarly to Southeast Asian and Ethiopian food."

Sean nodded sadly and Gia's stomach knotted. "Had I known you planned on preparing an entire pig for her I would've warned you sooner."

He grinned sheepishly and rubbed the back of his neck. "She's a tall lady. I thought she would appreciate the bulk."

Gia laughed. "No meat for her, but thanks for the enthusiasm."

"Is it a her-thing, or a cultural thing?"

"It's a cultural thing."

"But you eat meat."

"Orphanages scraping by don't have the luxury of catering to individual meal preferences, especially not during that time period."

"You never told me that."

"Was ages ago. I quickly learned to eat what I got or risk starving. Eventually I got used to it."

"Sometimes I forget that you're an old woman."

Gia grinned and nudged his shoulder with her own.

"Did you get sick from the food there?"

"Really badly, though the meat was mostly meat flavour from the bones in soups. Or used to make broths and stews. My mother had shown me the glamour and cast a spell to help me understand the language…I—she was hardly in her right mind. I know that now, but there were a lot of things I had to adjust to. And my sunny disposition wasn't really screaming adoptable."

He pressed a kiss to her head. "Do you want to be more vegetarian around here?"

"You smother your vegetables in meat."

"Well, I meant I would support you buying more vegetables and prepare my meat separately."

"I've actually started a garden patch out behind the nursery. It wouldn't hurt to have more veggies on our table, especially with your longevity issues."

"Longevity issues? We can't all be gorgeous immortal beings, you know."

"A pity," Gia said, and laughed at his overembellished scoff. "We can see how it goes. You're getting older, we should be taking better care of you."

He hummed and removed vegetables from the fridge while Gia amusedly watched.

"You know, other people's wives have secret meth labs," he said, "not secret gardens in hopes their partners live longer."

"I enjoy keeping you on your toes."

He flashed her a toothy grin and shuffled the vegetables around, organising them according to colour on the counter.

"So, what am I supposed to call her?"

"*Gerlari Iluna, lur Ederraren Ezpata.*"

"Okay, I try my best to be racially and culturally sensitive, but there's no way I'll be able to learn how to properly pronounce her name before she arrives."

"It's easy to avoid saying someone's name and I'm sure she'll tell you to call her Luna."

"So what I'm getting here is that I shouldn't call her Luna until she tells me to?"

"It's not appropriate without permission, especially when you're not family. It's the standard way non-Guardians address Guardians in Ederra."

"Got it," he said, looking a little green. "Anything else I should know?"

"You're probably the most tactful person I've ever met—"

"You're such a charmer."

She laughed. "And I know how you enjoy playing Elves in those online games and have a fascination with them, but we're not Elves and it's rude to call us that."

He nodded sincerely.

"Most importantly, don't mention her ears. I know you would never, but don't ask to touch them. Don't even look at them if you can help it."

"Is she sensitive about them?"

"No, it's just not appropriate. Like the name thing. It's about manners and being polite."

"Okay, I won't. But do you know why?"

"No, it's something my mothers told me. When I was a baby, I used to suck my thumb and rub the earlobes of whoever was holding me, to fall asleep."

"Aw."

A pang shot through her chest but Gia smiled through it. "They explained that it was okay because we were family, but not to do it to other people. It's just one of those body parts that are private."

"I wish baby pictures of you existed."

"My aunts have paintings and photos. My grandmas too."

"Oh, wow. Am I not allowed to see you even then?"

"It's not that you aren't allowed, Sean…"

"Yeah, yeah, I know. You don't want to bedazzle me with your pretty." He softly smiled. "And you do realise that now you've told me not to look at her ears, that's probably where I'll focus, right?"

Gia laughed again, because yes, that was probably true.

"She's gonna set me on fire, isn't she?"

"Luna's great. It's going to be okay."

"Yeah…" He dubiously said and stared at all the vegetables. "What am I supposed to do with these?"

Gia laughed, having waited for him to admit it. "Go put your ribs on the grill. I'll make the vegetable dishes and a salad for you. Would you like some potato wedges?"

"Yes, please. You're such a good housewife." He pecked her cheek and jumped out of the way before she could hit him.

Sean Williams wouldn't stop staring at her.

It was perhaps easier to tolerate the man who shared a home with her Arima when he looked at her with that idiotic expression. Luna sat at the head of the table where she'd been offered a seat by the Human while Gia was engrossed in the Ederran Black Tulips Luna had brought her, arranging them in a large crystal vase at the centre of the table. Luna found it excruciatingly difficult not to look at her with the same simple wonder he had on his face.

Thankfully, the food that was uncovered offered some distraction. Small and dull looking vegetables and a strangely coloured curry were presented and Gia anxiously watched her for a reaction.

"It smells delicious, Gia," she overstated to offer reassurance.

"Gia?" Sean Williams wondered.

Luna decided not to react and dished some food into her bowl and ignored the animal carcass he placed on his plate. He ate like a starved Dwarf.

"It's a shortening of my name."

"So, short for Argia?"

Gia smiled at him and Luna tensed, not liking that she'd shared her name with him. It was bad enough Luna had to speak his ridiculous language. The words rolled thick and uncomfortably across her tongue.

Why had she ever agreed to come?

Hazel eyes glittered at her and the reciprocal flutter in her stomach reminded Luna of how weak she was.

"I hope you'll like it," Gia said and pushed the plate of flatbread closer to her.

Luna carefully eyed the utensils next to her bowl and reached for the bread.

"Oh shit, wait!" Gia shouted, jumped up and knocked over her chair in the process. "I forgot, sorry," she awkwardly told Luna and hurried toward the kitchen.

Bread hovering over her plate, Luna turned to Sean Williams already watching her, and at her questioning look, he shrugged.

"We'll find out soon enough," he knowingly said and chuckled like he understood Gia in ways she never would. That was the truth, but it didn't stop Luna from wanting to strike him with her magic.

Gia returned, breathless and smiling sheepishly while she carefully placed down a bowl of warm water containing citrus slices, and two neatly folded white cloths. Luna's cutlery was removed too.

"Thank you," she softly said after Gia sat back down and they began eating. The vegetables were adequate and the spices duller than she was used to, but Luna understood there was only so much Gia could do and she had made the food more palatable than expected.

When Gia kept looking at her in concern, Luna smiled. "The meal is wonderful."

She got a bright grin that left her brain spinning, and Sean Williams thankfully stopped her from dumbly basking in it for the rest of the evening.

"I think it's amazing that the Guardians protect Tristea even when it was us who sent the Darke to you in the first place. I'm honestly surprised you didn't just send it right back through the Veil."

"Unlike your kind, we have honour."

"Lu," Gia reprimanded.

"It's fine, Ree. I sort of agree with her. Ederra and Tristea were once mirror worlds, right?"

"Lur Ederra."

"Pardon?"

"Our home is called Lur Ederra. Not Ederra."

"Oh. Okay. Sorry. I didn't mean to offend you."

"Yes. The worlds were once the same."

"And all the magical beings here died?"

Luna bit back her frustration.

Why did he bother asking her things that Gia had evidently already told him? Gia herself offered no input and instead sent him an encouraging smile he anxiously returned. And what exactly did he have to be anxious about when he had *everything*?

"Yes."

"And everything in Ederra—Lur Ederra—is made of magic?"

"It's our life essence. Some of us can wield it, in others the magic is passive. Like unicorns who may heal injured hunters and travellers on occasion, or Dwarves who live for centuries and are immune to most illnesses. The trees pulse with magic. Some, in the most isolated corners of Ederra, are even sentient, as old as the world itself."

Sean Williams's mouth hung open in awe while he listened. "It sounds incredible…Are the Humans there magical too?"

"There are no more Humans left in Ederra."

"Oh…"

"Though before their extinction, a few were able to cast spells and brew potions."

"Maybe I could give it a go." He lightly laughed and Gia did too, which only made Luna less inclined to join them.

She chewed on the miserable piece of orange thing in her mouth, wanting to ask Gia what everything was she'd been served and how she'd prepared the meal. What the vegetables had looked like before she'd chopped them up into unrecognisable pieces. But like with Bo and Ukitu, and with her mothers, like it was everywhere she went, Luna was the odd one out. She only hoped they would allow her to leave after the torturous meal completed.

Sean Williams's kind green eyes still sparkled at her, but he seemed to have overcome some of his compulsory awe.

"The Humans of Tristea don't intrinsically have magic," she told him. "Some have been gifted the ability to cast spells, needing to draw from their environment to give them power. I believe they call them witches."

"You aren't a witch?"

"Do I look like a witch?"

"I don't know what witches look like."

"They look like Humans. As I just said, they are Humans gifted with the ability to cast spells."

"So not all magic was destroyed when they banished the Darke to Lur Ederra then?"

"It was."

"But you said there were still witches here."

"There are."

Sean Williams's brows earnestly furrowed. And despite herself, despite how the evening was going, Luna found that she liked him. He was trying so hard and seemed to possess the patience and determination of a seedling during winter.

"Stop teasing him, Lu."

Gia seemed amused, though, and smiled at her, causing some of the tension to leave Luna's shoulders.

"The Red Mother gave power to a few witches here in Tristea."

"The Red Mother?"

"She's the first Guardian. Her Arima was the one who made the ultimate sacrifice to save us."

"What do you mean?" Gia asked.

"*Elurra Erortzen*, have you heard her name?"

Gia shook her head.

"She was the Elf Queen at the time the Darke was sent through the Veil."

"The Mother of Light?" Gia asked and looked pleased when Luna confirmed with a nod.

"How long ago was that?" Sean Williams asked.

"About ten millennia ago."

"Wow."

"When the Humans of Ederra fell to the Darke, the Elves were targeted next. Elurra Erortzen knew that like the Humans who had sacrificed all magical beings in Tristea to save themselves, she too would need to make a sacrifice to save our world."

"She sacrificed the Elves," Gia whispered as though remembering her lessons.

"The Elves were powerful and Elurra Erortzen only intended to keep the Darke trapped, as destroying it would've required more magic than she could safely harness from our world."

"And so she trapped it beneath Lake *Beltza*," Gia said.

"But she knew that the spell had its flaws, that there were cracks in the containment where some creatures could escape. Thus far, we have only needed to deal with the Husks, but who knows what creatures lurk beneath its surface? And so to protect Ederra, Elurra Erortzen selected three hundred of her best."

"Her best what?" Sean Williams asked, hanging on her every word.

"Her best and strongest warriors. When she drew all of the power from the Elves, she cast her spell on the Darke and bestowed a gift onto her warriors. She made them stronger than they'd ever been and blessed them with longevity. In honour of *Sua Orro*, who she needed to leave behind, she made sure that no Guardian would ever be alone. That she would have a partner to fight beside and protect. From that time forward, each Guardian would forever be born with an Arima to complete her."

"She died? That was her ultimate sacrifice?" Sean Williams asked.

"She'd asked for volunteers and every single one of her people stepped forward. The Sacrifice was made by the entire Elf nation. They died heroes, forever glorified each time the sun rises over an Ederra not plagued by Darkeness. There's no misery in death. Only peace. It's those we leave behind who suffer. Her ultimate sacrifice had been breaking her Arima's heart."

Gia's gaze bored into her own and they both jumped at a loud vibrating sound coming from beside the meat platter on the table.

"Sorry," Sean Williams said. "I know it's rude, but I'm on call at the station and I need to take that."

Luna nodded, confused about what exactly he meant, and watched him walk out with the device pressed to his ear.

Gia had stopped eating and Luna left her to the thoughts of her mothers she was no doubt having, and hoped she hadn't hurt her with her blunt words. She couldn't help but be angry at Gia's mother for sending her away. Sure Gia could understand the language, but Tristea had many things they didn't even have words for. Gia would've needed to learn so much from people who wouldn't have understood why she didn't know.

Sean Williams returned with an apologetic look.

"Drunk and Disorderly down at the docks," he told Gia. "Bunch of college kids have been getting on everyone's last nerve over the long weekend." He then looked to Luna. "It was nice meeting you and really incredible talking to you and learning about your world."

Luna nodded and found a slight but genuine smile curling her lips.

"Maybe next time you'll tell me more about the magic Sorro gave Tristea's Humans to help us restore balance."

She cringed internally and Gia visibly winced at the flippant and incorrect way he addressed the Ama Gorria. His genuine want to learn, though, made it difficult to be angry with him.

"Perhaps I will. There's not much to tell, though. These beings are all still Human with Human vices and flaws. She regrets the power she gave them and could only remedy it by making them foils for one another."

"What kind of beings?"

"Vampires. Werewolves…"

"Are you teasing me again?"

"Perhaps. Perhaps not."

"No seriously, you need to tell me, but next time." He grinned brightly.

"Next time," Luna agreed, unable to say no to him.

"I should get going. Maybe you'll still be here when I get back?" He seemed uncomfortable with that and Luna understood.

"I'll be leaving soon," she reassured. "Be safe, Sean Williams. Thank you for inviting me into your and Gia's home."

"Please call me Sean and you're welcome here any time," he said. Luna was about to extend him the same courtesy of her name, when he kissed Gia's temple.

A sharp pain pierced her chest and she clenched her jaw shut, focusing back on her food.

Dinner had gone much better than expected. Sean was less dazed than expected. Luna was predictably uncomfortable but mostly pleasant. Gia wanted to hug her again for being willing to compromise, but it felt too good to be in Luna's arms and she wasn't entirely sure whether that was appropriate, especially with Sean not there.

Friends hugged, of course, but they didn't hug and have their magic surge and blend and soothe, filling them with so much warmth, comfort, and safety they forgot the outside world existed until the sky started to blaze over the horizon.

Luna quietly washed dishes while Gia dried and packed them away, unsure how to handle Luna in her home. She seemed too big, figuratively, but also very literally. And no matter how elegantly she moved around, she still had to duck through doorways and made their furniture seem small and inadequate.

Impulsively, Gia kicked off her shoes and loosened her clothing before she dropped her glamour. Luna turned to her, pleasantly delighted and smiling as stunningly as she had after their long hug on Luna's balcony the night of the Naming

Ceremony. The mood instantly lightened and they easily spoke about Bo and Ukitu and the sleepless nights they were having, and Gia's visit to her aunts' home in the alpine tundra of the Northern Lands.

They finished in the kitchen too soon and Gia walked her to the door, remembering almost too late that Luna was going through the Veil. She paused in the living room, wanting to ask her to stay, but knowing she shouldn't.

"Thank you for coming tonight," she mumbled.

"Thank you for having me."

She bit her lip, afraid to look at Luna, who she could feel studying her.

"He's a good Human."

"He is."

"If this is what you choose, I'm comforted, at least, that it's with him."

"Thank you, Luna," Gia breathed and hugged her.

They both were controlling their magic, but a pleasant buzz still vibrated between them. It lasted far too long again and Gia was happy that she'd lost the glamour so she wouldn't feel like a child because of her size. Now she could press their cheeks together and curl her arms around the far too familiar frame. Their bodies aligned perfectly and she found her face pressed into Luna's neck inhaling that familiar earthy scent. Her eyes fluttered at the fingers that caringly traced down her back.

Fighting the release of a contented groan, she stiffened and quickly stepped away, staring into Luna's dark smouldering eyes. The urge to kiss her hit her out of nowhere, as did images of that dream which had reoccurred a few more times, though it seemed to flip between different settings around their Rift. They would fly around on their pegasuses before landing at a picturesque spot and instantly grab at each other, kissing feverishly.

"I should go." Luna's voice was low and raspy and she stared at Gia's mouth before she blinked and took a step back. "If you ever have questions about our history, or our present, ask me. Or ask Mom. We'll be happy to tell you."

"Thank you, Luna," Gia replied. She had lost count of how many times she'd thanked Luna that evening, who was only there because Gia had asked her to be.

A melancholy smile tilted Luna's lips. "Anything for you, Gigi," she all but whispered and stepped back through the Veil.

CHAPTER SEVENTEEN

Lust was a foreign feeling for Gia. It was distracting and confusing, often times inconvenient, yet it was also fascinating the way her body would heat at the mere thought of Luna or in remembrance of one of the dreams she'd been constantly having of the two of them together. Her days were spent longing for intimacy and drowning in guilt, this despite her relationship with Sean seemingly better than ever.

Life was strange. When she wasn't being distracted by Luna or dodging wedding planning with Sean, she spent time in her garden at the nursery, either practising her magic or tending her plants. It was a warm day, yet dark clouds had gathered and thunder sounded in the distance. She couldn't wait for the storm to finally reach them, hoping she would still be outside when the rain started. In contrast to many of the Human children she knew of, thunderstorms had always calmed her when she was younger. They still did.

"Do you know what love is, Argia Erretzea?"

Gia jumped at the sudden voice behind her where she'd been carefully tying a Nigra Hollyhock to a stalk. She turned to the Red Mother standing tall and out of place in her garden and immediately knelt again.

"Rise up and answer me, child."

Gia obediently rose, eyeing the red robes and hair that made the Elf look like a medieval Tristean cult leader. "Why are you asking me that?"

"Do you know how to recognise it in others?"

Gia frowned.

"Are you able to recognise it in yourself?"

"Why are you here, Ama Gorria?"

"Curiosity."

"About me?"

"Certainly. And how this world has dulled you."

Gia scowled.

"No offense intended but Guardians are intuitive beings."

"We are."

"And yet here you are."

Gia's scowl deepened. "Have you come here only to insult me, Ama Gorria?"

"I have come to thank you."

Taken aback, Gia could only stare.

"Had you not encased yourself in layers upon layers of sorrow and fear, I would never have had the opportunity to get to know my little warrior."

Gia's spine went rigid. "What do you mean 'get to know' her?"

"I mean what I said."

"What—were—are you two…have you been—"

"Spending time with her while you hide? Yes."

"And how have you two been spending your time together exactly?"

"Now, why dear, would you feel yourself entitled to that information?"

"*You* brought it up!"

"I only thanked you."

"Please leave. I don't need this in my life on top of everything else."

"From reverent to insolent. You are a unique creature, Argia Erretzea. Perhaps your time in Tristea has prepared you for the future."

"You see the future?"

"I learn. I predict. I revel in surprises. And you have certainly been a pleasant one."

"I have?"

"Hm. Do you know what love is?"

"What is it with you and love?"

"Do you know how it sparks? How it grows? How it's sustained?" She stepped closer, towering over Gia. "You were taken from us too soon."

Gia hung her head.

"Have you not learned the difference between love and sex?"

"I know the difference."

"Then tell me, when does a Guardian fall in love with her Arima?"

"After our Initiation, when we meet at our Rift…"

The Ama Gorria shook her head.

"No?"

"You know when. You know why. You know how."

"We meet at the Sanctum or at our Rift where we touch and it sparks our attraction."

"You insult the memory of my Arima."

"What? How? I'm sorry, but I didn't—"

Sua Orro laughed lightly. "Our love was pure."

"I'm certain it was, Ama Gorria."

"It was also dark and passionate."

"Oh."

"It was desire and anguish." She looked Gia over. "How does love grow?"

"Through spending time together and getting to know each other."

"And when do you learn to know your Arima?"

Gia knew it wasn't the answer she wanted to hear, but it was the only one she had. The Red Mother really was as mad as they said. "After the Meeting, when you start your life together."

Her breath caught when the Ama Gorria stepped forward and placed a hand over her heart, effortlessly removing Gia's glamour who then stood two feet taller. She didn't remove her hand and Gia's heart raced, not out of fear, but at the raw power radiating from the ancient Elf.

"When do you learn to know your Arima?" Sua Orro softly asked, a pale finger lightly tapping against Gia's obsidian chest.

Gia gasped and the Red Mother smiled before stepping away. A large circular portal appeared beside her, edged with red flames.

"May you have sweet dreams, Argia Erretzea," she said and stepped through the Veil.

* * *

"Wait! They're still—" Gia sighed when Sean sucked a sharp breath through his teeth, jerking his hand back from the hot tray. "Come, let me see."

He reluctantly held out his hand and looked forlornly at the cookies. "You're making them for Luna?"

"How'd you know?"

"She mentioned liking them after dinner the other night. I think she liked that red wine too."

Gia studied his face. He didn't seem angry or jealous, only curious. "Yeah, she did like the wine too."

"Does she have a birthday?"

"A Name Day. Dated from when she was assigned her role and given her name."

"I think I'll get her a few bottles for her Name Day. When is it?"

Gia was about to stare at him some more, when she sensed the foreign magic on his skin and tilted her head, studying his fingers that should have at least been reddish and swollen.

"Is there a shield on you?"

He pulled his hand back and awkwardly grinned. "A protection spell."

"Who?"

"Luna came by the station last night, almost had me falling off my chair in surprise because she appeared out of thin air. Luckily Sarah was out getting us some snacks."

"Guardians don't cast spells, save for glamour and cloaking in case they need to come to Tristea and hunt down the Darke. And though I've seen her cast before, this isn't Luna's magic, Sean."

"She told me that. Said you were wielders not casters," he said with a dopey grin, still mildly starstruck.

Dropping his hand, Gia latched onto her braid. "You two hang out now?"

"No, that was the only time I've seen her aside from the two times she came for dinner here."

"So she showed up randomly at your place of work and somehow cast a protection spell on you with someone else's magic?"

"She brought a redheaded woman—Guardian—with her."

"The Ama Gorria?" she asked, recognising the magic.

"Yeah, sorry. It's really difficult to remember the names and you say them so fast. Maybe it'll help if you wrote them down for me?"

"The Ama Gorria cast a protection spell on you?"

His smile dropped and he must've noted her agitation. "Yeah. Was that a bad thing?"

"Why would they do that?"

"Um, should I be hurt and offended that you don't want me to have a protection spell?"

Some of the tension left her at his teasing smile and she lightly laughed while she made sure his fingers really were okay. But if it was the Red Mother who cast it, he would definitely be safe. "I was just wondering about their reasoning. I've heard that the Red Mother doesn't really mingle with people."

"She seemed close with Luna. Do you think they're seeing each other?"

Gia scowled. "I told you, we can't be attracted to other people."

"Sexually," he said and took his hand back.

"You know what I meant, Sean."

"Actually, I'm not sure why you're acting so slighted by this."

"I just want to know why things are happening and would appreciate people not being cryptic about it!"

"Why is this a puzzle to you? You love me, they care about you, so they wanted to protect me. At least, that's what Luna said. Why does there have to be more to it?"

"People don't just do nice things for no reason."

"I knew you were a cynic, but come on, Ree, are you that blind? Do you really not see when people love you and want you to be happy?"

"Why does everyone keep asking me whether I know what love is?"

He shook his head. "I'm going to work."

"Please don't leave like this." Her constant confusion and guilt wasn't his fault.

"I'm not mad."

"Yeah, but your face says you're disappointed and that's far worse."

"Do you know why I'm disappointed?"

"Because I questioned the actions of a couple of good Samaritans?"

"Think about it, because I really do need to get to work. We can talk tomorrow," he said, already walking to the front door with Gia following after him.

"How strong is this spell?"

"Luna said it's only some light healing and shielding. Won't stop a bullet to my chest from doing damage, but it could keep me alive longer than usual. Should prevent me from getting sick, too. Apparently, they can't just make me invincible and leave me to become a medical miracle, or a government lab rat should anyone find out. Which is probably for the best, or I might've been compelled to get a spandex outfit and become a superhero." He placed his fists on his hips in a power pose and flashed his dimples at her. Gia's entire mood lifted, laughing even as she shook her head at him.

"Okay, Superman. I'll thank Luna when I see her in the morning. Whatever the reason, I'm glad she thought to do it."

"Ah, that's more like it," he said and pulled her into his side, kissing her head. "Remember to take pics of your armour when you get it, since I'm forbidden from seeing you in it."

"You know why you can't see me."

"Not sure how I can be any more in awe and in love with you than I already am, but okay."

"Very smooth."

"I know."

Gia laughed and stood in the doorway after he exited.

"Stop worrying so much," he said from the pathway. "I think this is working out."

"Looks like it, yeah," Gia agreed, though she seemed the only one to feel unsettled by Sean and Luna's...*contentment* with the situation.

"You've been sleepwalking less."

"Yeah, I have," she agreed stiffly, knowing he thought it meant that she was settling in Bluewater Bay with him, but she was starting to suspect it was because she'd been spending her nights with Luna in her dreams.

* * *

Her armour wasn't ready yet and the Rift was quiet. She had no reason to be in Ederra, and yet there Gia was, a basket under an obsidian arm while she picked the giant yellow tomatoes that grew in Luna's garden. The Guardian herself was dressed in a pair of black breeches and vest, her long silver arms dirty and glittery with perspiration as she planted seeds in a freshly treated garden patch.

Gia bit her lip and continued her search for ripe tomatoes, attempting to condition her brain that the red ones were too young to pick.

"How do you keep animals out of your garden?" she wondered out loud, staring through the fruit trees in the orchard to the forest just beyond, teeming with wildlife.

"Sua Orro has placed a shield around my house to keep them out."

Gia swallowed down her jealousy at the name and focused on the way Luna's sinewy arms flexed as she picked up a basket laden with the vegetables she'd harvested, then followed her to the back porch where two basins sat on a long counter.

"You and the Ama Gorria placed a protection spell on Sean."

Luna paused from setting vegetables in one basin to be rinsed. "Did I overstep?"

Gia shook her head. "I was only wondering why you would go out of your way like that."

"He's important to you." She passed Gia the large green equivalent of what she thought was a pumpkin, or might have been a squash. It was all so very confusing and felt like learning her vegetables all over again. She hadn't paid that much attention when her mothers had prepared meals, opting to rather play outside until she was called in for dinner.

"Well, thank you for doing it. Humans are very fragile," she said and examined the supposed pumpkin, trying to remember what it tasted like. After finding no rot, she placed it in a basket on the counter and tilted her head at Luna. "Does the Ama Gorria also keep the insects from destroying your crops?"

Luna softly laughed and Gia's insides quivered at her smile.

Stepping further down the long counter, Luna retrieved a glass spray bottle filled with shiny purple fluid from the cabinet beneath the sinks.

"I use this magical repellent the Faeries make, but the alchemists in Erdiko have some potions too that they use on their crops. Those are mostly for large-scale farming, when you'll need to use a lot of it."

Gia nodded and continued to sort the vegetables into three baskets. "And what do the Faeries require as payment? My mothers warned me to leave them as a last resort."

"Perhaps they meant the Pixies? They do tend to try and trick you as you believe them harmless because of their size. The Tuatha Dé Danann, however, trade in precious and rare metals as payment for their potions and spells. Sometimes they'll settle for a favour if they have a problem that needs solving. Well, the Fae of Falias, Gorias, and Finias are open to trade. Murias has been closed to outsiders for nearly four millennia."

She *had* confused them with pixies. Gia remembered learning about the Pixies because a couple had tried to nest in their flower garden, which had resulted in a week-long negotiation to get them to leave and Gia being heartsore, not seeing the problem with their presence. They were cute. Tiny. The size of an adult Guardian's thumb with dragonfly wings. One had played with her and enjoyed eating passion fruits nearly as much as she did.

Nodding slowly, Gia swallowed the knot in her throat and quietly continued her vegetable sorting, grateful when Luna let her be and focused on her rinsing. She wracked her brain for recollections of her childhood. She'd suppressed so much, but the more time she spent in Ederra and with Luna, the more memories would invade her mind at random.

"What do you do with the ones that have too much rot?" she asked to get out of her head.

"I'll add them to my compost heap later," Luna said and picked up one of the baskets Gia had separated.

They walked around the house toward the stables where the trough stood that Gia had crafted with Luna's help. She was grateful to have been allowed the contribution and was proud that something she had made was there.

Luna handed over the basket and she grinned, filling the trough with vegetables while the pegasuses trotted over in excitement at the treat.

"Have you named him yet?" Gia asked, brushing her fingers down the beautiful black pegasus's flank.

"Trumoi," Luna murmured. "You?"

Her throat tightened. "Tximista."

"They match."

"They do," Gia agreed, not the least bit surprised.

"I need to go to Erdiko to pick up some armour pieces I'd left for repairs. Your armour isn't ready yet, but would you like to come with me?"

And just like that, Gia's day got even better.

They exited into what looked like the fancy lobby of a bank without windows. A grey marble floor, white pillars, and various potted plants were set up throughout the large square room and stood directly opposite a set of double doors. Behind them was the mirror they'd just exited, the length and width of two Guardian-size doorways. It was the biggest free-standing mirror she'd ever seen.

"Wow," Gia mumbled when the rippling surface settled and reflected the two of them in their matching robes. She had to look away at how good they looked together, like a two-piece puzzle.

"It's to easily transport large items home. Furniture, for example."

"Does it matter if you don't have a big one like that at home? Or would you get stuck if you tried to squeeze through too much?"

Luna smiled. "Imagine this room as being the inside of a bottle. It squeezes you like a sponge through a bottle neck that is the mirror portal and pops you out safely on the other side with everything you entered with intact. The only consideration you would need to worry about, would be having enough space for your cargo on the other side."

Gia hummed in understanding and followed her to where the sun shone through the stained glass in the wooden double doors. Luna held one open for her and she stepped through, mechanically descending the steps while gawking at her surroundings and halted on a paved sidewalk.

Erdiko was not a village but a bustling city.

Gia wasn't sure what she'd expected, but the engraved sign on the small building they'd exited read *Erdiko Village* and she had to accept that it was simply a name and not a designation.

The street was lined with storefronts that had neat signage on their front windows, product displays behind them, and buildings made of stone, some towering at least forty stories high. For all the colour in Ederra's plant life, the architecture was all sleek greys or dark browns, framed by silver or gold. Simple yet elegant. The roads were lined with prettily patterned paving stones, the surfaces as flat and smooth as the walls of the buildings.

Bicycles, motorcycles, and cars—or maybe she should call them automobiles—passed them by. The city was glamourized in an Art Deco design reminiscent of 1920's France, yet somehow modernised, as everything looked shiny and brand new, made with the most lavish materials.

"What do you use for fuel?" Gia asked, having noticed how soft the vehicle engines were as they drove past.

"Enchantments," Luna proudly answered, lips curled in a smile, patiently waiting for Gia to finish taking in everything.

The people gave them a wide berth, but it was obviously out of respect rather than fear. The sidewalk was full of pedestrians glancing in their direction and then promptly away again. Most were dressed in tunics, wraparound dresses, cotton-like suits, shirts and jackets made for comfort and luxury. Everyone seemed wealthy and healthy.

Across the busy street, on the front steps of the tailor's shop, a small green goblin child wearing an orange sundress unabashedly stared at them. Gia flashed her a smile and her eyes grew wide before she let out an excited squeal and ran into the shop, peals of laughter reaching them over the din of the crowd.

The Dwarves and Goblins made up half of the crowd but when Gia's stare made brief contact with a pair of amber eyes and slanted pupils, her gaze flickered across the people she'd thought of as Human, forgetting for a moment that Luna had said they were extinct in Ederra.

"When I was younger," she softly said, "I visited a few villages with my mothers. When I arrived in Tristea, I thought the people I'd seen there were Human. It made the Tristeans feel less foreign to me."

They weren't Human, though. Their ears were larger, pointed to various degrees, blunter at the tips and shorter than a Guardian's, arching away from their heads. Some were really tall and slender with sharper facial features, but most ranged between five and six feet, all with Human-like skin and colour tones.

"Halflings," Luna said, lowering her voice for what Gia could only imagine was discretion's sake. "From a time when Humans lay with Elves in secret. It was taboo. Some of their offspring that survived until birth and could pass as either Elf or Human remained in society, but those with the eye mutation, especially, were left in the forest to perish, while the fortunate ones were discovered and raised by the Tuatha Dé Danann."

Gia blinked dumbly, not having expected such a morbid origin story.

"Nice of the Faeries to take them in."

Luna shook her head. "They raised them to be…servants. That word best describes what they were, I think. Once they were old enough, they were sent about on errands, often assigned to be gatekeepers intercepting those in search of Fae help."

"Oh."

"They received food and shelter in return and could leave whenever they pleased. But where would they have gone when their existence was seen as an abomination? That was until the Darke Blight spread across Ederra and the Faerie wards kept them safe from the Corruption. Once there were no more Humans and Elves to reject and ridicule them for simply existing, they found each other and built villages and started families. They're not much half of anything anymore, a people on their own. But they go by that name to remind themselves, and I suppose us too, of their history and the reason they'd been spared."

"Good for them," Gia said.

Luna smiled, hooked their arms together and set off down the street while Gia practically floated beside her at the touch. The armourer was situated in a quiet street and Gia wondered whether it would be okay to take pictures on her phone so she could show Sean. She would need to remember to bring the device with her next time.

"Guardian Luna!" a Dwarf greeted when they entered his shop, bowing to them both, which was weird and a little cringy.

"Torsten," Luna returned with a smile, placing a hand on his shoulder. He seemed to grow taller beneath the touch. "Please meet Argia Erretzea, Shield of Lur Ederra."

"A pleasure to finally meet you Argia Erretzea, Shield of Lur Ederra."

"Please, call me Gia," she said. "Luna tells me you're the best armourer in all of Ederra."

Torsten seemed to bloom under the praise. Short and stout, he stood nearly as tall as their hips, and let out a hearty chuckle as he stroked his long red beard that hung down to his navel. Did Dwarves have navels? "You will be able to judge that for yourself once I complete your armour, Guardian Gia."

"I'm sure it will be perfect."

Noticing the line forming outside as people waited to enter, presumably only after the two of them had left again, Luna and Torsten got down to business.

Payment was made in runestones from a small velvet bag Luna retrieved from the leather satchel that hung across her shoulder and where she'd placed her repaired gear pieces. They sounded like marbles, which alerted Gia that they weren't the gold coins she'd expected.

The coins weren't a worldwide currency, but merchants accepted them from Guardians as they were exchangeable at any bank. According to Uda, they were easiest to gather and store in bulk at the Sanctum and distribute as stipends amongst the Guardians to assist their cost of living.

"Where do you get runestones and is it the preferred currency for armourers?" Gia asked when they were out on the street again.

"Not usually, some of the runes served as payment for the repairs, but most will be used to make enchantments for your armour so Torsten may complete it sooner. I saved him from waiting on their arrival by travelling to a few reliable merchants to trade for them myself. Though if you don't want to trade for them, you may attempt to mine our land or apply for a permit to become a miner. Then you'll need to get them enchanted too."

"What can I do to repay you?"

Luna smiled softly and shook her head. "A Guardian's armour is always a gift. You're simply receiving what's owed to you."

Gia's heart tightened, understanding dawning. Her mothers or zaindarias would've gotten her the armour. It was a rite of passage during the Initiation Ceremony when a Guardian was assigned to a Rift.

"Thank you," she softly murmured, nearly stumbling over thin air when Luna's fingers entwined with her own, like it was something natural they often did.

"Are you hungry?" Luna asked.

Gia finally looked away from their hands to see they stood in between a park and a row of street vendors on the broad sidewalk. She'd skipped breakfast in her rush to get to Luna, and by the looks of the sun, it was already nearing dusk.

"I could eat. Why don't you pick for us?"

Luna brightened at the challenge and marched off, the amber eyes of the six Halfling vendors glowed with anticipation. She chose a dark-skinned Halfling with a red painted cart to offer her patronage to and stood behind two dwarves waiting in the queue. As one, they casually turned and went to stand behind Luna, staring up at her back in awe. The Halfling woman was equally as starstruck with her lovesick eyes, and Gia wondered whether she herself looked that pitiful.

Spending time with Luna was dangerous. Her reasoning at first had been to desensitise herself to her presence, but it had the complete opposite effect. The more time they spent together, the more time she wanted to spend with Luna. She'd tried telling Sean, but he was so happy with the way everything was seemingly going that Gia decided to give it a bit more of a chance.

Thinking about it made her mood plummet fast, guilt settling like a rock in her stomach.

Luna appeared in front of her again, smiling tentatively and holding out a wrap, and instantly Gia's insides lightened at the mere sight of her face. She nearly rolled her eyes at herself, only stopping because she was afraid Luna would misinterpret it as a slight against her.

They strolled down the pathway beside the park while they ate in comfortable silence. The wraps had been made to accommodate their size. The vegetables in it were bright, colourful, and strange looking, so she decided to simply take a bite, humming softly when she tasted avocado, persimmon, something like garlic, lemon and ginger. Perhaps some corn and…mushrooms? She wasn't entirely sure, but it was delicious.

"Good?" Luna checked and Gia immediately nodded.

"Very. Thank you."

Seemingly pleased, Luna went back to her own wrap, leaving Gia to her curious staring around the city. She tried to find something lacking, something Tristea had that Ederra didn't, and when the blazing red sun disappeared behind Mount Bularreko, casting the city in its shadow, streetlights flickered on and soft lights glowed in the building windows.

"Dwarves are amazing engineers," Luna proudly stated, before she could even ask.

Uncertain whether it was coincidence, or if Luna had timed it that way, they entered the building with the large mirror just as Gia finished her last bite. Crumpling up the wrapper, she looked for a bin and threw it in the one she saw near the door. On the other side of the entrance was what looked like a large chalice, coming up to her hip, filled to the brim with gold coins and nuggets she hadn't noticed on their arrival.

She rose her eyebrows at Luna, who was already watching her.

"Donations."

"To the Guardians?"

"We don't ask, but the Guardians who train and live at the Sanctum are all tasked to monitor mirrors around the world for attacks by Darke Husks and Thralls. The less we need to worry about farming, gathering and mining, the more we may focus on protecting the people of Ederra. I assume that's their reasoning. Perhaps some just need to show some form of gratitude."

Gia frowned. "I'm sorry if this is a stupid question, but I thought the Darke escaped Lake Beltza and then went to the Rift that pulled them most?"

"Those are the ones headed back to Tristea. We've always had our own Darke to deal with here in Ederra too."

It made sense and Gia nodded, but she froze when Luna stepped closer and her thumb brushed the corner of her mouth. Softly gasping, she watched Luna place that same thumb in her mouth, licking off the sauce she'd presumably removed from Gia's face, and then Luna's eyes widened. "I'm so sorry, I don't know why I did that."

Laughing through a tight throat, Gia shook her head. "It's okay." It really shouldn't be, but at least they hadn't kissed each other again and it was only natural for slip-ups to happen. Right? Gia didn't want to obsess over it. She could leave that for the following day or even later that night when she was back home.

"Thank you for bringing me with you today. I had a great time."

Luna immediately lightened, though she still seemed a little tense and wary. "It's been a while since I enjoyed the city. I can't remember when last I wasn't simply in and out of whichever shop I came to."

"We should definitely come again. I would love to see more of the park."

She regretted the words the instant they left her mouth, not because she didn't mean them wholeheartedly, but because she knew she shouldn't have said them out loud. The smile Luna gave her though, made it worth it.

CHAPTER EIGHTEEN

Gia's face was adorably scrunched in concentration while she intently listened to Uda explaining something in the training yard at the Sanctum. A small smile tilted Luna's lips, entirely captivated by the way Gia moved. Her magic surged to life, an aura of pink glowing around her silver robes, beautifully contrasting against her obsidian skin.

Uda was attempting to teach her how to turn her naturally defensive magic into offensive attacks. It took Shields decades to learn the technique and even longer to master it, but already Gia showed immense progress and promise.

Chest expanding along with her grin, Luna remembered too late that she wasn't alone in that little corner of the training yard, and she slowly turned toward Saso, copper eyes watching her with a clear look of worry.

Clearing her throat, Luna picked up the blanket they'd brought and spread it open across the patch of soft grass beneath a large, blue-leafed maple tree. Saso joined her, placing the picnic basket down beside the blanket and they silently unpacked the food.

"She's powerful," Saso said. "It must be all those repressed feelings longing for escape."

Luna's shoulders hunched and she bit her lip, concentrating on gathering the plates from the basket.

"You may say what's truly on your mind, Mama," she said, carefully placing the jug of passion fruit juice on a wooden board.

"What are you doing, Lulu?"

For a moment she considered being flippant and stating that she was packing out their lunch, but that approach had never worked on this particular mother.

"I honestly have no idea."

"This can't be good for you, darling. Are you two friends now? I'm sorry, but I just don't understand how that's possible."

"We're building a friendship."

"And you're all right with that?"

"I don't have much of a choice, do I?"

Saso stared at her for a long moment. Luna had run out of things to unpack and warily met her concerned stare.

"What about what you want?"

"I can't have what I want."

"And you want this?"

"I want her to be happy," Luna mumbled and crossed her legs beneath her on the blanket. "A part of me hopes that if she spends enough time with me, she will eventually come to love me," she admitted, her throat tight over the words. "Another part dreads that she never will and I'll have to watch her build a life with someone else, probably start a family. I know they can't have children of their own, but they could adopt. She would be a child's mother that wasn't mine."

"And what will you do then?"

"I don't know, Mama. It hurts being apart from her and it hurts to be with her and not hers. What are my other options?"

"Lulu," Saso breathed, her gaze filled with a pained sorrow. She reached for her but stopped when she saw Uda and Gia approaching. Uda's arm was slung over Gia's shoulders and both were grinning broadly. Even that caused an ache in Luna's chest, yet she smiled when Gia dropped into a sitting position on the blanket beside her, so close their shoulders brushed. She couldn't look at Saso and instead focused on filling a plate when the scent of Sweet Alyssum warmly embraced her.

"She's getting better," Uda announced.

Saso offered no comment. She hardly ever addressed Gia unless absolutely necessary.

Gia tensed though and frowned at the blanket. "I need to practice more," she said and Uda took her hand, Gia's shoulders loosening at the touch.

"No need to push yourself so hard, darling. You're making excellent progress."

Gia smiled at Uda, then looked to Luna through silver lashes. "Well, someone needs to protect this one while she attempts to save every single magical creature enthralled by the Darke." Gia nudged her shoulder against Luna's and her skin burned where they briefly touched, her cheeks growing just as hot. Wordlessly, she passed the plate of food to Gia.

"Thank you," Gia said and sent her the softest of smiles that made Luna's heart ache all over.

"Honestly, it's what worried me most with her alone out there," Uda agreed. "She would risk her life to save them."

"It's what makes her so wonderful," Gia carelessly remarked and popped a piece of fruit between grinning teeth.

Feeling heat to the tips of her ears, Luna looked down at her own plate and continued to avoid Saso's intense gaze on her.

* * *

A slight breeze rustled between the purple leaves of the Passion Fruit tree and fluffy white clouds floated against an orange sky. Their robes lay spread out across the golden grass to dry beneath the blazing red sun.

Gia sat in a pair of white shorts and a vest, with her back against the tree. Luna lay stretched out on her back, dressed similarly, with her head in Gia's lap. They'd gone swimming in the river and decided to eat some fruit and let themselves dry before they went back home.

"My mothers loved swimming," Gia murmured, running her fingers through Luna's hair who intently stared up at her and listened. "They met when they were children and grew up together."

"Part of the same Circle?"

Gia nodded. "The Circle of the Sanctum. They grew up as neighbours in the cabins by the lake," she said and attempted to keep the tension from hunching her shoulders. She had visited with her grandmothers the day before and they had pictures of her mothers and a young Gia everywhere. More memories had come flooding in and Gia had left their pretty home against the slopes overlooking Lake Beltza feeling emotionally drained, her mood only lifted when Luna had taken one look at her and decided they needed to go swimming.

"Their mothers made sure they saw each other often. They went to do their Practicum together as they'd been born only weeks apart and had their Initiation Ceremonies on the same day. Their bond was strong."

Luna took Gia's hand that wasn't stroking her hair and entwined their fingers on top of her stomach, lightly squeezing.

"The day the Darke attacked I was obviously at home, big enough to not be taken to my grandmothers or zaindarias. They hadn't been gone long and I was playing outside, the wyverns guarding me, when they grew restless, clearly in distress. I climbed on one and they flew to the Rift. A Husk floated in the air and a Dragon Thrall lay dead beside my mom's body—"

She swallowed thickly, watching the gold-tinted tears that silently streaked down Luna's temples, dark irises reflecting the sadness in Gia's heart.

"My mama stood frozen and staring at Mom, her armour was mangled and she was clearly injured and bleeding. Her wyvern swooped down and pushed her out of the way when the Husk attacked and she only lay there when the wyvern covered her with his own body. The one I rode landed beside my mom and I jumped off and screamed for Mama to get up. Her eyes were glazed and she stared right at me as though I wasn't there and when the Darke screeched again, I put up a shield. Some of the Darke lightning got through and hit her, but it seemed to snap her out of her trance and she looked at me in terror, got to her feet and then drew her sword. I tried to shield her best I could…"

"You did great," Luna thickly rasped. "You both survived."

Gia nodded shakily and wiped her tears with the hand not desperately clinging onto Luna's and took a deep breath, before lightly laughing. "I don't know why I'm still crying about it."

"You can allow yourself to be sad sometimes."

Gia smiled and gently brushed Luna's tears away too.

"We buried Mom. Mama explained to me what would happen to her. We spent three days at home after that while she made preparations for me. She made me food, but didn't eat herself. I don't think she slept at all. I heard her speaking to my grandmothers and lying to them that everything was fine. I thought about calling them too but Mama forbade me and I listened. Part of me was afraid of her, I suppose. Of how she increasingly wasn't feeling like my mama anymore. She taught me the glamour spell, took me through the Veil, and told me that she wanted me to live a good life, free of the Arima bond."

Luna drew their entwined hands up to her lips and kissed Gia's knuckles. "I'm sure there were many, but what was the biggest thing you needed to adjust to?"

Gia thought on it a moment. So many things had been new and foreign. "Visually? I think the sky was startling the first time I saw it. Maybe in combination with the lack of colour."

Luna nodded as though she might have experienced the same.

"Emotionally…I had never been around that many people so consistently before and yet I felt more alone than ever…"

"I wish I could've protected you."

"You were a child too, and I survived."

Luna shook her head and placed their hands back on her stomach. "I should've searched every corner of Tristea. I should've trusted what the bond was trying to tell me."

"You didn't think any Guardian would willingly live in Tristea."

"I didn't, but I should've done more instead of only waiting."

"I would've run from you then too."

Luna smiled. "You're aloof like that. It's one of my favourite things about you."

"That I hurt you?"

Luna shook her head. "That you stand your ground in the face of everything and everyone."

"You like that I'm stubborn?"

"Very much. It's how I know that any time you spend with me is because you want to, and I treasure it even more."

Gia huffed. "Why do you say things like that?"

"True things?"

"You make it so difficult, Lu."

"I make what difficult?"

"Staying away from you."

"Do you want me to apologise for that?" she asked with a gorgeous grin that made Gia's stomach swoop. "Watching you discover our world anew makes me feel young again."

"I feel young again, too. I didn't realise how much I missed Ederra. How much I didn't know."

Luna hummed. "I love seeing our world through your eyes."

Gia sighed and ran her fingers through the inky abyss of Luna's voluminous hair. "You're too beautiful," she whispered. "Sometimes it hurts just looking at you."

Luna's smile tilted sideways and she placed their hands on her chest where her heart steadily thumped away. "You don't know the things you do to my heart."

"You have my stomach in constant knots," Gia confessed. "It aches when I'm missing you, or thinking about you."

Luna laughed lightly, squeezing Gia's hand and her stomach did another painful swoop.

"It's funny, isn't it?"

"What's funny?" Gia whispered, lost in the serenity of Luna's face.

"How quickly it can go from feeling great and exciting to a terrifying, yearning desire."

Gia hummed. "Do you yearn for me often?"

"Every single moment of the day. Sometimes so much I can't stop touching myself."

"What?" Gia gaped and stared into the dark eyes that heatedly met her gaze.

When she remained dumbstruck, Luna tilted her head and her brows furrowed. "Is that not appropriate?"

"Is what, exactly, not appropriate?"

"Pleasuring myself to thoughts of you."

Slowly closing her mouth Gia began stroking Luna's hair again, as though she was a house cat curled in her lap. Those twinkling eyes made her feel abruptly warmer. "A-Are you asking for permission to think of me when you do it?"

"I guess so. Had I known I needed permission, I would have asked you sooner."

"I don't think you need permission, but thank you for asking." Another bright grin made Gia's breath catch and her brain stutter. "W-What do you think about?"

The grin grew lopsided and Luna shyly glanced away, playing with Gia's fingers still resting on her chest. "Things…"

Gia laughed and awkwardly bent down to place a kiss on her brow. "Sounds very salacious."

Luna hummed, her eyes shutting at the brief kiss before they lazily fluttered open again. "I think of you kissing me."

"On your brow?"

"Everywhere."

Gia drew in a sharp breath, eyes raking over Luna's damp body. "What else?"

"Your hands on me."

"Where?" she whispered.

Against her hand Luna's heart beat faster before she moved Gia's hand and placed it over her breast.

A strangled whine squeezed past Gia's nose and throat.

Biting her lip, Luna dazedly nodded and pushed her breast into Gia's trembling hand. "It feels so much better when it's your hand."

"Is it okay, would you mind…" Dark eyes twinkled up at her. "May I touch myself too, thinking of you?"

"Yes," Luna breathed, raising up and kissing her in one smooth motion.

Gia's hand twisted into Luna's hair while her other palmed the breast it keenly cupped. Luna's nipple strained through the light fabric of her vest and pressed against her palm. Gia lightly pinched it and trembled when Luna moaned into the kiss, moving closer, making Gia's stomach pleasantly tighten. She squeezed her thighs together, hot and aching.

"Wait," Gia said and frowned, not ceasing the movement of her hands on Luna's breasts. "Why do you need permission to touch yourself thinking of me when you can just touch me and I can touch you?"

Another gentle kiss was pressed to her lips before Luna pulled back and sadly smiled as she stroked Gia's cheek. "Because this is only a dream, Gigi."

Gia's eyes tore open, heart hammering and chest heaving. She glanced next to her where the bed was empty and it took too long to remember Sean was on night shift. Rubbing her thighs together, her arousal had yet to abate and she was uncertain whether it was more exciting to be touched in the dream or the idea that Luna might be masturbating at that very moment, thinking of her.

Without thought, her hand slid into her underwear and she nearly cried out when her fingers slipped over slick wetness. She removed her hand and got out of bed.

Awkwardly and quickly, she padded out the door and down the hall, lowering her glamour when she stepped into the guest room. She locked the door, pressed her forehead to her arm resting against it, and shoved her hand into her too tight underwear.

* * *

Luna wasn't home yet when Gia arrived at the cottage. She could feel her and there was no call of distress, so she didn't worry too much. Instead, she walked to Luna's bedroom and opened the wardrobe where the choice of clothes Luna had given her hung on the left side in a space of their own.

She absently pulled on a silver dress, eyeing the window seat and a second armour display stand that had been set up. Both were empty, matching perfectly, and Gia wasn't comfortable with checking the drawers to see if Luna's leg and arm pieces were in there.

She frowned when she remembered the first home she'd bought in Tristea. It was a small apartment, and she had hated everything about it, save for the window seat, where she'd spent countless hours reading and staring out over the harbour.

Feeling Luna's approach, she attempted to school her features and walked down the hall, out the front door and onto the porch. In the sky, the black pegasus approached with blue-tipped wings expanded. Luna was beautifully illuminated in the flames and the moonlight, hair blowing back from her face during the gliding descent. They landed down the pathway and Luna dismounted in a gorgeous flutter of black robes, a large trunk in her hands.

Gia sucked in a breath and mechanically returned the happy grin she received when Luna floated up the path, lugging the trunk along that no doubt contained Gia's armour set.

"Sorry to keep you waiting. The Tuatha Dé Danann don't like mirror portals in or near their lands so I was forced to fly there," she explained and walked up the steps, kissing Gia on the cheek before making her way inside.

Slowly recovering from the shock of the casualness and realisation that they'd greeted each other like that for a while now, mostly accompanied by a hug, Gia followed after her into the living room.

"I thought you went to see Torsten?"

"I did," Luna replied, placing the case on the coffee table. It covered more than half of the length and hung over the edges. "His enchantments are excellent but I had the Faeries place some additional wards and protection spells on the pieces."

She was still smiling but Gia's frown was back in full force.

"Are you all right, Gia?"

No, she wasn't all right and was on the brink of a full-blown meltdown when soft hands cupped her cheeks. Silver fingers brushed her jaw and slipped behind her neck and Gia helplessly leaned into Luna's forehead when it tenderly pressed against her own.

When had they grown so used to touching each other?

"What's wrong, Gigi?" Luna asked, worriedly searching her eyes.

She gently squeezed Luna's hands before she took a step back. "Just hungry, I guess." She smiled and Luna dubiously returned it.

"I could make something? Or are you due back?"

"You've been travelling for most of the day. I'll make dinner and you can go take a bath. I'll try on my armour afterward."

Luna scrunched her nose and flashed a lopsided grin that made Gia's chest ache and her legs grow weak. "Do I smell?"

Luna, in fact, smelled far too good.

"I suggested it more for you to rest a while before dinner."

"All right, I'll have a bath and then come help you," Luna agreed and gave her a hug that Gia couldn't help but fall into before she headed toward the bathroom, the one with the exact same tub design Gia had once fallen in love with through a storefront window, but hadn't had the space or money to purchase it.

She set about stewing vegetables and cooked some rice on the stove. The flames burned with magic and the icebox in the corner noiselessly cooled with freezing charms. When she was younger, Gia hadn't questioned how the appliances worked, but she had definitely wondered when she'd learned about electricity in Tristea. There was no electricity in Ederra, only the Dwarves and their ability to enchant almost anything they touched.

Luna was right. Life was comfortable. There was no need for more. She hadn't seen a single homeless or impoverished-looking person on her trip to Erdiko, unless they kept their poor out of sight, which she doubted. Luna would take their existence as a personal slight against the glory of Lur Ederra and immediately build homes for them with her bare hands or get her best friend, the Ama Gorria, to simply use her magic and provide them with shelter and sustenance.

The sound of bare feet padding down the hall and over the kitchen floor had Gia's heart skipping a beat and starting to race. Luna wore that black thin-strapped dress again and entered the kitchen in a cloud of sweet flowery fragrance that left Gia's head spinning.

She could barely focus on her effort to clean while the food simmered on the stove. It had three settings, low, medium, and high, and it had taken her a while to figure out how much heat certain meals required, especially when to switch between settings. Always high for the kettle to make tea, that much she remembered from watching her mothers. It was on low now and filled the cottage with a mouth-watering aroma of herbs and spices.

The kitchen smelled homely and right, and Gia shuddered when Luna's breasts lightly pressed against her back to remove two bowls from the cabinet above her head. She was gone as quickly as she'd appeared, but the feeling of warmth and magic buzzed across Gia's skin for a few startling moments after.

In a daze, she finished dinner, Luna tasking herself with setting the table and taking out the passion fruit juice she made especially for Gia's visits, then dished the food into serving bowls and plates.

When had they fallen into this domestic routine?

The usually delicious Ederran vegetables tasted like nothing in her mouth and Gia sat absently dipping the sticky rice into sauce.

"What's wrong, Gia?" Luna softly asked, carefully watching her.

A week ago she'd dreamt of them sitting on the beach at the bottom of the cliff while she listened to the story of the first Husk Luna had fought.

"Do you remember the first Husk you fought?"

Luna laughed. "I doubt I would ever forget it, no matter how much I might want to."

"What happened?"

"I thought I was ready. I was only fifteen years old and a full decade and a half from starting my Practicum. But my mothers took me with them to one of the Rifts after I begged them for months on end. I managed to hit the Husk a few times with my fledgling magic, but that did little to it, and then it screeched its lightning at me and I ran on instinct, slipped and fell off a cliff and into a lake." She grinned. "If my mothers weren't there, I don't know what would have happened to me."

Gia's laugh was a lot more subdued than it had been in the dream. Because then, Luna had pulled her close and deeply kissed her to shut her up. Now though, her brows furrowed in concern and she searched Gia's face.

"Sorry. I'm just tired, I guess."

"It is late," Luna agreed, still carefully studying her. "I'm sorry you had to wait for me."

"No, it wasn't long. And I was excited to see the armour." She reached out and covered Luna's hand with her own, unable to stop herself from seeking the connection. "Thank you again for getting it for me."

Luna smiled prettily. "You're welcome, Gigi."

* * *

Trumoi landed in the snow, black wings flapping once in agitation, before he raised one that allowed Luna to slip off his back, her bare toes curling when the soft ice welcomed her feet. She grinned at the annoyed snort from Trumoi, puffs of steam blowing from his nostrils.

"I thought you would like it," she said with a smile, her hand brushing along his flank.

He stomped his hooves into the snow and shook his fiery mane.

"Fine, go home to Tximista's warmth. I'll use a mirror," she murmured and patted his neck, placing a kiss against his cheek. He nuzzled her back, nearly knocking her over, before he grandly trotted a few feet and smoothly lifted up into the air.

Twin howls followed his departure and Luna glanced toward the icy cliffs where Askarra and Zuri sat, the white wolves blending with their surroundings, pink tongues lolling out as golden eyes stared at her.

Luna walked up the gentle slope, watching them lithely make their way down the ridge, gracefully jumping from rock to rock and coming to flank her in greeting. Their heads came up to her waist and she gently scratched behind their ears, her fingers sinking into the thick and warm fur at the scruff of their necks.

Bo stood waiting on the doorstep of her large wooden cabin, little Bree in her arms and smiling widely.

"Certainly took you forever to come visit," Bo complained, walking forward and bowing her head when Luna wrapped her fingers behind her neck and pressed their foreheads together with a soft laugh.

"I thought I would give you time to bond with my favourite Guardian," she said, her grin growing when Bo handed Bree over.

The baby was dressed in yellow robes to match her hair, green skin glowing with her magic the instant Luna touched her. On instinct Luna let her own magic flow to Bree, who gave a delighted gurgle, small chubby arms flailing excitedly.

"Believe me, we've bonded more than enough," Bo dryly said and led Luna through the house, the majority of which consisted of floor-to-ceiling feature windows.

"Where's Ukitu?"

"We ran out of flour and sugar so she went to the market."

Luna nodded, making faces at a drooling Bree, who had two fistfuls of her black hair in a tight grip. They exited the back door where tall flames from a roaring firepit were surrounded by cushioned benches that overlooked a misty canyon, and sat down beside each other.

Luna reluctantly passed Bree to Bo when the baby reached for her mother.

"Are you sure she isn't cold?" Luna asked. It was her first time being acquainted with a baby as an adult. She thought she knew what to do with them but had grossly overestimated herself. From listening to Bo and Ukitu, they required a lot of maintenance compared to their relative size.

"She's far more protected than us. I could probably throw her into the ravine and she'll be fine."

"Bo!" Luna exclaimed and her friend only cackled, gently handing over her daughter when Bree leaned forward, grabbing toward Luna with tiny hands.

"Look at the little troll," Bo said, shaking her head. "Can't even make up her mind about what she wants. Drives me mad."

Luna rolled her eyes.

"And speaking of beings who can't make up their minds—"

"Such a subtle segue," Luna mumbled.

"You and your Tristean Arima disappeared for the entire evening during Bree's Naming Ceremony."

"You know very well she's not Tristean."

"And you know that I know."

"We were only talking."

"According to your mothers, *talking* up in your room. Locked away from prying eyes."

Luna grinned and Bo matched it. "So, it's going well?"

"I don't know, Bo. I'm not sure what to do or what's going on half the time I'm with her."

"That's normal."

"It is?"

"Yes. After our Meeting, all Kitu and I did was lose track of days and spend hours talking while we lay in the snow and watched the clouds and the stars."

Zuri jumped onto the bench and laid her big wolf head in Bo's lap, eyes closing when she received a scratch behind her ears. Bree let out a screech of joy, nearly throwing herself out of Luna's arms to grab Zuri's muzzle, causing the wolf to sneeze, get up and move to lay beside the fire.

Bo sighed and took Bree back, whose bottom lip trembled as she forlornly reached out toward Zuri.

"See? She ruins everything good in my life," Bo said and tenderly kissed Bree's forehead before laying her on her shoulder and gently rubbed her back. "I can't touch Kitu without her noticing and demanding attention instead."

"Aren't babies supposed to sleep a lot?" Luna asked, knowing full well Bo's love of hyperbole.

"She wakes up the second I've enticed Kitu into pinning me against some surface or another. Like she knows my neglected body will finally get some release and needs to ruin it for me."

Luna laughed even as her cheeks grew hot. She stared into the roaring fire, lost in thought of the dreams she kept having of Gia. Then her face fell, because what did it matter if they were only dreams? Dreaming of Gia wasn't anything new, though they had never been as vivid as they were now. Most likely a result of them spending time together and having shared magic whilst fighting the Darke at their Rift.

"You all right?" Bo asked, pink brows drawn together, while searching her face.

Luna nodded.

"I know today's a bad day for you, Lulu, but I'm happy that you chose to visit me."

"You always make it easier."

"Because I'm amazing and I made your favourite stew. Kitu will be baking some fresh bread when she returns."

Shifting closer and smiling softly, Luna wrapped her arm around her friend, eyes on the sleepy child on her shoulder. "You're the best, Bo."

CHAPTER NINETEEN

Gia stood on the lip of a gradual slope against a range of lilac-coloured, grassy hills. The sky was overcast with heavy grey clouds and gentle rain fell like a light mist. Higher up, a bluish grey mansion stood beside a rushing river that ran all the way down and tumbled over a cliff.

She was dreaming, but whereas before it had always been sunshine while Luna showed off her favourite places, this time felt different. Aside from the gloomy weather and Gia's quick awareness of her reality, stranger still, was Luna not beside her, laughing and talking. Instead, she stood a few yards away, completely drenched and far too close to the cliff's edge for Gia's liking.

Dressed in silver robes and without her glamour, Gia warily made her way closer. Even through the rain, the golden glitter of tears was visible on silver cheeks and Gia's breath hitched, the sorrow on Luna's face forming a lump in her throat.

Luna sighed, a cloud of condensation leaving her mouth as she stared out over the misty valley below. "Perhaps I wanted to tell you."

"Tell me what?" Gia warily rasped.

"Do you think you're here because I crave your comfort?"

"I don't know why I'm here, Lu."

She nodded. "I don't want to need your comfort."

"Why do you need comfort?"

"I'm sad."

"About?"

Dark eyes ran over her face as if contemplating. "Why do I do this to myself?"

"Do what, Luna?"

"Dream about you. It's already too much and now you're here when I need you."

"What happened?" Gia asked, taking her hand.

Luna stared down at their entwined fingers. "It happened a long time ago. My sadness is manageable now. I don't know why I need you here."

"Maybe you want to tell me about what happened?"

"Perhaps," she nodded. "My sister died. Today is the anniversary of her death. Her Arima passed a few days after."

The fingers in Gia's hand gently squeezed and she realised she'd gone entirely rigid thinking of her confession to Luna under the Passion Fruit tree. Luna's distress, though, seemed to be centred on Gia's presence in her dream, rather than the loss she'd suffered.

"When did you lose them?" Gia asked, and immediately brought her free hand to her chest at the pang of remembrance. "Forty years ago," she gasped, then sadly smiled at Luna's surprise. "I felt you," she explained. "I was working as a librarian and had learned to change my glamour to a Human woman because I met a vampire who helped me get identification documents. Life had finally seemed to settle. I was as content as I'd ever been and then it was just pain and lethargy. I spent a week in bed, barely able to eat—"

"I'm sorry," Luna said.

Gia wrapped herself around Luna's arm, pressing in closely, and shook her head. "I shudder to think what I put you through over the years. I only wish I'd been strong enough to make you feel better then. But like you said, sometimes it's okay to allow ourselves to be sad."

Luna smiled and Gia placed a kiss on the damp cloth covering her shoulder. She wrapped her arms around Luna's waist and they held each other, heads tilted close.

"They lived here," Luna said, breaking the comfortable silence. "Another pair have made it their home, so this place remains preserved only in my mind. I often wondered if it would've been better if they'd had a daughter, a part of them left behind for us to love and cherish and remember them by. But now that I know you, I feel selfish and cruel for ever having thought that."

Gia had met plenty of orphans she'd envied for never having had a taste of home and family. They adapted a lot easier to their circumstances. And after reuniting with her aunts and grandmothers, she couldn't help but wonder at the life she could've had. Even if her family hadn't wanted her and she'd gone to live at the Sanctum where Luna was, her life would have been so different. *She* would have been different and she had yet to decide whether she regretted that or not. Tristea had been awful for a long time, but she had carved out a life there. It had shaped her into the person she had become.

"I know it doesn't compare," Luna continued, "but I'm your family, Gigi. Sean, too. Mom and Mama will always be there should you need them. You will never be alone again as long as you have us."

Overwhelmed, Gia sunk to the wet ground, unable to release her hold on Luna, who easily went down with her until they sat wrapped together in the rain. Gia closed her eyes, rested her head on Luna's shoulder, and wondered if she could fall asleep within a dream.

She needed to confess that she was real, but it hardly seemed the time to do so. She was certain the instant she told Luna, the easy intimacy they shared in their dreams would stop. And what if they never shared a dream again? It would most certainly influence the tentative friendship they'd managed to build. Luna would withdraw from her entirely. Gia had no doubt about that.

"I think I'm losing you," Luna softly said.

"What?" Gia dragged her head from the comfort of Luna's shoulder to look at her face. "No. Why do you think that?"

"You acted strangely yesterday, caught up in your mind. It's been months since you've sleepwalked to me. We've been spending so much time together and I love it, but perhaps I'm crowding you? Am I selfish for cherishing every moment, for wanting to keep you with me for as long as possible?"

"You're not losing me. And you're the most selfless person I've ever met."

"Something was wrong and you wouldn't tell me. You left without trying on your armour and flinched when I hugged you goodbye, as though my touch made you uncomfortable."

"Maybe I've been feeling guilty about how close we've become."

Luna considered it seriously and the urge to kiss her was immense.

"I think we've been *dating*," Gia confessed.

"*Dating*?"

"Like getting to know each other."

Luna frowned. "Is that wrong?"

"It's meant in a romantic sense. Almost like a test run to see if we're compatible to bond."

"How have we been *dating*?"

"Whenever we weren't fighting Husks, you've been showing me the best spots around your home. We've been eating food together and sharing stories about our lives."

"Friends do that."

Gia couldn't help but smile at Luna's earnest befuddlement. Sighing, she placed her head back on Luna's shoulder and closed her eyes when Luna's cheek rested against her hair.

"Talking to you is so easy," Gia said through a soft groan.

"Because this is a dream?"

Gia shook her head. "Even when we're awake together, I want to tell you everything. I want you to know everything I am. I want to know everything about you."

"I don't think I can handle knowing more of you, you're already everything."

Gia pressed a soft kiss to Luna's jaw, because that was how Luna always was in their dreams: open with her words and feelings. Free with her touches and kisses. Losing her like that would hurt so much.

"Are you happy?" Gia asked.

"More than I've ever been."

"You don't want more?"

Luna tilted her head. "More what?"

"You don't want me to live here with you always? You're happy having me visit and then leaving to another world? Another life?"

Luna played with Gia's fingers while pondering the question.

"I have more now than I had last year. I have you in my life and fighting at my side."

"And that's enough?"

"When you leave me to go through the Veil, it's jarring. It's as if my heart breaks a little each time."

"It's become increasingly hard to leave you," Gia admitted and looked up at the wry chuckle from Luna's lips. "What?" she whispered, their faces close.

"At least I have this, right?"

"This?"

"You. Each night in my dreams, being perfect for me and remedying my intense longing."

Luna pressed their lips together and Gia forgot about a reply and pushed aside the fear curling in her gut, because she knew she couldn't take these dreams away from Luna too—not when she'd taken so much from her already.

CHAPTER TWENTY

She hadn't really been sure how to offer comfort, but Luna hadn't seemed to require much aside from Gia sitting with her in the rain, holding her close, and allowing her to be sad for a little while. Perhaps if she'd allowed herself to grieve instead of trying to simply forget Ederra and her mothers for decades, she would've adjusted a lot sooner.

Luna's family all differed like night and day, and yet they all seemed to look at her and know things Gia struggled to understand. Uda was the most confusing. Some days she would show up for an hour or two and simply help Gia tend to her plants, seemingly content to wait for Gia to talk if she wanted, never minding the long silences when Gia became lost in her work and at times forgot she was there. She never asked anything about Luna. She didn't push Gia into being with her and she'd come to value Uda so much that she was certain Uda could guilt her into doing anything.

In a weird way, Uda reminded her of Sean—patient and careful, always waiting and trusting her to make the right choice. Allowing Gia to dictate how much she shared at her own pace, which often had her blurting things at them without really meaning to.

"Do Arimas share dreams? I mean, we do vaguely dream about each other before the Meeting, but after that, can Arimas consciously share dreams with one another?"

Uda straightened, lifted one golden brow, and dusted the soil from her copper hands. "It's possible. Are you asking for any particular reason?"

"Does Luna know it's possible?"

"I'm not sure. It's rare. It's been documented to happen when Arimas spend significant time apart. As you can imagine, that hardly ever happens."

Gia nodded and even though she knew the answer already, she needed the extra reassurance. "You won't tell Luna what we discuss?"

"I won't. And she won't ask. She barely speaks to us about this…situation."

"I'm sorry. I never meant to come between you."

"Oh, it's not you, darling. Lulu has always marched to the beat of her own drum. Rather resolutely." She fondly smiled and Gia did too. "She was determined to show us she could guard the Rift on her own and has come to embrace that a bit too much for my liking."

"She has Haize Bolada, though, to speak to?"

"Bo is thankfully the type of friend that understands that Luna needs to get away from everything and deal with her own emotions in her own way. Well, Bo and the Ama Gorria."

"How did that happen? I thought the Ama Gorria was a recluse? That she sleeps for centuries at a time to avoid losing her mind?"

"She remains a recluse and seems to be in one of her wakeful periods for the last two centuries. We were surprised when she appeared to perform Luna's Naming Ceremony."

"Well, at least you didn't need to do it yourself and could participate as her mother."

Uda smiled. "It had been a welcome honour and I had newly Ascended to Apaiz Nagusia of the Sanctum, so our family had twice been blessed by the Ama Gorria that year. She left after

Luna's Naming Ceremony, though, and only appeared to us over a decade later when Luna began sleepwalking. But we suspect Luna had been sneaking off to visit her long before then."

"Sleepwalking?"

"Yes. Saso and I barely slept that year. One of us needed to constantly watch her."

"But she stopped?"

"One night, we needed to banish a Husk at a Rift in the Eastern Lands. We asked the Novitiates to watch Luna. They were respectful of her privacy and stood outside her bedroom door—"

"She went over the balcony?"

"To this day, we don't know how she got out. The Ama Gorria brought her back to us. She had somehow made it all the way to the Rift outside of Erdiko."

"How long was it until she stopped sleepwalking?"

"That same night. The Ama Gorria bound her, only allowing conscious travel."

"Why would she be going to the Rift? Children can't sense the Darke. My mothers said I wouldn't be able to until my Initiation Ceremony."

Uda smiled sadly. "You already know where she was trying to go, darling."

Gia was jealous. She felt left out. Luna and Sean seemed to have bonded through a shared caring of her. There was no hate between them. Luna had smiled widely when Sean opened another bottle of her favourite wine and poured it in the large wineglass he'd bought especially for her so it would fit better in her hand. She still teased him and he was still a little dumbstruck around her, but they got along and Gia wasn't sure how to feel about that.

Had she wanted them to be possessive? To fight over her? No, she definitely didn't want that. Why then was their growing friendship so difficult to accept? Knowing both of them, she was confident that neither was doing it to mess with her ever-dwindling sanity, but to make the entire awful situation easier on everyone involved.

They sat on the living room couch, side by side, two tipsy peas in a pod, and stared at the screen of Sean's laptop. Gia could only watch them from her chair at the dining table across the room. She didn't need to be that far away, but seeing them like that was as disturbing as it was perplexing.

"What about kittens? Do you guys have kittens over there?" Sean asked after they finished watching about ten cat videos in a row.

"We do. They grow a little bigger and we have a few at the Sanctum."

"How about dogs?"

"Halflings seem to enjoy having dogs as pets. The Dwarves keep them to protect their goods. I think we have a few of the same domestic and farm animals, though we don't have quite such a wide variety of them as you do in Tristea. From what I've gathered, insect, plant, and sea life seem to be where we share the most similar species."

Sean looked at Luna as though she'd hung the moon, and Gia knew he couldn't help it, but she had the intense urge to go sit between them.

"But you have no vampires or werewolves?"

"Logically, since we have no more Humans, we can't have vampires and werewolves, can we?"

She grinned cheekily and Sean returned it. "Fine, I blame the wine for not being *logical* right now."

"Of course," Luna agreed good-naturedly. "We do have a considerable selection of creatures you seem to label as mythical."

"Gia told me about the dragons and griffins and pegasuses. Does that mean we used to have them here too?"

"You did. Before the Humans drained all of their magic to power the spell that banished the Darke and split your world into continents."

"Wait, so no Big Bang? No dinosaurs?"

"They existed when the worlds were still one. Magic fell from the sky and split us in two, destroying all life and creating us anew."

"Twenty millennia ago?"

"Twenty millennia ago."

"And the Blight was ten millennia ago?"

"Correct."

"So we had the Big Bang, then the dinosaurs, then the magic comet that created the mirror worlds and then the spell that split the continents?"

Luna smiled. "Yes."

"Are you messing with me again?"

"I would never."

She grinned charmingly and Sean laughed. "So we covered it up? That we once had magic here?"

"Uh-huh."

"Why?"

"To absolve you—absolve Humans—I suppose."

"Are we very awful compared to Lur Ederra's people?" he sadly—drunkenly—asked.

After taking a sip of her wine, Luna tilted her pretty head, waves of dark hair falling beautifully to one side and sent him a lopsided grin that made Gia's stomach flip.

"You're a good Human, Sean Williams," she said and Sean accepted the complement as gracefully as any drunk person could, with a hearty fist pump, and then promptly showed her some puppy videos.

Caught up in staring at Luna's laughing face, Gia startled when dark eyes shifted to her.

"Why don't you wear an engagement ring, Gia?"

Gia looked down at her bare fingers as though she might find one there, and maybe she'd had a little too much to drink too, which explained her intense feelings of being left out. Luckily Luna had potions to sober them up should any Darke approach their Rift.

"She didn't want me to get her one," Sean answered. "But we'll both wear our wedding bands."

Gia nodded that yes that was true. Getting an extra ring seemed strange and a waste of money. It had made much more sense to contribute that money to a deposit on their home.

"Will you be coming to the wedding?" Sean asked. Gia's spine almost snapped the way it straightened with tension.

Luna took another long sip of wine, throat bobbing as she swallowed. "I wouldn't be comfortable there, Sean. And it would make me very sad."

He didn't even blink at the honest response and immediately accepted it. "I understand," he sadly said, while Luna's stare burned into Gia. "Do you guys have these types of whales?"

He drew Luna's attention again and Gia was released from the hold. She immediately went for another beer and lingered—hid—too long in the kitchen. It was becoming too much. She was feeling so much all the time. It couldn't be healthy and it most certainly wasn't right. Emotional cheating was a thing, and since the dreams were real, wouldn't that mean she was physically cheating too? Was she having an affair with Luna?

When she gathered the courage to go back, Luna and Sean were near the front door, and even when she was relieved that her torment was over, Gia still found that she didn't want Luna to go.

"Will you be okay crossing realms after you've been drinking?" Sean worriedly checked and got a reckless grin in response.

"Opening the Veil is second nature, innate to all Guardians. It's not a conscious thought or we might end up inside of objects on the other side." She laughed. "Imagine how easy it would be to open a portal over the ocean, or on top of a mountain, or inside a boulder. We tend to go to the safest possible...*landing spot*, for lack of a better word."

"So you're sure you won't get trapped between dimensions or anything?" His concern was so genuine that the hug Luna gave him was less of a surprise. He looked ready to pass out, though, still very affected by her as he dazedly grinned and rested his head against her chest. "I'll be all right, Sean. Thank you for a nice evening."

"Always great having you, Luna."

Luna's face softened on Gia and she forgot her jealousy and willingly fell into her hug. Gia hated that she had the glamour on. She'd grown so used to being without it around Luna that she felt wrong in her skin, pressed up against her. She hated herself for relishing the fact that her hug was far more intimate than the one Sean had received. And she just barely resisted the urge to snuggle her cheek against Luna's breasts.

Letting go was hard but she managed, and after Luna stepped through the Veil, she and Sean made their way up the stairs, but a ping from his phone had him stopping partway up to check it.

"Mom wants to come visit," he said, causing Gia to halt too.

"She can come visit anytime she wants. It's after midnight. Is she really messaging you this late? Is she okay?"

"That was just a reminder of a meeting I have with the sheriff tomorrow afternoon. She sent the message earlier."

"Okay, well, I make my own schedule so she can come whenever she likes and I'll keep her company."

"She asked if we had a date for the wedding yet. I'm pretty sure she's coming to hurry things along." He anxiously chuckled and continued up the stairs.

When a shock of dread twisted in her gut, Gia knew that things couldn't continue the way they had been.

CHAPTER TWENTY-ONE

Gia wasn't sure when the dream had started, but her clothes were off and she was only in a pair of panties. Luna's warm mouth greedily sucked her nipple and Gia's stomach dropped and clenched. Groaning in pleasure, her head fell back onto the soft pillow of Luna's ridiculously comfy bed.

Was it a shared dream again? Or was it only her own fantasies manifesting? It felt different somehow. Luna's magic felt stronger, and Gia's legs fell open when silver fingers slid into her underwear. She let out a whine and threaded her fingers into Luna's hair, keeping her against her breast, unable to think while her hips canted into Luna's touch. Heat curled in her lower belly and she was already so close, unsure how time worked in dreams, but her body was miles ahead and her muddled brain unable to keep up.

"Please don't stop," she panted.

"Never," Luna promised and slowly entered her with one long finger.

Gia cried out, shaken by how good it felt. "Where—*How* do you even know what to do?"

Luna chuckled, her voice low and sexy, sending a throb of want through Gia's core. "I've read many books, and Bo gave me some very explicit descriptions and advice," she said and kissed Gia's mouth, sucked on her tongue and slipped in another finger.

Gia's back arched and magic erupted from her body. When she realised her eyes were screwed tightly shut, she opened them to the sight of Luna glowing brilliantly blue, dark eyes sparkling in awe while she took in Gia's body mindlessly moving to meet her thrusts.

"Are we dreaming again?" Gia wondered out loud.

Luna went rigid and Gia nearly swore at her for stopping, but a deeply frowning Luna spoke before she could voice her displeasure. "Are you here, Gia?" she asked, and in a blind panic, Gia woke up, breathless on her back, instantly mourning the loss of those perfect fingers and the palm that had warmly cupped her.

She briefly squeezed her thighs together, pink flames covering her black skin, and froze when her knee bumped against warm flesh, the contact causing a spark of delicious magic.

"Were you there with me?"

Gia turned to face a very naked and confused Luna, glowing blue while a silver hand rested on Gia's obsidian waist. Gia herself was dressed in a pair of panties, her baby blue sleep shirt straining and rucked up to reveal her long toned stomach. A now familiar pulse throbbed between her thighs, more insistent than it had ever been.

They lay so close that their lips were inches apart.

Had they moved? Had Gia moved?

The air was thick, heavy with the scent of gentle rain over a field of flowers blooming beneath the sun as it broke through the clouds. Warm and pleasant, and Gia dazedly inhaled, their magic blending so seamlessly she couldn't tell the difference between Luna's and her own anymore. She was feverish, her heart thrumming and insistently pulsing in various parts of her body. She ached so badly, and now knew that her only respite lay in Luna's touch and kisses.

In touching Luna back…

Shaky obsidian fingers tucked a dark strand of hair behind Luna's ear, who gasped when Gia lightly stroked from the pointy tip, all the way down to the lobe. Dark glittering eyes grew hooded, and Luna's warm body shivered beneath the delicate caress. Gia traced down a sharp jawline and gently swiped the tip of her index finger across a dark bottom lip.

Luna remained still, save for her laboured breaths through parted lips, as though she was trapped under a spell when Gia was the one entirely enraptured.

Her finger continued to trace Luna's bottom lip, then dipped inside a warm wet mouth, baffled as to how it could feel so suggestive when it made her stomach tighten in response. A moist tongue licked at the digit and Gia's hips jerked against Luna's thigh.

Luna sucked in a sharp breath and searched Gia's face.

All Gia could do was desperately press their mouths together.

Luna's mouth readily opened for her, accepting Gia with a needy moan. In contrast to the eager explorations in their dreams, the kiss was slow and deep, and Gia's brain swam when Luna came to life beneath her. Silver fingers caressed her body and removed Gia's panties and then her shirt. Luna pressed a trail of lazy kisses across the newly revealed skin of Gia's torso, before returning to Gia's mouth and pulled her into an embrace.

Their breasts pressed together and Gia moaned at the dizzying sensation, Luna gasping against her lips and drawing the breath right out of her lungs. Gia wished for more hands to touch Luna everywhere at once, but focused on Luna's breasts until she grew bold enough to press Luna's back to the bed and slip a hand between a pair of silver thighs, entirely unprepared for what she found there.

They both cried out, Gia startled by her own visceral reaction even when she immediately stroked the slick velvet in a blissful stupor. She dragged her eyes away from Luna's hypnotically rocking hips to the euphoric expression on her face.

Gia repeatedly found herself entranced by everything Luna did. Whether it was the way she fought the Darke, tended her garden, or simply walked with her hands folded behind her back, asking about all the Tristean flowers in Gia's greenhouse... Luna would be curled up on her couch reading to Gia from a book on Ederran history, and Gia would be entirely enchanted by her.

"Sometimes I struggle to believe that you're real," Gia dazedly murmured between kisses. "That I actually met you. That I got to see you and know you more."

Luna deepened the kiss, her magic enveloping Gia in a cocoon of warmth and pleasure, and they slickly slid together, as naturally synchronised as when they fought the Darke.

Gia desperately rubbed herself against Luna's thigh, feeling like she was going mad, and loving every second of her spiral as Luna ardently matched Gia's increasingly frenetic pace.

As with all things Luna, it was too much and still not enough.

Gia was addicted to her smooth curves and the taste of her hot skin and tongue. Forever changed by the exquisite sound Luna made when she climaxed with a hoarse cry. Gia barely needed the clumsy silver fingers that slid down her stomach to touch her, before her body stiffened and she came with a shuddering moan.

Tears filled her eyes when Luna immediately hugged her close while they breathlessly rocked together for a few long moments after. Featherlight kisses pressed over her face and hair, and it was pure ecstasy and serenity. Luna's magic soothingly cradled Gia with the same tenderness as the silver arms she never wanted to be released from again.

"I love you so much," Luna rasped against her hair.

Gia's head had cleared enough for the words to have her flash back to when Sean had said them to her earlier that evening, when he'd wished her goodnight.

Luna hummed while her everything pleasantly buzzed, but the abrupt tension in Gia's previously boneless body had her stiffening too. Warily, she pulled away from the arms tightly clinging to her and looked at Gia's face. She wasn't surprised by the remorse reflected in sad, silver eyes, but she was entirely unprepared for just how much it hurt to see it. Worse still, was how easily Gia let her go when she shifted away.

Sitting up, she rested her feet on the floor, placed her elbows on her knees and covered her face with her hands, trying to breathe through the constricting pain in her chest.

"We—I shouldn't have—that shouldn't have—"

"Please stop talking," Luna croaked past the thick knot in her throat and pressed her fingers to the bridge of her nose, attempting to stave off the burn in her eyes. She was so stupid.

Had she really thought Gia had chosen her?

She should never have allowed things to progress that far. Her mind had been muddled by the dream and all rational thought dissipated when Gia had kissed her.

The bed creaked and her stomach dropped. Squeezing her eyes tightly shut, she bit the inside of her cheek. Gia didn't leave, though, and instead walked over to stand in front of Luna, still stunningly naked. Luna looked up at the shimmering tears that ran over Gia's obsidian cheeks. She now knew how smooth every inch of Gia's body was and how perfectly the two of them slotted together.

Luna's magic glowed across her skin. "Leave," she roughly rasped, warm tears spilling down her face.

"I can't. Not like this."

"How many times have you been in my dreams?"

"Lu, I swear, I didn't realise it at first."

"When did you realise, then?"

"That day I asked about the first Husk you fought. I knew for sure then that the dreams were real."

"And what? You decided not to tell me? Decided to allow me to lay myself bare for you when you had so much of me already?"

"It wasn't like that."

Luna inhaled a shaky breath. "You're selfish."

"I know." Gia's voice shook and she hiccupped through a sob.

Luna pressed her palms into her eye sockets to keep from comforting her.

"I can't"—Gia's breath hitched—"I can't leave Sean."

"Please go," she begged, her shoulders shaking while she silently cried.

"I'm so sorry, Lu," Gia shakily rasped.

Feeling Gia's magic approaching, Luna took hold of her wrist to stop Gia from touching her. She rose from the bed, flames blazing in contrast to the gentle pink glow that emanated from Gia's body.

"You came here."

"You know I can't help that."

"Funny how you're able to fight your very nature only when it suits you." She threw Gia's wrist away when she realised she still gently held it.

"I can't live this life—"

"But you have been living it, Argia! You've visited with your family. You've fought at my side. You've shielded us. What you can't live with is *me*."

"It's definitely not you. Luna, you're amazing, but I made a commitment to Sean."

"You felt me!" Luna yelled, magic surging so powerfully it blew her hair wildly away from her skin. "You knew I was waiting for you! You understood that every single part of me was yours. That loving you, for me, is as easy as breathing. Make no mistake, Gia, your betrayal was to me first and with none of this consideration."

"I was a child—"

"You haven't been a child for a very long time. Your actions are unforgivable."

"We can work through this—"

"We can't!"

"Luna, please. I know it's selfish, but please, we can work something out. I can't imagine not having you in my life somehow. I can't even manage not showing up here in my sleep. We can go back to the way things were before we had sex."

"Sex? Is that what you choose to call it? Or is that what Tristean culture had told you to flippantly dismiss it as? A lack in judgment? A one-time mistake?" Luna shook her head. "You think I frivolously lay with every warm body I chance upon? Do you think that I could?"

"I haven't either and there's nothing wrong with people who do."

"Spare me. We aren't *people*. We're Guardians. You've desecrated something that has been sacred for millennia, rejected something beautiful about our race. And why? To prove that you could?"

"Say what you like about Tristea, but at least I can be whoever I want there."

"Yes, you can be anyone other than yourself! Leave. Now."

"I can't leave things like this."

"I can't ever not love you! So, go. Do at least that much for me."

"Luna, please, our emotions are all over the place. We can talk once we've calmed down."

She shook her head. "I'm done. I don't ever want to see you again. You are no longer welcome in my life. In my home. In my dreams! You are no longer allowed to take what you want and then leave me here!"

Luna's fists clenched at her sides, chest tight and straining. Through her blurring vision she saw Gia's stricken look, teary silver eyes frantically flicking across Luna's face. Then Gia drew a quivering bottom lip into her mouth, bit it and nodded, more tears falling free. With trembling fingers, she took Luna's robe from where it lay across the vanity chair and pulled it on.

"I'll try to speak to you again tomorrow," Gia whispered, and walked out of the bedroom door.

Luna stood fuming and aching, feeling Gia moving further away from her, out her front door, then released a shuddering sob when the Veil closed between them.

CHAPTER TWENTY-TWO

Luna desperately searched the forest in the dark, unable to calm herself long enough to allow her magic to guide her on her stumbling path. The Novitiates on guard duty had stared at her with wide eyes when she'd arrived at the Sanctum, her cheeks tearstained and hair still messy and knotted from her time with Gia. No doubt her mothers would hear about it in the morning if they managed to sleep through her current distress.

"Sua!" she called into the night, unable to focus on finding her hiding places. And Luna didn't know how Sua Orro managed it, but she appeared in a swirling cloud of flames soon after, like she had some tracking spell on Luna. Immensely grateful for it in that moment, she sunk into the arms that instantly wrapped around her.

Sua let her weep and quietly listened to Luna's garbled retelling of what had happened.

"Will you help me?"

"You shouldn't make decisions when upset."

"I can't anymore."

"You can't what?"

"Every day hurts, Sua. Pretending hurts. I want to share a life with her, build a future, but I'll never have that and the pain will never end."

Sua frowned. "How do you think I can help you?"

"You can remove the tether. I've seen what your magic can do."

"It will kill you."

Luna sucked in a shaky breath. "She's bound to me when she doesn't want to be. She was physically intimate with me when she didn't want to be. Do you have any idea what that knowledge feels like? I *violated* her. I can't continue like this. It's not right to force her to be in my life when she has no choice."

"It will kill her too," Sua said and Luna's already aching heart painfully clenched. "Severing the tie will feel like losing her. You will go into Mourning and so will she."

"You can't stop the Mourning?"

"The Soulbond is ancient magic, strong and powerful. Nearly sentient in how it adapts to fullfil its purpose. You can't simply remove aspects of it without consequence. It affects all Guardians and unless you want to change the fate of every bonded pair, present and future, it will be difficult to do what you ask."

"Difficult but not impossible?"

"Iluna—"

"You have to trick the Soulbond somehow, instead of changing it…"

"I've always been proud of how quickly you took to understanding aspects of magic, but today I despise that trait in you."

Luna stared at the ground, holding her aching stomach while her heart painfully thudded against her ribs. "You could trick the bond into thinking Gia had passed, and I will go into Mourning. Will that spare her? Will that be enough?"

"You don't wish for me to trick the bond into believing you passed as well?"

Luna smiled sadly. "Can you?"

Sua hung her head. "Even if I trick the bond into believing your Arima has passed, she will still go into Mourning—"

"Why? I don't understand, Sua."

"You have been growing together all your lives. You've shared magic and experiences. Tethered or not, she will feel your loss, because you are an integral part of her."

"Then you need to transfer her Mourning to me."

"Luna—"

"Will that be easier, Sua? Can you keep her safe if I take her Mourning?"

"You're not thinking clearly."

Luna helplessly sunk onto the forest bed, shoulders hunched in defeat. "I can't live like this anymore." Each day felt like a clawed fist around her heart, always painfully gripping it, sometimes squeezing so tightly Luna could barely breathe. It was torture. Even in her dreams where she should have felt some reprieve, the ache had persisted. And now she'd lost that sanctuary as well. "I'm so tired, Sua. It hurts so much."

Sua sat down beside her, a caring hand threading the knots out of her hair. "Take a moment to consider what you're asking me to do."

"I'm asking that you free her of me, so she may live the life that she chooses, the one that she wants."

* * *

Gia couldn't stop crying and she couldn't go home and face Sean. She hid in her shop and wept, her head throbbing and her heart sore. Un-glamoured and dressed in Luna's robe, she was unable to move from the counter to go find the spare T-shirt and jeans in her office. She needed to go back. Luna had been so hurt and Gia knew she'd really messed up. Things had been going great and she'd ruined it.

She needed to calm down, though, and get her words in order before going to speak to Luna again. It was morning already, so she would need to text Sean that she wasn't missing and then go beg Luna to forgive her for being a selfish asshole.

And then hope that Sean could find it in himself to forgive her too…

Her chest clenched and she felt Luna before the door to the shop opened. She braced her hands on the counter and waited for Luna to lower her cloak.

"Lu," she wetly breathed, her lips quivering into a hesitant smile when she finally saw her, but frowned when the Red Mother uncloaked herself a moment later. She looked every bit as cold as Saso ever had, and Gia's chest tightened because there was no way Uda would visit her now after what she'd done. Luna had made every compromise for her and Gia had thrown it all away because she couldn't control herself. She'd always wondered how people could ruin lives because of cheating, and there she was, hurting the people who loved her, because she was weak and selfish and greedy.

"Lu, can we talk in private, please?" Gia carefully asked. She'd seen Luna angry before, but the look she received in that moment could only be described as glacial. Luna stood tall, her chin lifted, blue flames brilliantly lighting up the shop.

"No." Gia flinched at the icy dismissal. "The Ama Gorria has agreed to sever the tie that binds us."

Her heart flipped and she looked to the Red Mother, sage ruby eyes carefully studying her. "You can do that?"

"I just said that she could!" Luna hotly interjected and Gia bit her lip.

"With no side effects?"

"You'll be fine and free of me."

"Luna, that's not what I want."

"I don't care what you want. I want to be rid of you."

The words hit hard and Gia's chin trembled. She searched Luna's stoic face, dark eyes brimming with tears. Perhaps she was being cruel in her delivery, but Luna wasn't lying. She wanted the tie severed.

"Sua, please. I can't stand being here much longer," Luna tightly whispered.

The Red Mother nodded. "Come here, child," she directed at Gia, who for some reason felt afraid, like she was making a mistake. But she'd wanted to be free of the Soulbond almost all her life. She wanted Luna to be free from its restraints too.

Frowning, she walked closer to the odd pair.

"Take each other's hands."

Luna unceremoniously lifted her hands between them and Gia gasped slightly when she felt her again. Their magical bond had definitely grown stronger since they'd been intimate. Her body still sang at the memory of Luna's hands and lips against her skin.

"This won't hurt her?" Gia asked the Red Mother.

"*You* hurt me!"

"Lu, maybe we should talk about this before we decide to do anything we might regret."

"Now you worry about actions you might regret?"

Gia flinched.

"Do you want this or not?" Luna asked through gritted teeth. "Or do you wish to keep me here until I give in to your will? I don't want to talk to you. I don't want to see you again. The Ama Gorria is granting your wish to be rid of me. Be grateful and stop wasting her time."

"I don't want to be rid of you. I only want to have a choice in who I love."

"And you will have it. Sua, please, do it. I need to leave."

The Red Mother turned to her. "Do you want this?" she asked and Gia gave a jerky nod, unable to draw her gaze away from Luna. "No talking. No moving," the Ama Gorria instructed and began to slowly circle them, muttering words beneath her breath that Gia couldn't understand. Had she known the language, she doubted she would've paid attention to them as she was transfixed on Luna's face. Her dark gaze was pained and silent tears streamed down her cheeks.

Gia squeezed her hands in reassurance and Luna trembled, nostrils flaring and more tears spilled from her eyes. The urge to embrace her was overwhelming. Only the glow of their bodies distracted her enough to remember she'd been ordered to remain still.

When the glow faded, Gia frowned, because she felt no different. Luna, on the other hand, looked on the verge of collapse. Sweat dusted her forehead and her skin looked dull and pasty.

"It's done," Sua Orro said.

Gia barely heard her. "Are you okay?"

"Yes," Luna croaked and weakly pulled her hands free from where Gia still clung to them. The loss of contact hurt for some reason, but then Luna's fingers cupped the back of neck, and Gia shivered. Their foreheads rested together and Gia's eyes fell shut. Breathing Luna in, she attempted to find the words to express her gratitude, but all thoughts left her when Luna's lips trailed the bridge of her nose and tenderly pressed a kiss between Gia's brows.

She exhaled, falling into the caring gesture. "I won't give up on you, Lu. I hope you'll agree to talk once you're not so angry at me anymore. The last thing I ever wanted was to hurt you."

Luna stepped back, seeming to take all the warmth with her. She then took hold of the Red Mother's hand and disappeared through the Veil.

The shop was unnaturally quiet and Gia's brows knitted, bringing her hand up to her heart. Without Luna physically there, she immediately noticed the difference. An ache contracted over the sudden hollowness in her chest and more tears flowed from her eyes.

Filled with an immense sense of loss, she went to her office to change and shakily made her way home.

As soon as the Veil closed behind them, Luna fell to her hands and knees, and *screamed*. Her fingers dug into the dirt and the pain in her chest burned like dragon fire.

"Let it out, little warrior," Sua Orro calmly murmured, rubbing her back while Luna wailed and her body wracked with uncontrollable sobs.

She'd thought it had hurt before, but the pain was immeasurable. She couldn't move and thought of simply lying down in the dirt and never rising again until she remembered her mothers. They deserved a goodbye. She would beg them forgiveness for what she'd done. Perhaps they would now have a chance to conceive and raise a better daughter, one who could fullfil her duty without being overwhelmed by emotions. One whose Arima would accept her and save them the burden of constant worry and disappointment.

Cool magic washed over her and Luna nearly collapsed at the slight relief attempting to soothe her fevered body.

"Shush now," Sua softly said. "Let's make you more comfortable."

* * *

Her joy at not being cursed any longer had lasted for all of five seconds, and by the time Gia walked into her living room, the only thing she could think of was Luna saying she never wanted to see her again. Before, their Soulbond would've made that difficult, but now... Now Luna could disappear and go anywhere in Ederra. Gia wouldn't be able to find her or sense her. She'd be unable to feel whether she was all right. She might actually never see Luna again if that was what Luna wanted.

A sob escaped her and it was like the floodgates opened. Gia sat on the couch and pulled her knees to her chest, smothering her cries into them as sorrow and panic filled her aching lungs.

"Ree?"

She cried harder at Sean's concerned voice. The couch dipped beside her and she went rigid when he wrapped an arm around her, which he instantly removed at her severe reaction.

Gia couldn't look at him.

"What's wrong?"

"Luna broke our Soulbond," she cried into her jeans.

He seemed to ponder that for a moment.

"Is it hurting you?"

"Yes," she croaked and turned to his worried face. "I can't feel her anymore and it's strange and I feel empty. Like I've lost her forever."

"Must be hard considering she's been there with you all your life."

She buried her face back into her knees, her body wracking with sobs. She'd been terrified of the Soulbond because of how her mother had reacted to it, but Gia had also been comforted to know that a part of Luna was always with her. Grateful for the dreams she'd had of Luna and Ederra. When she'd been isolated and scared in a new world, Luna's unerring presence had reminded her that she was still connected to someone. That no matter what, she wouldn't ever be truly alone when she had her Arima.

"Why did she break it off?" Sean asked. "Did you know it was possible?"

She drew in a trembling breath and tried to calm herself. She wasn't the victim here. She was the one who ruined everything.

"I had sex with her."

He stiffened and then got up from the couch. Fear gripped her heart at the thought of losing him too and Gia had to smother down her sobbing not to make it all about her.

Sean drew in a breath, visibly putting aside his pain and sense of betrayal in order to listen to her first. As though anything she could possibly say would make what she'd done okay.

"When?" he rasped.

"Last night."

"Why?"

"I don't know, Sean. You know I can't help it when it comes to her."

"You had been helping it, though."

"*You* insisted I stay here. You said we should try to make this work. I failed. Clearly your trust was misplaced."

"You've been helping it for months. Why last night?"

"I don't know why! I—she—I was dreaming that I was kissing her and I'd sleepwalked over there. I woke up in her bed and she was looking at me and she looked so...I—it just happened, Sean. I couldn't help it."

"You made it happen."

"Sean..."

"Luna has made no secret of her feelings for you and I know I'm half dazed most of the time when I'm around her. I really don't know her at all, come to think of it, but one thing I do know is that she wouldn't have crossed a line that *you* didn't want crossed."

A sharp pain shot through her chest. "It was me. It was all me," she sobbed through her words. "I could've stopped it at any time."

Sean let her cry and watched her with watery eyes. "I think we should break up."

"What?" She was about to jump up and go to him, but he'd already taken a step back at her movement, so she remained seated on the couch, silently willing him not to leave. "Sean, I know I was weak, but I left and I told her that I choose you. That it won't ever happen again. And she did the spell and we're not bound anymore. This won't be a problem again."

"You slept with her, told her you chose me, and then you left?" He looked pained.

"I didn't mean to hurt her, to hurt either of you."

"I know you didn't."

"You do?"

He nodded. "But I still need to end this relationship."

"I'm sorry, Sean. I promise it won't happen again. I love you."

"I know you do. But I'm in love with you and you love me as a friend."

She frowned. "We've been together for almost four years! How can you say that? I haven't ever been with anyone the way I'm with you."

"I know you believe that, Ree."

"Of course I believe that. It's the truth. It's only ever been you."

"You barely noticed that we were dating, only asking when my sister made a comment over five months in."

"I told you it was because I never dated anyone before."

"And because you thought of me as friend."

"Plenty of couples start out as friends first."

"They do. But we need to break up."

"She doesn't want anything to do with me, Sean. I promise it won't happen again. The bond is gone. *She's* gone!" Her heart beat furiously and she was suddenly breathless.

"This isn't about Luna."

Gia stiffened. "What else did I do?"

"I suspected it for a while, even before Luna. I thought it was okay because it was comfortable and you seemed happy and you really are my best friend. Sounds perfect, right? I think I've been fooling myself…Things with you were safe and fun. What more could I want? Who doesn't want to marry their best friend?"

"So marry me then!"

"I can't, Ree. That won't be fair to either of us."

"I don't want to lose you."

"You won't lose me…at least not permanently. I just need to take some time for myself."

"Sean, I don't understand."

"I want someone to be in love with me."

"I don't understand what that means. We go on dates and we share a home. Do you need me to be more romantic? Do we need to do things together that we haven't done before? What do you need me to do? Just please tell me and I'll do it."

"And that's why I fell in love with you."

"What?"

"You step out of your comfort zone for me. You supported my career in that hellhole of a city. You make me feel good about myself, like I can do anything I set my mind to. We're great friends but you don't love me romantically. You've never looked at me the way you look at Luna."

"That was the Arima bond."

"Was it?"

Gia frowned.

"She was respectful enough of our relationship to school her features around me. You seemed entirely unable to do the same."

Gia grew nauseous. "I didn't mean to disrespect you. I wasn't aware that I was doing it."

"I know."

"It was the bond."

"Does the bond grow stronger over time?"

"It does, but because we have that connection from birth, we only activate the sexual attraction when we're adults and ready to start our lives together at the Rift, and our bond grows stronger the more time we spend together and share magic."

Sean stared at her incredulously.

"What?"

"That has nothing to do with love, Ree...The spell only made you horny for her, the rest sounds like your choice."

Gia's brows furrowed. "Yes, that's what I said. I care about her but the sex was a physical side effect of the bond. One I admit now I could've avoided. I take complete responsibility for that, Sean. Just give me one last chance. Please."

"If you admit that you could've avoided it, how can you blame the bond for anything that's happened?"

Gia's mouth fell open, struggling for a response.

"For months now, I've watched you go through the Veil every day with a smile on your face. I watched you progressively become happier than I've ever seen you. I had to watch you fall in love with her, Ree. I guess I've been waiting for this moment for a while now."

"Sean, I *know* we can be happy together."

"No doubt we can. I know you make me happy, but now that I know that you need more and that you can be happier with someone else, it's not the same."

"I won't be happy without you."

"Even if it was the bond, Ree, you've never looked at me like you look at her. Not even a little bit, and that's how I knew for certain. Soulbond or not, if you and I ever stood a chance, I would've seen at least some of that same intensity directed at me at some point."

Her chest clenched so sharply that a sob escaped her at the sudden ache. "I'm so sorry."

He smiled sadly and knelt in front of her, placing a hand on her shaking knee. "Sleep on it. When you wake up tomorrow, be honest with yourself."

Gia wetly sniffed. "And then what?"

"Then I'll be here and we can talk. I'm not going anywhere."

She grew hopeful. "We'll still live together?"

"Well, you weren't with me for my money and we need to pay for this house."

"We?"

"Yeah, I could try to buy you out eventually, if that's what you want?"

"No, of course not," she hurriedly said and touched his beautiful face, frowning in confusion. "You're not sending me away?" she asked in a small voice that made her cringe.

Sean's expression grew pained and he instantly hugged her close. "No, babe. Not ever."

She exhaled and held him so tightly that it hurt her arms and probably him too, but he didn't complain. Gia eventually managed to let him go, but she gripped his hands, hoping it would somehow stop him from changing his mind.

"What do you need?" she rasped.

"Some time. And it's gonna take a while, so I'll probably be moody a lot."

"You can be as moody as you like for as long as you want."

"And you'll have to stay in the guest room."

Gia nodded.

"And I want you to get me a puppy."

"Really?" She tentatively smiled. They'd talked about getting a puppy, but pets weren't allowed in their apartment block back in Ridge City. "I'll email the shelter. Mrs. Goldberg's son from the coffee shop works there and it's over an hour's drive away, so maybe he'll send us some pictures."

He only nodded and stood, Gia following when she caught sight of his glistening eyes. She threw her arms around him again and hugged him tightly. "I love you."

"I love you, too," he hoarsely said and sniffed. Gia finally let him go when he shifted away from her and she watched him walk up the stairs until he was out of sight.

* * *

Luna woke in her bedroom, grateful she wasn't dead yet because her mothers would never have forgiven her had she not said goodbye. They still wouldn't, but at least she would have a chance to explain and convince them there was nothing they could have done to have prevented it. Hopefully Mama wouldn't blame Gia.

Movement at the window seat caught her attention. The orange red glow of either sunset or sunrise invaded the room and illuminated Sua's hair.

Luna swallowed hard, her tongue thick and glued to the roof of her mouth. An invisible weight pressed against her chest, heavy and suffocating, and her heart slowly thumped against it. Like it wouldn't be long until it gave up the effort of beating entirely.

How could everything hurt and yet make her feel numb at the same time? It made no sense, but enlightenment hardly mattered in that moment. She needed to go to her mothers, managing to lift only her head from the pillow, straining, before she gave up and fell back, heavily panting and unnaturally fatigued.

Was it too late? If she was already nearing the catatonic stage, the Mourning was well on its way. Arimas had been known to last days—miserable, agonising days—before they succumbed to their despair. She'd witnessed it once and it had been a relief when death finally claimed her sister's Arima.

"I need to see my mothers," she croaked, and Sua walked closer, sitting beside her on the bed. "Please get them for me, Sua. This is the last thing I'll ever ask of you."

"Have you really made peace with this? Won't you even try to fight?"

"I can't even get someone who can't help but love me to love me," Luna said, every part of her body aching, yet the emptiness in her chest where she'd once been comforted by Gia's presence, hurt the most.

"Who says she doesn't love you?"

"She chose someone else," Luna croaked, hot tears leaking down her temples.

"Did she?"

Luna scowled at Sua, who held an inscrutable expression while she studied Luna's prone form. "Do you love her?"

"*Yes*, Sua."

"Do you love her still?"

Her lips trembled, understanding the question for what it was. "Yes." Luna hated that she did, but her feelings hadn't changed. Not even a little.

"She needed a choice and now you have given her one, and instead of taking this chance, you want to lay down and die."

Luna felt unreasonably proud at the weak scoff she managed. "I don't have a choice in dying. At least Sean Williams is a good Human. I will die knowing that he'll make her happy."

"And people call me theatrical."

"You are. I need to say goodbye to my mothers before it's too late," she said and attempted to get up again but couldn't muster enough desire to make her limbs move. Maybe if she dictated a letter, Sua would give it to them. She was so tired, though… And her eyes fell shut.

"What if it's not too late?"

"I can feel it, Sua," she mumbled, sleep trying to claim her.

Was it sleep?

"I want to take your place."

Luna's eyes fluttered and she stared into Sua's solemn face through heavy lids.

"There's a very thin line between bravery and foolishness, and you, little warrior, are simply a fool in love."

"Love shouldn't hurt this way. I don't want such a love."

"It doesn't always hurt."

"It hurt you, too. It affects you to this day."

"But did I die?"

Luna sighed at the snark and tried to lift her head again, mumbling a "thank you" when Sua finally helped her into an upright position, propping her up with pillows. Along with a wave of nausea and pain, the scent of Sweet Alyssum wafted from her bedding, stuck in her nose and throat, and burned her eyes.

Why did Sua bring her here, to this bed that she should have burned the second after Gia had left her?

"My Elurra wanted to protect me with immortality and thrusted on me the burden of all this power I hold."

"You see it as a burden?"

"It is a burden, Iluna. No singular being should ever hold such power."

"You use it wisely, though. Few others would."

"Little I do changes much, and when I do too much it changes little. This magic is a curse."

"I don't understand."

"What use is this power if I can't decide how to use it? And if when I use it, I only make things worse? Nothing I did in Tristea helped."

"Why do you care what happens to Tristea?"

"Lake Beltza won't hold forever."

Luna tensed, her tired heart managing one final sprint.

"No spell is infallible and absolute. I thought if I could arm Tristeans, we may once again share the responsibility of fighting the Darke. But I'm tired of fighting, Iluna. I have chosen you as my successor."

Luna laughed shakily. "Chosen to give me your burden?"

"You're stronger than I ever was."

"I'm laying here dying because my Arima broke my heart. How is that strong?"

"You gave someone you love what she needed, despite the consequences for yourself."

"To save myself from hurt."

"We both know you've been hurting for a long time, and when it was only you who suffered, you bore your burden bravely. You could've asked me decades ago to sever the tie and you never did."

"Because I used to have hope that the pain would have been worth it in the end when I finally found her."

"The first time I held you in my arms, I knew you were meant for more."

"More what?"

"Who knows, only time will tell."

Luna shook her head. "I won't let you die."

"Well, if you choose not to take my power and save yourself, you'll be dead and I will still have made the decision to end my life."

She huffed. "How long have you been thinking about this?"

"I don't remember exactly, but I have been seriously considering it for about two thousand years."

"Why haven't you done it sooner then?"

"Someone needs to be Mother. Not only for the Guardians, but to ensure our worlds remain in balance."

"How?"

"However she decides to do it."

"How do you do it?"

"If anything, the Mother will become a keeper of this magic. If I die without transferring it, it will choose whomever it wants. I would die peacefully if you accept this gift from me."

"So you want me to be Mother and do nothing?"

"Ederra is stable. It's a safe time to transition."

"And Tristea?"

"With the limited magic there, it's difficult to find remedies for what ails Tristea."

Luna hung her head. "I don't know, Sua. Mom could do a great job. She's already in a position of leadership."

"She would, but I have a feeling that this will better suit you. Do you really want to die, dear one?"

"Dying seems fine, but I think of my mothers and how they would mourn me and I feel guilty. They already lost my sister."

She was so selfish. She should have spoken to them before severing the bond, but they would have tried to convince her not to go through with it. And she might have given in to them and then weeks from now Gia would somehow have ended up in her bed again and Luna would be too weak to resist her and would touch her and Gia wouldn't want her to, but would let her…

Another wave of nausea had bile rising in her throat.

"Then don't break your mothers' hearts," Sua said. "Come, I will heal you and give you time to decide whether you wish to succeed me."

"Wait," Luna said, trying to catch up with the conversation. It was very difficult with the dull throb in her brain. "You could heal me this entire time?"

"It's a remedy, not a cure. My magic is the only thing dimming your pain and keeping you alive and lucid right now. You would have died hours ago."

"Sua," Luna swallowed thickly.

"Either I die, or we both die. I'm simply granting you more time to decide."

Luna frowned, grateful for the opportunity to speak to her mothers, but it still felt too surreal to process. "You can't die, and I'm not worthy of this gift."

"But you passed the final test."

"What test?"

"That matters not, but you have passed it." Sua smiled and brushed a strand of hair from Luna's forehead and kissed her there.

"I—" Luna sighed when her body went limp at the cool relief of Sua's magic spreading through her aching bones.

"Take some time to rest. You've put your mind, body and heart through enough today. I have told your mothers what I would offer you. That is the only reason they haven't barged in here at your distress. I won't be able to save you from their wrath forever, though."

"I won't let you die," Luna sleepily mumbled, sighing heavily as the weight on her chest lifted, even when the usual heartache from loving Gia remained.

"Rest now, my little warrior, we'll talk more later."

CHAPTER TWENTY-THREE

The little German shepherd mix bounded across the lawn in their backyard, tail wagging, pouncing and yapping at the bone-shaped rubber toy Sean shook in his direction. He had a smile on his face, green eyes twinkling with a familiar merriment Gia had missed, and her gaze travelled to the stubble on his jaw where he was growing out his beard. She'd never liked facial hair, and though she couldn't remember ever having told him that, he must've somehow known as he'd been smoothly shaved for the majority of their relationship.

"Mom wants me to move back home," he said, not looking at her.

Gia's heart gave a painful thud and she pulled at the blades of grass where she sat cross-legged beside him. "Do you want to go home?"

"I like it here."

"Yeah, it's a nice place. But if you want to go back, I'll take care of the house, so you don't need to base any decision on finances, and we can move back as soon as you're able to leave your job here."

A stifling silence followed her words and Gia stared off at the Black Bearded Iris she'd planted, standing tall and proud. When Sean finally looked at her, the sparkle in his eyes had dulled.

"You don't need to prove a point to me, Gia," he said. It was still so strange, yet wonderful, to hear him say her name.

"I don't feel obligated, but I will do anything I can to make this easier for you."

He sighed. "Don't be scared to put yourself out there. She loves you."

"Why are we talking about Luna?"

"Because you're in denial and you owe her an apology."

"We just broke up, Sean. I'm not gonna go chasing after someone else. Besides, she got her all-powerful friend to break our connection. A literal *goddess*. The two of them are probably off happily *spending time* together. I doubt I've crossed her mind since we were untethered. She seemed in a hurry to leave me standing there in the shop like an idiot with my heart ripped right out of my chest!"

"Oh, wow." Sean laughed and Gia scowled.

"This isn't funny."

"No, it isn't, but this is a whole new side of you."

She drew back defensively. "What?"

"The intense jealousy."

"I'm not jealous."

"Just paranoid that you let your girl get away."

"I liked you better when you were my fiancé."

He hummed. "I liked it better when I was your fiancé, too. Please don't make me play matchmaker for you. It's far too soon, babe."

"I'm sorry."

"Go see her. Make sure she's okay. If I'm being honest, I'm worried about her."

* * *

When Gia had gone through the Veil three days prior, Tximista had bounded toward her, nickering excitedly and she had drowned in guilt while she petted the pegasus. Trumoi had only watched her where he stood out in the field and Gia couldn't look at him.

She spent hours there with no sign of Luna. Not feeling her was awful because she could've been right there in the cottage, ignoring all the knocking, and Gia would never have known.

She was also unable to sense the Darke any longer, and that was something that worried her too. Luna would be stubborn enough to continue guarding the Rift on her own, without her Shield, and what if she got hurt again like she did with the dragon? It was becoming increasingly difficult to push down her incessant worry and all the brutal images her mind would conjure of Luna's burned skin, and those claw marks on her arm the day of the Meeting.

Where was she? The day before, Gia had watered Luna's flowers and her vegetable patch, realising that Luna couldn't have been home if they were beginning to wilt.

It was only on the third day of her desperate stalking that Gia felt it, almost like she used to when they were tethered. The Call of Luna's magic was faint but achingly recognisable, and coming from inside the house. She had to have used the mirror and Gia had the sudden urge to flee back through the Veil.

Standing from the porch swing, she adjusted Sean's track pants and T-Shirt she'd borrowed. The pants were too short but the outfit was more comfortable than her own clothing in her true form. She wished she was wearing her silver robes, but they were inside the cottage that hadn't been locked that first day Gia had experimentally tried the doorknob. She had immediately paused and closed the door again, very careful not to enter uninvited.

She hadn't even had a chance to see her armour…

Inhaling a fortifying breath, she walked forward and lightly knocked on the front door. Luna's magic became stronger but the door remained closed for a few long agonising minutes. Gnawing at her lip, she debated whether she should leave or knock again. But the burning desire to see Luna's face had her standing there, staring at the door, which meant she visibly startled when it slowly opened.

Luna's expression was blank and she kept hold of the door, blocking the entryway.

"Hi," Gia croaked and tensed when Luna only stared. "I-I wanted to check whether you were okay—"

"I'm fine."

Well, weren't those the two words no one ever wanted to hear during an argument.

"I'm not with Sean anymore."

Gia winced, not entirely sure why she'd told Luna that. Not being able to feel Luna any longer made the lack of reaction to her statement even more prominent. She'd rehearsed what she needed to say, though, and desperately tried to remember.

"I know I don't deserve your time or forgiveness, but I wanted to apologise for the way I treated you after we were intimate," she said. "I was unfair and inconsiderate and you have every right to hate me right now, but I want you to know that I don't regret being with you. I didn't then and I don't now. I regretted that it happened while I was committed to someone else, because neither of you deserved that…And we may not be bound anymore, Luna, but I still feel something for you, and I was hoping you would give me another chance? That I could still protect the Rift with you even if you don't want anything more than that?"

She anxiously fidgeted under Luna's stare whose eyes watered. "Gia."

The soft whisper trickled down Gia's spine and caused her to shiver as her chest tightened.

"Loving you is terrifying," Luna hoarsely said. "It took me to a very dark place and I made an awful decision with no regard to myself or the people who love me."

Gia's heart heavily thudded at the grim look on Luna's face. "What happened?"

"I can recognise that loving someone that much isn't inherently bad. I grew up surrounded by love like that, only ever seeing it requited. I had been grossly unprepared for you entering my life."

"None of this was your fault. I never meant to hurt you," Gia softly said. "You've been perfect and I thoughtlessly took that for granted. I know how irrational it must seem to you, but I thought that staying away from you would protect us both. I didn't realise you were out here fighting on your own. I made a mistake because I was scared and I know it doesn't make it right, but I'm so sorry, Lu."

"I believe you're good. I know the way you made me feel wasn't out of malice, but my life is changing and I can't—I—my priorities have changed. I have responsibilities that require my full attention and focus. And I thank you for coming here and offering me this chance at closure."

"Lu…" Her voice cracked. Gia had no idea what was happening, but would Luna simply give up on them? "Please…"

"I don't trust you, Argia," Luna sadly said, "and I especially don't trust myself around you." She then took a step back and softly closed the door between them.

* * *

She missed Luna, and though they shared a house, she missed Sean too. Gia wanted to talk to them both about how she'd destroyed her relationship with the other and wasn't that just something that said a lot about her as a person and how selfishly she'd handled the entire situation?

Sean wasn't moody, but he avoided her, and Gia was determined to give him whatever space he needed. Luna's words to her had left her reeling and needing clarification, but she granted Luna her space too and didn't go trespassing on her property again.

She went in to work early and went home early, cooked dinner, placed a plate for Sean in the microwave and then went through the Veil to guard the Rift for a few hours.

She made sure to stay away from the cottage and hadn't run into Luna or any Darke Husks yet and wasn't sure whether to be relieved by that or not. Sometimes she would go there in the middle of the night because her sleep was restless and agonisingly dreamless, and she woke in the guest room feeling nearly as lonely and abandoned as when she'd first set foot in Tristea.

When she cashed-up early for the third time that week, Gia was forced to admit to herself that she was hoping to run into Luna rather than a Husk. She didn't plan on saying anything if Luna didn't want to talk, but she needed to see her and was certain that if she did, things would be better.

Caught up in her thoughts and distracted by the tentative hope knotting in her stomach, she startled when the shop's door opened, seemingly on its own accord and her chest expanded with a disturbing amount of joy when she immediately thought that Luna had come to see her.

The pitying look that Uda sent her once she'd lowered her cloak was therefore no surprise, as it took some effort to swallow the utter disappointment that must've been clearly written all over her face.

"Uda," she softly greeted, dread twisting in her belly when she remembered that despite the close relationship they'd built, this was still Luna's mother. Sean's mother wasn't speaking to her at all and she knew Sean had told Vanessa that the breakup had been a mutual decision. Vanessa seemed to suspect that Gia was the one to blame for it, though. "What brings you here?"

"I haven't seen you in a while," Uda said and placed the large familiar chest she'd been wheeling behind her onto the counter.

"I-I didn't think you would want to see me."

"Because you broke my daughter's heart?"

The words struck like a blow to the gut. "Yes," Gia rasped and tugged at the braid with the silver crescent moon.

Uda only hummed and clicked the chest open. "I brought your armour."

Gia carefully approached the chest, and sensing her apprehension, Uda stepped aside.

Gia assumed the leg and arm pieces were in the bottom of the chest, but up top was a stunning silver chest plate and next to it, a silky piece of inky black fabric neatly rolled up.

"It's your cape," Uda said and Gia drew in a sharp breath.

She reached out shaky hands and rolled out the fabric, reverently spreading it across the countertop. Her heart tightened at the fine silver embroidery of two pegasuses up on their hind legs, wings spread upward and hooves kicking at the air while they faced each other.

"When did she do this?" Gia whispered, eyes burning with unshed tears as her fingers delicately traced over the fine detailing.

"She brought it to Erdiko a day before the anniversary of her sister's death."

Gia nodded slowly and carefully rolled the cape back up. "Why aren't you angry at me, Uda?" she asked, busying herself by placing the garment back in the chest.

"Luna asked me not to be."

Gia closed the lid and sniffed, mustering up the courage to look at Uda. Her golden eyes were soft, but she stood a few feet away with her hands behind her back, guarded like she'd never been before. She might not have been expressing her anger, but her disapproval was evident.

"What did she tell you happened?"

"She hasn't said much. Seeing her sadness was enough to know that you hurt her terribly."

Wiping a tear from her cheek, Gia nodded. "I did."

"There's a ceremony at the Sanctum on the next full moon. You should attend. It's formal, so you must wear your armour with your cape."

Gia gaped in surprise at the invitation. "Will Luna be there?"

"All the Guardians of Ederra will be there."

"Do you think she'll be okay if I show up?"

"Do you think she would forbid you this time with your people?"

Gia shook her head. "She wouldn't."

"Good. I'll see you then, Argia," Uda said and stepped back through the Veil without a smile or a hug. The growing emptiness in Gia's chest was only negated by a little bit of hope that she hadn't been shunned entirely.

CHAPTER TWENTY-FOUR

"I don't understand why we need to make a big show of it," Luna grumpily complained where she sat reading through a spell book in the Sanctum's library. The Ama Gorria didn't care much for crowds and Uda had made sure they would have their privacy while there.

"People take comfort in rituals," Sua answered from the other side of the table laden with books, her feet propped up and leaning back in her chair. "They accept change more readily when it's wrapped in a pretty bow of ceremony."

"I'm only one hundred and twelve years old; they won't accept me."

"Since when do you care what they think of you?"

"Since I have all this responsibility now to do right by them."

"I've told you, you don't need to do a thing."

"I can't have the power to change lives and then not use it when they need changing."

"Sometimes you can only guide choices, watch them hurt, offer alternatives that make no difference or make things worse. It's exhausting. The sooner you make peace with the fact that more often than not you will fail, no matter your good intentions, the better."

Luna huffed and propped her cheek against her fist. It wasn't the first time they'd gone over how useless Sua's powers apparently were. She was surprised, though, at how patiently Sua kept on repeating herself. Her usual snarkiness had taken a backseat and that only added to Luna's apprehension.

"And why do I need to learn all these spells if I'll be able to cast at will?"

"Spells focus your magic," Sua replied, open and forthcoming like she'd never been before. No teasing. No infuriating riddles. Luna's heart hurt as though she'd lost her already.

"They set parameters and exclude variables from interfering with your intent. Simple things like summoning a book"—a red book appeared in her hand in a light red magical mist—"will become second nature once you learn control. You try that right now and there's a very good chance hundreds of books, perhaps the same colour as this one, may come flying at you at once. Understood?"

Luna nodded, but apparently Sua didn't believe her.

"For example, the protection spell I cast around your home. Had I ever asked you who you wanted to have access to your front door?"

Luna shook her head.

"Exactly. I took my time and instead of simply placing down a shield, I cast the spell to bind with you and your needs. Allowing it to recognise what and who you perceive as threats and who you want in your home. Imagine if the shield would simply block all life from getting in. It would be as though you were encased in an impenetrable glass dome. You would have needed to call on me each time to lower it and let someone in."

Luna smiled. "I understand, Sua."

"Good," she said and slid the red leather-bound book across the table toward her. Luna felt her magic on it before she'd even picked it up.

"I journaled some events I've been responsible for and witnessed over time and documented their consequences. I hope those retellings will at least save you from making the same mistakes. And perhaps assist you should you be faced with similar challenges."

Luna brushed a finger over the cool leather, the white unicorn engraved on the cover, then picked up the book and hugged it to her chest without opening it. Her heart beat frantically against the cover and she looked back to Sua when she continued speaking.

"We'll need to start preparing your body to accept this power tonight. I will gradually be transferring the magic to you up until the next full moon, and then you'll be given the remainder."

Luna swallowed thickly. "If not even a Guardian body can hold this power without preparation, why do you fear where it will go should you not give it to someone?"

"The magic will seek out a vessel, perhaps one that can wield for a while, until the power simply drains them of their energy. And so it will go from body to body, destroying it, driving it mad. And in their madness, they may wreak havoc. This is all speculation, Luna. You will be my first. It's you alone I trust."

Luna gave a jerky nod.

"You'll be gifted with immense power that will require time and focus to learn and master. You let it overwhelm you, and you may destroy villages, entire civilisations. I know you're patient when you believe, little warrior. I'm asking you to please believe in this."

"I believe, Sua. But I don't believe that I'm the right one to do this."

"Think of something you want to change."

"The Soulbond. We should be allowed to choose who we want to be with."

"And how will you accomplish that?"

"I'll simply stop it. No new daughters born will be tethered to anyone."

"There are currently five hundred and ten adult Guardians in Ederra. Six hundred and twenty-four Rifts. How will you ensure that they're all guarded?"

"The way we have been?"

"What if the Guardians don't want to live together? What if one wants to go look for love and guard a Rift with her chosen partner instead of the one where she was assigned? What if two Shields fall in love?"

"There will be no Shields and Swords. Individuals will be able to do both themselves."

"It takes time to find someone to love and the current birth-rate is extremely low as it is."

"I'll make it easier to conceive."

"So Guardians have sex and will become pregnant each time?"

"Yes."

Sua laughed with sparkling eyes and Luna couldn't feel embarrassed that it was apparently at her expense. "So much to learn. Not all people who have sex want to raise children together."

"We will raise the daughters they don't want here at the Sanctum."

"It sounds like you're planning to farm Guardians."

"No," Luna said, horrified. "I didn't mean it that way."

"Aside from the ethical considerations of your orphanage for warriors, the reason the rate of reproduction is slower is to prevent too many Guardians, considering their natural lifespans. Too many Guardians reduces the threat of the Darke. Without that urgency and need to protect and defend, they will become idle, bored, and start seeking other endeavours. In theory this seems harmless. Honour is in their blood but the allure of power is an evil temptress. Ederrans hold Guardians in high regard, but that awe and trust can easily be manipulated."

Luna nodded.

"Now, how will you control that magic to avoid that a pair of Guardians have hundreds of children during their lifetime?"

"I'll make it so that daughters can only be born from love."

"How will you stipulate in your spell what love is? What if others don't have the compulsion to search for it? What if some are together simply for the companionship? Happy, but not in love, because it's better than living in isolation at a Rift? What happens if a daughter isn't born and they realise they've been lying to each other? They fight. They neglect their duties? Love is a messy business. I'm certain you can attest to that."

Luna snorted her agreement.

"With the danger out there and the search for love, you will have more Guardians dying than you do daughters being born. How will you fix that? Guardians were born from Elves, but you are not Elves. My Elurra had been pressed for time, casting the Arima bond had been severely influenced by her affection for me. The spell mirrored the type of love of its caster, subsequently preventing the birth of any males to your race."

Luna frowned. She'd known that the ancient Elves had been more diverse in their genders, but it hadn't been something she'd ever thought to question. Guardians were a race on their own, comparing them to Elves was senseless. Sometimes she forgot that the Elves were their ancestors, too.

"I know that hadn't been Elurra's intention," Sua continued, "and therein lies the complex nature of magic. In how your implicit intent can breathe life into a spell and transform it into something else entirely. Whatever well-intentioned changes you make to the Guardians might mean that, in essence, an entire people, an entire race and culture, will cease to exist as you know it. You may very well destroy the Guardian population because of something you thought would only be a small alteration."

Luna sighed. "I don't know, Sua. This only proves that I'm not the one to accept this gift."

"I understand why you feel you want to change the way of the Guardians, but you need to understand one simple truth, Iluna. I'm uncertain whether this is something that's unknown because the Soulbond has been universally accepted for millennia, but magic cannot create love as it's impossible to clearly define and unique to each who experience it."

Frowning, Luna tilted her head in question.

"The spell my Elurra casted, pairs Guardians based on compatibility. The Soulbond opens a connection between them from birth. The intensity of this connection changes from pair to pair. When they're of age, touch opens them to a physical connection. Sharing magic, in general, heightens what's already there and strengthens the bond. The Binding Ceremony seals it. Guardians have every capability to stray, no magic keeps them together, though a lifelong awareness of each other does make it extremely difficult. Regardless, whatever two Arimas feel, is very real and good and dependent on *them*."

Mouth agape, Luna stared at the table, her heart racing while she thought on the implications. Scenes of her time with Gia flashed in her brain like a montage of happiness and contentment. It had never felt one-sided or forced. Gia had come to her doorstep of her own volition even after the tether was cut. She hadn't known what it meant then, and even with this new knowledge, Luna was uncertain what it meant now. But Gia repeatedly choosing Tristea and Sean Williams was proof of what Sua said, though, wasn't it? Which meant that Gia spending time with her had been a choice too…

"Finding solutions takes time." Sua thankfully saved her from her spiralling thoughts. "Your final test showed how you held no desire for power and that's another reason I know I can entrust you to protect this magic and pass it on responsibly if you ever need to. I'm confident that you will thoroughly explore your options and their possible consequences if you ever feel the need to act."

Luna stared at her—this person who had been a constant during her entire life—always there when she was needed and never asking anything in return.

"I don't want to lose you, Sua."

She received a sad smile and the Elf got up and rounded the table, kneeling beside her chair and earnestly gazed up into Luna's eyes. It was bizarre to see her like that. Even during the direst times, Sua would have a mischievous twinkle in her eyes, her lips slightly tilted into a teasing smirk.

"Is that why you're fighting so hard against this and finding reasons why I shouldn't choose you?"

"If I embrace this, if I prepare my body and mind and study these tomes, it means accepting your death and it doesn't feel right."

"I know I'm asking a difficult thing of you, dear one," she said, taking Luna's hand. "And I apologise sincerely for it. You've been a light in my life when all I knew was darkness. I know I would use all the power I had to save you and it honours me that the thought of my death grieves you so." Luna lowered down beside her, clasping her hand tightly, the journal still pressed to her chest. "But I make this decision with a heart full of peace and hope that *you* have placed there. I make it knowing that you love and protect in a way that is fierce and frightening, and our worlds will be that much safer with you as vanguard."

Luna ducked her head, but Sua's fingers lightly pressed beneath her chin and lifted her gaze again. "I make this decision, little warrior, because no soul should survive for as long as I have. It is the very nature of things to end and make way for the new to arise and bring about change."

* * *

Stepping out of the mirror at the Eastern Courtyard where the Naming Ceremony had been held, Gia's stomach anxiously twisted and she had to inhale a steadying breath in a futile attempt to calm her racing pulse. If Luna didn't want her there, or looked even the slightest bit uncomfortable at her presence, she would leave immediately.

The sound of her armour rhythmically clinking as she walked up the stone path to the courtyard entrance, made her spine mechanically straighten out of her shameful slump. The long dark cape that perfectly matched her skin billowed behind her and a sad part of Gia was excited to see Luna wearing her own matching one.

Would she be wearing it, though?

The various enchantments Luna had requisitioned made Gia's armour feel as weightless and untroublesome as a tank top and yoga pants. Her magic was heightened, flowing more easily and focused through the gauntlets and made her shields that much stronger and longer-lasting. Gia had little experience with armour sets, but the way hers made her feel practically invincible spoke volumes of the craftsmanship and magic that had gone into its creation.

Lost in thought, it took her far too long to notice that the courtyard was deserted. The pink cherry blossoms that covered the ground like a sheet lay undisturbed.

The full cerulean moon hung low and smiled down on her nearly above the Sanctum on its trajectory across the clear night sky, which meant she wasn't too early nor so late that everyone might have gone home already. Frowning, she walked out and by chance spotted two Guardians holding hands while they walked down the stone path a few yards ahead. Another pair was a few feet in front of them, their armour shiny and capes fluttering, shoulder-to-shoulder with their Arimas.

Feeling awkward and suddenly alone, Gia quietly trailed after them until she could hear the droning of a large crowd where they entered a different courtyard. She was stunned by all the armoured Guardians gathered there, their young daughters standing amongst them, dressed in their respective robes.

Gia felt proud to be in their midst, these warriors of the Veil, who devoted their lives to protecting entire worlds.

She hadn't fully understood the purpose of the Soulbond before. For as long as she could remember, she had rejected and despised it. Tristea had shown her how difficult it was to fall and stay in love, but looking at the Guardians now, wasn't it the least they deserved? To have a guaranteed soulmate who joined in her fight? Who offered companionship when a lifetime at a Rift would otherwise mean one of potential isolation? To bring happiness to each other while they risked their lives day after day?

There were hundreds of them, and still Gia spotted the striking visage of Saso making her way over in her set of copper armour, a beautiful golden cape fluttering at her back.

"Welcome, Argia Erretzea," Saso stiffly greeted. "My Arima requested you wait with me."

Gia nodded and followed her down the stone path that split the crowd in half. Saso's cape was embroidered with two copper Griffins, clawed paws up and facing each other. She was led into the front row before a white marble stage. This courtyard seemed to be made of the softest and greenest grass, surrounded by grey stone walls, and lined with green-leafed shrubbery and trees.

Gia only had a quick glance around, waving at her grandmothers after they excitedly caught sight of her, before her attention went back to the stage. A statue of the Mother of Light, seated on an ornate throne as though presiding over the event, stood upon it. Right in front of the statue, standing centre stage and wearing a glittering silver cape with her shiny black armour, was Luna. Her hands were folded behind her back and that gorgeous mass of hair was thick and windswept, and begging to be touched. The moon shone on her like a spotlight as she stared intently at the stage floor. Gia's stomach swooped at the sight of her even as it filled with dread.

"What's happening?" she asked, and a wild thought had her almost stumbling despite her stationary position. "Is this a Binding Ceremony?"

Saso snorted out a laugh and tilted her head at Gia before softening her features.

"I'm not entirely sure how to describe this ceremony."

Gia frowned and looked back at Luna, who seemed lost in thought and oblivious to the crowd gathering below her.

"I guess it's both a funeral and a coronation, but funeral seems incorrect."

Her heart leapt into her throat. "A funeral for who?"

"Does it matter to you?"

And okay, *ouch*.

"Itsaso Amorratua, I understand your anger. I'm angry at myself too for the way I handled everything. But you need to know that I care about your daughter very much. And I do it without compulsion—for who she is and not who she's supposed to be to me. And I will make every effort to make it up to her, if and when she allows me to do so."

Saso stared at her for a long moment, so long in fact, that Gia seriously considered going home.

"You make life unnecessarily difficult, Gia," she eventually said, looking back toward the stage and Gia felt like she'd won a battle. "My daughter has been chosen to become the next Mother."

Saso's chin raised and her eyes glittered. Gia wanted to ask more, because *what*? But a flash of golden armour and hair hurried toward them. The crowd parted for Uda to reach their side and Gia almost cried when she was wrapped in a quick, but affectionate, hug and was then flanked by Luna's mothers.

Silence fell and Gia bit her tongue, the two groups of warriors seemed to tighten ranks as the path that split them cleared. From the back, each row of Guardians took a knee, heads bowed as the Ama Gorria, dressed in a set of simple ruby-red robes, walked up the pathway.

Gia slowly lowered too when Saso and Uda did, but remained fixated on the Red Mother as she ascended the steps of the stage toward a kneeling Luna. Sua Orro took a moment to stare up at the statue of the Mother of Light, then directed a fond grin at Luna's bowed head. She slipped a pale finger beneath Luna's chin, who looked up and beautifully smiled at her before she stood.

Gia ached for that smile to be directed at her, the jealousy only tempered by her utter confusion about what was happening and the repercussions thereof.

It was an odd ceremony and it began as unceremoniously as Sua Orro was known to be. Gia smiled softly when Luna's eyes twinkled in amusement at the uncomfortable shifting and low murmurs from the confused crowd that quickly quieted when the Guardians focused on the Ama Gorria, who had her eyes closed as she circled Luna, softly muttering under her breath.

The air grew thick around them, saturated with the most powerful magic. The Ama Gorria continued her circle chant and the longer she did, the stronger Luna glowed with beautiful blue magic. She seemed to overflow with it and her body rose a few inches from the floor. Her back arched, hair falling behind her, arms hanging at her sides. When she let out an agonised scream, only Uda's strong yet shaky hand on her shoulder kept Gia in place.

"She'll be fine, darling," Uda murmured, though her expression was tight and equally worried.

Gia decided that Luna's mothers wouldn't stand by and let her get hurt, so she released a breath when Luna lowered onto her feet, magic still brilliantly blazing from her body. The air smelled like a fresh thunderstorm and Gia's own body glowed in response, her magic coiling in her stomach like a knot of excitement and anticipation.

The Ama Gorria completed a last circle and stood in front of Luna. The words they shared were private and brief, before Luna wrapped her arms around her friend, tears streaming down her cheeks. Sua Orro's body went limp in the embrace and Luna released a loud sob, tenderly picked her up, and held Sua to her chest.

Seeming to remember she was in front of an audience, Luna looked up, body still lit like a blowtorch. Even her eyes swirled with magic despite the tears pouring from them. As one, the Guardians knelt again, and Gia belatedly followed, momentarily struck dumb when Luna's anguished gaze met hers.

The new Mother didn't say a word, though Gia supposed some sort of speech had been expected. Instead, perhaps as an homage to her friend's abrupt nature, they disappeared from the stage in a swirling blue inferno.

It took a while for people to recover from the scene. Of watching someone lose their life while the other was elevated. It was the end and start of something extraordinary, and Gia's emotions were conflicted. She felt breathless for some reason. Her fists clenched and her chest filled with longing while her stomach twisted anxiously, her magic having dully settled with Luna's departure.

Luna as the new Mother had just pushed her that much further out of reach.

"Will she live here now?"

"She will live wherever she pleases," Saso replied.

"I want—I would like to continue protecting the Rift." Gia glanced between them. "My and Luna's Rift…Without Luna, I'm unable to sense the Darke."

"You want to go through Initiation?" Uda asked.

Gia nodded. "If—if that's okay?"

"Of course. We need all the Guardians we can get. I can perform your Initiation tonight or on the next full moon?"

"Tonight. If you don't mind. My family's here and I don't want to infringe on Luna—"

"That's a matter you two will need to discuss between yourselves," Saso interjected. "You are a Guardian. Ederra is your home. That will always be so."

It had been instinct, born from an intense need not to be on that stage with the entire Guardian population gawking at her any longer. Like Sua had warned, magic was as simple as breathing now. Luna could feel it all around her, practically tasting the magic in the particles of air she breathed. With it came a new awareness of the world and on that stage she'd been struck by over five hundred Guardians and their individual magical signatures all at once, none more so than the familiar presence of Gia, who stood in the front row, looking too beautiful in her armour. To once again experience such a consuming awareness of Gia on top of everything else was almost too much to bear.

Luna was tethered to every living magical thing. And as overwhelming as the thought was, and as frightening as it could have been, she forced it to the back of her mind and focused on Sua's lifeless body in her arms. Sua seemed suddenly small and frail. Despite being at least two feet shorter than the average Guardian, "small" and "frail" had never been words Luna had associated with her. She had struck a larger than life figure throughout her extensive and remarkable existence.

Her chest tightened and new tears sprung in her eyes. Luna had felt it the instant Sua had left the world, as though the tether that bound them had been cut and an emptiness remained in its place. She was determined to fill it with all the memories and adventures she had shared with Sua throughout her life. Over a century of recollections and yet it was still too little time. It left her feeling bereft and abandoned.

A stone altar had been set up in Sua's favourite place, where the herd of unicorns lived in the forest atop Mount Bularreko. When Luna gently laid Sua on it, the herd walked out of the trees and surrounded the altar. She shook with silent sobs while she watched each of them gently nuzzling Sua's body. They'd been like children to Sua, bringing her joy when she'd lost all interest in the rest of the world. Luna had grown up amongst them and hadn't understood until much later what an honour it was that they'd accepted her in their midst.

Fat tears blurred her vision while she waited until even the littlest filly had her turn to gently nudge Sua's body in farewell. Luna then drew in a shaky breath, knelt on the ground, and dug her fingers into the earth at the foot of the altar.

As though they were sprouting from her own person, vines grew from the soil and wrapped around the altar, threading across Sua's form. Luna was left dumbfounded at how, with only a thought, the red roses came into bloom, stunningly decorating the green sarcophagus she'd created. A softly muttered spell she'd practised for the past three days straight, ensured they would bloom forever. She'd seen the roses in Gia's garden behind her greenhouse; she had called them Blaze of Glory Climbing Roses. They'd instantly reminded her of Sua.

Frowning at the tiny pinpricks at the back of her neck, Luna rose and stiffened when she turned toward the presence she sensed. "How are you here?" she asked, surprised and relieved, but also confused by the intruder in this sacred place.

"Sua placed a mirror here for me to use, which you are instructed to destroy once I leave."

The unicorns that would usually have scattered at the intrusion still stood around Sua. Luna swallowed thickly and allowed them their privacy, joining Bo where she remained standing a respectful distance away.

"She said that since you forbade your mothers to be here, it was no betrayal of your confidence to ensure that someone else was available to offer you comfort. We might never have understood your relationship with the Ama Gorria, but we all respected it as something genuine and profound."

"She had no reason for concern and neither do you, Bo. I will mourn her like she deserves and I'll make her proud."

"You know, each time we spoke you said you were fine." Bo carefully took a step closer, searching Luna's face. "You were carrying on an unheard of friendship with your Arima and now you've been chosen as our Mother. I guess it's true what they say, once you have a daughter you miss out on what goes on in the world." She lightly laughed, but her magic was stormy and Luna recognised it as Bo's emotions swirling within her.

It was too much, this newfound awareness, and Luna finally understood why Sua had kept to herself and sometimes slept for centuries at a time. She'd only been exposed to it for a little while and perhaps it was her sorrow adding to it, but she already felt exhausted.

Instead of giving in to the need to lie down and cry, she straightened and the effort to smile was immense, but she managed. "You love your daughter."

"I do. And I love you too, Lulu. You don't need to hide your pain from me. I've been forced to learn being better at soothing, which can only be a benefit to you right now."

Luna laughed huskily. The more emotional she became, the more the power inside of her stirred. Bo was transported into her arms and even though it gave Luna a fright at how, with a fleeting thought, she'd made the embrace happen, Bo laughed quietly and held her tightly when Luna instantly began sobbing into her shoulder.

CHAPTER TWENTY-FIVE

It was a Sunday afternoon and Gia stood in her bedroom in Sean's house staring at the armour she wore in the full-length mirror. She bit her lip, lightly hopped on the balls of her feet and shook out her nerves before she went to show Sean, halting at the top of the stairs.

"Are you sure about this?" she asked his back where he stood at the foot facing away from her as he'd been asked to.

"Yeah, it's about time, don't you think?"

It was. Gia wasn't sure why she was so anxious when showing herself to him was something she'd been wanting to do ever since she realised she loved him and wanted him in her life forever.

Revealing herself to him as magical had been an accident. He'd broken his arm when he tackled a mugger and fell awkwardly. When she saw him that night, his arm in a cast, eye horribly bruised and swollen as though he'd been punched, she'd panicked. Ever dreading the fragility of Humans when it came to Sean, she'd healed him without a thought. He'd stared at her as though she was alien and listened to her fearfully telling him she was from another world. Since the concept of a parallel universe existing had been as much of a bizarre concept for him to process as magic, his reaction hadn't been unexpected.

He'd excused himself and went to his bedroom, closing the door behind him. It was a year into their friendship newly designated as something more, and Gia still had her own place. She'd gone home, heartsore and certain she would never see or hear from him again. Yet the next morning, he'd showed up at her door with a sheepish grin and a bouquet of pretty Stargazer Lilies, full of curiosity and questions.

Gia descended the stairs and stood behind him, inhaling a steadying breath. "Okay. You can turn around now."

Perhaps it was the wariness of her voice that made him uncertain, because he hesitated a moment, before slowly turning around. His eyebrows rose in surprise and his mouth fell open.

"Oh," he managed softly. "You're beautiful, G."

She flashed him a grin and twisted a strand of silver hair around her finger.

"No piercings?" he asked, carefully walking closer and stopped more than an arm's length away to unabashedly stare up at her face.

"They were part of my Human glamour. It's a bit difficult to pierce my actual skin without magical help. Plus, Guardians don't really express themselves in that way."

"Pfft." He waved a hand in the air in front of him. "About time you added some flavour to the Guardians."

Gia giggled at his wide grin, not sure how she'd somehow managed to love him even more.

"Would you like to see Ederra?"

For a while she thought he was having a medical emergency because he froze in place and stared at nothing, an expression of shock stuck on his face.

"Sean?"

He snapped out of his stupor as though the soft query had been a shout.

"Uhm, yeah. Okay, yes. If it won't get you into trouble?"

"Well, as Uda told me, Ederra's only a secret because the lack of magic in Tristea makes it difficult for people to believe. Then there's the fact that only Guardians can travel between worlds. It's less complicated to remain secret, but given the source of the Darke Blight, there remains a general distrust of Humans and Tristea."

"Not inspiring confidence here, babe."

Gia laughed. "We're only going to be around the Rift. No one in a hundred-mile radius to know you're there. And even if someone did find out, I'm certain it wouldn't matter as long as you don't cause any trouble."

"You know," Sean said, puffing his chest a little, "when Luna heard what my job entailed, she said that in a way *I* was a guardian too."

"You are," Gia easily agreed, heart melting at how small he seemed now to her.

"I know it's in no way the same thing," he bashfully continued and scratched the back of his neck. "But I think if I can grow on Luna, I could grow on anyone, right? At least enough so they won't kill me with their magic."

"I'll protect you."

She wasn't sure why that made him stare up at her in wonder and open his arms. It was like hugging him for the first time and he rested his head on her chest plate. They basked in this new aspect of their friendship, something finally settling after weeks of awkwardly living apart in the same space.

She took hold of his hand. "I've never actually transported anyone through the Veil."

"Again, not inspiring confidence here, G."

"I discussed the possibility with Uda and she said that you should be fine since you don't have any magic to counteract mine. All you need to do is not let go of me, okay?"

"Okay."

"Close your eyes."

"Is that part of it? I won't be torn into particles if I opened them on accident? Or come out the other side with my arms and legs swapped around?"

"No,"—she chuckled—"but I think it would help you if you closed your eyes and held my hand."

He did so with a trust that brought a lump to Gia's throat and with a gentle tug, he blindly followed her through the Veil.

"You can open your eyes now."

He inhaled a breath and fluttered open his eyes and Gia stood back, watching the awe in his face as he took in his surroundings.

"Oh wow, you weren't kidding, this place is like walking into a dream," he said, and Gia allowed him a moment to process it all. He blinked up into the sky in wonder, green eyes skidding over the cottage and the thick forest surrounding it. "It's literally as though we're neighbours."

"Yes, so I can come see you whenever I want or whenever you want. It'll be like I'm still living there and if you start dating anyone, it won't be weird that you're sharing a house with your ex."

"Not many dating options in Bluewater Bay. Gonna need to expand to other towns in the county." He flashed her his dimples but his gaze soon wandered across the colourful landscape once again, before he looked up into the sky. "Do you think it's the magic in the air that reflects the colours so beautifully?"

Gia's brows lifted. "Huh. I actually never thought of it much, but that's most likely the reason."

"Do they have science here—?" He paused when Tximista trotted up and distracted him entirely.

Tximista was gentle with Sean, as though sensing Gia's affection for him. She scanned the forest for Trumoi and finally spotted him in the shadows at the edge of the forest, silently watching her and refusing to come closer. He and Tximista remained at the cottage together and Gia hated herself for being jealous of them.

Thankfully, Sean's enthusiasm about going for a ride lifted her spirits again. She climbed up behind him, holding him steady when Tximista flapped her large wings and climbed into the air. Sean let out an excited whoop, leaning to the side to watch the view when they glided over the forest surrounding the Rift and the sparkling magenta ocean that stretched for as far as the eye could see.

She laughed at his rollercoaster scream when she urged Tximista down toward the field of golden grass where she'd left the disassembled tent she'd bought in Erdiko beneath a tall orange-leafed tree.

After dismounting and lavishing Tximista with attention, Sean quickly helped her set it up.

"Will it be safe for you out here on your own?" he asked, dubiously eyeing the tent.

It was large and the canopy high enough for her to stand, and she could easily fit a nice comfy bed and some luxuries inside. "I have magic," she assured him.

"Yeah, but so does everything else here."

"Magical creatures powerful enough to harm Guardians tend to stay in their own territories. None of the Ederran races will attack us since our lives are dedicated to protecting them."

"Then they should come build you something more solid." Sean scowled at the tent as though it had offended him.

Gia smiled. "I can still escape through the Veil to hide if there's any real danger I can't handle. Uda gave me a mirror too, so I can even travel around Ederra. I doubt she knows my plan was to camp out here, but it will have to do until I can build my own place."

"If you're sure…" he warily conceded. "I'll come help you with that when I'm off. We can start drawing up plans at dinner tonight. But you need to check in with me at least once a day so I know you're okay."

"I will, and I'd love your help…What?" she asked at the soft look on his face.

"It's nice that you've found your place in the world."

"It was a lot easier taking all these leaps with you at my side."

He grinned but it fell away when Gia touched her stomach and stared in the direction of the Rift. "There's a Husk on its way."

"Uhm…"

"We need to get you back. I'm gonna take you through the Veil from here and since we're away from the cottage, you might end up somewhere in town. I don't know how to cloak you so you may scare a few people by appearing seemingly out of nowhere." She took his hand. "I'm still learning how to aim with the portals. That does take some practice, otherwise I could've dropped you directly at home."

"Okay, that's fine, but what if I stayed here and out of the way?"

Before she could scold him for that terrible idea, the hair at the back of her neck prickled and Gia looked up into the sky where a streak of blue fire hurtled toward the ground like a meteor. Her stomach swooped when Luna landed in a crouch on the grass a few yards away, then raised up to her full height. Even from that distance, Gia could feel her almost as strongly as she used to.

She stood immobile when Luna glared in her direction, only dragging her gaze away when Sean gently tugged his hand from hers.

Oh.

"Yeah, she's probably gonna jump to the wrong conclusion."

"Sorry," Gia murmured.

He shook his head. "Don't worry about it. You two are like a negative photo of each other."

"Yeah." She softly smiled. "I guess so…"

"How long has it been since you've seen her?"

"Four weeks. Let's get you back to Tristea."

"Okay, but come see me as soon as you can so I know you're okay. We really need to find some cross-dimensional communication device."

Gia lightly laughed and took his hand again, relieved when they ended up in the empty park only a few miles from the house.

"I'll be back soon," she told him and stepped back through the Veil only to see Luna disposing of the Husk, the field smelling like a thunderstorm had hit. A delicious shiver travelled down Gia's spine at the welcomed familiarity of the scent. Her stomach fluttered and she quickly made her way over.

"Hi." She felt stupid and couldn't believe that was the first word she shared with Luna. It seemed too casual and wrong despite it being a perfectly normal way to greet people.

Luna didn't answer and instead glanced at the tent in the distance. She didn't seem angry or very sad, just distant in a way that pained Gia.

"You may have the cottage."

"I can't—"

"I built it for *you*," Luna angrily hissed and disappeared in a magical blue inferno.

CHAPTER TWENTY-SIX

Gia woke with a smile, the gentle linen against her cheek feeling woven by a million threads. She squinted at the morning light filtering through the curtains that covered the window seat and shifted her gaze to her polished armour glinting in the sunrays, the display stand beside it starkly empty.

With a sinking heart she sat up and sighed, the silky black nightgown she wore delicately gliding over her obsidian skin. She climbed out of bed and walked over to the wardrobe, removing Luna's robe from a hanger and slid it over her body.

She'd been at a very low point the first time she'd slipped on Luna's clothes. Aching with longing, it was awkward and invasive, but after weeks of Luna not coming to collect her things and Gia growing increasingly shameless in her desperation, she'd taken to sleeping in Luna's night clothes, soothed by her scent still lingering on some items and her residual magic pulsing in certain spots around the cottage.

She entered the bathroom and stood at the twin basin set behind the porcelain sink she had claimed as her own. Luna's toothbrush remained undisturbed in a glass holder next to a jar of toothpaste beside the other sink. Gia herself continued to use Tristean toothpaste. The strong minty taste had conditioned her brain into believing that the product cleaned better in comparison to the bland paste the Ederran alchemists swore by. Luna's teeth were perfect, though, and her mouth delicious, which left no doubt that it was the truth, but old habits were hard to break.

She finished freshening up and walked into the living room, peeking over the couch where Sean lay sleeping on his back, lightly snoring. His beard was long and thick and Gia missed seeing his dimples, but he was proud of his progress so she was sure to complement him on it often.

The large couch allowed him enough space to move around and he had assured her that it was comfortable too. She'd briefly considered adding a guest room to the cottage, but the thought of Luna not planning the expansion with her felt indescribably wrong and Gia had been forced to accept that her new home would never feel like a place solely intended for her.

Sean's puppy, Mr. Bones, lifted his head from where he lay on the carpet in front of the couch, one ear up and the other folded down, and tilted his head. Gia grinned when he got up and ran over. She bent down to scratch behind his ear and below his chin, before dragging herself away from the cuteness and walking into the kitchen.

With a spark of white magic, she started the coffee machine. She preferred tea herself, but Sean had fast become addicted to the Southern Lands coffee beans she'd gotten for him in Erdiko.

Some of her gardening tools had made their way over, as well as some crockery and utensils. But there was little lacking in the cottage, and while Sean's coffee brewed, Gia stepped out onto the perfect porch and went to sit on the perfect swing, breathing in the crisp morning air and smiled at the perfect pegasuses lazily grazing in the golden field out toward the cliff.

Mr. Bones ran out toward them and bounded around their long legs while they barely acknowledged his existence. Gia wished with her entire heart to see Luna with the puppy. With any puppy. Or to see her at all. Especially back in the cottage.

Signs of her remained everywhere. Lingering most notably in the spaces she'd frequently occupied. Like in the kitchen, where Luna had often smiled and laughed beside Gia at the stove, adding spices and taste-testing food from spoons Gia had mindlessly fed her. And seated at the table after a morning spent gardening together, devouring the wraps Gia had taught herself to make after learning they were Luna's favourite thing to have for lunch.

They hadn't shared a bed and yet Luna's absence in the bedroom felt the most glaring. No doubt a result of memories of that one night of intimacy they'd shared that would haunt Gia's thoughts the second her head hit her pillow each night. She'd been avidly avoiding going anywhere near the Passion Fruit Tree...

And yet despite the yearning, Gia was the happiest she'd ever been in her life. The most content in her skin and her wants. Her free time was spent either exploring Ederra, tending the garden and orchard, or entertaining Sean and her family when they came to visit her. Saso and Uda miraculously insisted on falling into that category too. Saso was still distant, but she had joined Uda on a few occasions and would quietly watch them while they trained on the lawn.

Everything was great save for her relationship with Luna, who had left an aching void in Gia's chest that no amount of sheer happiness seemed able to fill. She'd come to accept the pain as her punishment for all the hurt she had caused.

Soft footfalls sounded from inside and Sean walked out onto the porch, arms stretched in the air and yawning widely, before sighing and scratching his beard. Both Trumoi and Tximista looked up from their grazing and trotted over to meet him at the foot of the steps, Mr. Bones running after them and failing to keep up.

Sean fed them sugar cubes he always seemed to have on him these days and affectionately patted down their flanks with a big grin he finally directed at Gia.

"Morning," he said, and picked up a panting Mr. Bones before making his way over and sitting down beside her, then staring at her face until Gia lifted her brows. "Sorry," he mumbled, and dragged his gaze away, petting the puppy in his lap.

"Good morning," she said, laughing softly. "I thought it was getting better?"

"It comes and goes. The more time I spend with you the easier it gets, but I haven't seen you in a few days, so it's like that first time all over again."

"I thought for certain you'd get used to it."

"Ah, it's not that bad. Well, unless it makes you uncomfortable?"

Gia shook her head. "Only if you are."

He waved her off. "I'll survive your pretty, don't worry. Are you okay, though? You got all sad drunk last night. Is it Luna?"

Her chest tightened and she looked away.

"It's okay to tell me, G."

"Feels rude to," she mumbled.

"I'm still your friend, aren't I? You should be able to tell me when you're hurting."

Gia sighed, unwilling to make him feel like he wasn't still her best friend, or maybe that awful selfish part of her desperately needed to talk to someone about Luna.

"I've missed her all my life," she said. "But this? Knowing it's not the Arima bond dictating my feelings? It makes it that much harder to deal with."

He nodded and tilted his head. "It's good to know your feelings are real, though?"

She chuckled bitterly. "My feelings were always real, because she was always real. I just didn't realise it and now I feel like an idiot for wanting to be with her so much, yet when we shared the Soulbond, I couldn't accept it."

"Because of what happened to your mothers. It was a realistic response to a traumatic event."

"And because of my commitment to you. But yes, I'd decided not to be with her long before you and I met. Not going through the Veil and finding her was a persistent struggle. I grew up with a fear for both Luna and myself. Of being bonded that irrevocably to someone. I know I was scared of the Mourning, but getting to know Luna after the Meeting, all that fear quickly shifted onto her. I worried that I wouldn't be good enough at protecting her and our Rift, or end up dying and dragging her down with me." She shook her head, throat tight, and looked into Sean's eyes. "I'm sorry."

"For falling in love with her?"

Tears pooled in her eyes. "For being such a mess and hurting you both. I don't know how you could forgive me. And don't see why she ever should."

He shifted closer and wrapped an arm around her as best he could, and Gia rested her cheek against his head. Mr. Bones settled in the space between them and Gia absently stroked through his fur.

"For someone so guarded," Sean said, "you've always worn your heart on your sleeve. It was difficult to be mad at you when I could see what you were going through right in front of my eyes."

"I wish I handled things better."

"You definitely could've. But I think things were bound to get intense the second you and Luna met, no matter the circumstances."

"I've come to realise that too."

"She'll come around, G."

"I don't deserve—"

"You deserve to be happy as much as Luna and I do. Do you think she's worth fighting for?"

"Of course she is."

"Then allow yourself to have some hope of happiness. I can't start dating if you're moping around this cottage in another dimension. So look at it as a personal favour to me."

Gia smiled and pressed a kiss to his head. "I love you."

"Love you too, babe, which is why it's going to be hard to leave in a couple of weeks."

"Are you sure I can't come with you?"

"Mom's been attempting to fly down to see me. Promising to go visit her instead was the only way to keep her away."

"You don't need to keep us apart. Vanessa's allowed to be angry on your behalf."

"You haven't seen her really angry yet."

Gia's stomach swirled uncomfortably and a cold chill ran up her spine. The hair at the back of her neck raised. "She can't be worse than the Darke," Gia murmured and stood, straightening to her full height while her heart raced with adrenaline. "Speaking of..."

"I'll get breakfast ready."

Gia grinned. "Thanks. See you soon."

She went to change into her armour, the enchantments making the pieces click into place with ease. Hurrying out the door, she jumped onto a waiting Tximista and flew to the Rift.

Luna kept showing up to fight Husks and Thralls with her. Sometimes she would make a few snide remarks, only to disappear the second Gia attempted an actual conversation. Any interaction felt like a gift though, and it made Gia wish for the Darke to show up at their Rift more frequently, a sentiment that caused even more feelings of guilt and shame.

She stood in the open field and waited in anticipation of seeing Luna's gorgeous face again. An ugly twenty-foot-tall Cyclops Thrall showed up first, though. It was the first time Gia had seen one in person. It had thick limbs, dull grey skin, and a bald wrinkly head. A giant eye above a large fat nose only made its disproportionately small ears more noticeable. Animal hides of various shades and textures were thickly stitched together and hung over its body like a dress.

The cyclops roared, showing off the razor-sharp teeth it used to tear through creature, Halfling, and Dwarf flesh alike. Because they made a habit of terrorising Ederran citizens, they'd been hunted to near extinction. Gia had read in one of the books Uda had given her that a pair of cyclopses could devastate an entire town, killing hundreds.

She was stunned by its sheer size and notoriety, drawing up a shield a split-second before a massive log—the size of a tree— was swung at her head like a baseball bat. The blow reverberated against her shield, causing her to shuffle to the side, her shield disintegrating at the powerful impact.

She was built primarily to combat magic. Cyclopses were all brute physical strength, though, and Gia could only do so much offensively.

She ducked below another barbaric swing, the cyclops a lot faster than its size would suggest. Not willing to risk it escaping to Tristea if she ran away, Gia continued the deadly game of cat and mouse, ducking and weaving and blasting it with shields she used as moving force fields. She had hoped to tire it out, but instead sweat ran down her own temples and her breaths grew laboured from the rapid bursts of magic she was using in a way that was only intended for emergencies.

Where was Luna? Had she finally given up on her?

Gia's stomach dropped at the thought, but knowing Luna, even if she had abandoned Gia, she wouldn't abandon her duty. Had something happened to her? A stab of fear struck Gia's heart so sharply, she faltered and her only saving grace from the cyclops taking advantage was the wild nickering and stomping of hooves that drew its attention.

No, Luna was the new Mother. She was powerful. And bond or no, Gia believed she would feel it if anything happened to her.

Trumoi had joined Tximista at some point and both pegasuses flapped their wings and trotted around the cyclops, effectively diverting its attention. Drooling at the mouth, it stormed Trumoi and Gia's frantically beating heart jumped into her throat. She quickly formed another shield and when the cyclops raised its log, blasted it at him. The cyclops staggered on impact, nearly falling, but righted itself and turned to her. Bending at the waist, it roared its anger, saliva flying from its wide open mouth and gleaming on its teeth.

Gia attempted to slow her strained breaths and focus her magic like Uda had taught her. The perspiration on her face cooled in the light breeze and with every last bit of energy she could muster, she formed a shield that reflected a near solid pink.

The cyclops was nearly on top of her and Gia boosted her magic outward in a blast that had her hair fluttering back and screwed her eyes tightly shut, readying for impact.

A loud thump shook the ground beneath her feet and a moment later, a familiar screech had Gia's heart still with a dull ache when she remembered the Husk that needed to be defeated.

Her magic sparked weakly and her eyes opened to the sight of the cyclops dead on the ground and purple lightning headed her way. She managed to raise a flickering shield and hoped Uda would visit soon to tell Sean what had happened. Her final thought however, was of how grateful she was that the Arima bond had been broken and that Luna would be spared the Mourning.

A brilliant blue shield covered her own, stopping the Darke lightning, and Gia nearly collapsed to the ground in relief. Another streak of blue blasted the Husk into nothingness and black armour blocked Gia's view where she was hunched over and trying to catch her breath.

Luna wrapped her up in a protective embrace as though belatedly attempting to shield her despite the danger being over.

Gia melted into her. Into the welcome feel of Luna's magic. Dizzy with fatigue and respite. Their armour made the contact she sought impossible, so Gia nuzzled her face into Luna's neck and inhaled her scent like it was the oxygen she still struggled to get into her lungs.

Quiet settled around them, save for Gia's heart pounding in her ears. She tightly held on to Luna who seemed to cling to her just as desperately. Luna's magic was wild and consuming, yet soothingly filled Gia's chest and settled there with a pleasant warmth, like it had always done. Like it belonged there.

"I'm sorry I wasn't here," Luna thickly croaked against her hair. Gia was so overcome by her proximity she couldn't speak and only snuggled closer. "I had to go meet the Valkyries, and Freya, she—well, she's something. Are you hurt?"

Gia shook her head to quell the concern evident in Luna's voice and held her impossibly tighter.

Luna lost some of the tension in her frame and softly exhaled. "You killed a cyclops, Gia..." she murmured with a smile in her voice.

Gia's chest expanded. "I miss you," she rasped, pressing a soft kiss to the racing pulse in Luna's neck.

Luna stiffened and Gia froze too, before jumping out of her arms.

"Sorry!" She winced at her loud volume, her hands raised in supplication. "Sorry," she repeated in a softer tone. "I didn't mean to make you uncomfortable. Thank you for saving me."

Luna stared at her with an unreadable expression.

Unsure whether she'd ruined everything again, Gia hurriedly continued. "And thank you for the use of your home. It's really helped with guarding the Rift, and I mean, it's just perfect, Luna. More perfect than I could've ever imagined it would be. Everything I've ever dreamed of and wanted in a home."

Luna didn't say anything, but she didn't seem angry or impatient. She only searched Gia's face, brows lightly knitted together, as though she was attempting to solve a puzzle.

Gia continued, "I know when I asked you to leave me alone back when we first met, you tried your best to respect that. When I asked to be friends, you did the same and compromised to take my feelings and needs into account. I'm therefore very much aware of what a hypocrite I'm being right now for disrespecting your wishes. But I know that I hurt you badly and I don't want you to think that I'm not willing to fight to make things right between us."

Luna blinked, then scowled. "So you only want to ease your own guilt?"

"No, Lu. I want to show you how I feel, because I miss you very much and you deserve to know that you're cared for and wanted, even if you end up rejecting my affections."

"You're confused."

"You know that's not true."

"I won't be late again. The Valkyries are ancient and assist in protecting Ederra when needed. Sua instructed me to maintain relations. I wasn't prepared—I won't be late again. You don't need to fear that I'll abandon my duty."

"I know you won't. And what happened today didn't influence my feelings. I love fighting alongside you."

Luna still fought the same way, despite holding back most of her power for some reason. Her magic reverberated with each strike, tugging at Gia's bellybutton and leaving her tightly coiled and breathless during, and for a long time after, each quick battle. They synchronised instinctively, ducking and weaving in tandem, and it felt good. Right. Perfect, to fight beside her each and every time.

Luna shook her head. "You need some time to recover from the bond."

"It's been over six months, Lu. I don't want you to go on believing that me walking away from our bond was in any way a reflection of the extraordinary person you are, but rather insecurities about my own life and wants."

Luna looked pained, then frowned at the ground, hair falling across her face and Gia itched to shift the inky black strands behind Luna's ear.

"You don't need to decide anything now," Gia softly said. "I don't mind working on earning your trust back. I only need you to let me know whether I should stop bothering you, because I don't want to keep pushing when it's something you honestly don't want. You may tell me to stop now or at any time in the future, because if it's up to me, I won't ever stop fighting to have you back in my life and show you how much you mean to me."

Obsidian irises shifted back to her and Luna was quiet for so long, staring so intently into Gia's eyes, that she felt stuck. Her stomach dropped when she sensed the teleportation spell surging around them and the scent of a thunderstorm washed over her like a downpour.

Gia slumped and stared at the ground, fighting down tears and the disappointment gripping her heart.

"Don't stop," Luna murmured. Gia's gaze snapped up in time to see a tentative smile before Luna disappeared in a magnificent swirl of blue magic.

CHAPTER TWENTY-SEVEN

It was nighttime and heavy grey clouds encircled Mount Bularreko about three quarters up the high slopes. A thick fog had settled over Lake Beltza, casting the Sanctum in an eerie gloom.

Out in the Northern Courtyard, Luna bit her lip and waved her hand, the heavy mist drawing back and dissipating to reveal a clear night sky and a bright full moon. Sua had advised that it would help at first to accompany any wordless casting with hand gestures.

Luna was still wary of using her new power, but as time passed, she grew confident in containing it without accidentally exploding a nearby tree or potted plant—or her bed while she was on it. That had been very embarrassing at the time. Her mothers were visiting her in her room in the Tower and Luna had just finished reassuring them that she had everything under control.

An additional marble statue had been erected in the Northern Courtyard that held the one of the Mother of Light.

Sua had insisted that if they were going to memorialise her in any way, she be placed separately and not beside her Arima as had been suggested by Uda. A grin spread over Luna's face at the large statue of Sua riding a unicorn, her robes and hair flowing behind her, a sword in her hand raised into the air, as though she was charging into battle. She would've loved everything about it, especially the way the statue's gaze was directed at her Elurra.

Luna's stomach swooped, and even without her new magical awareness, she would have recognised the magical signature of the Guardian who hurried into the courtyard and looked around confusedly until she spotted Luna in front of Sua's statue.

The Guardians didn't understand her and Gia's relationship. Many assumed their separation was as a result of Luna's Ascension. Her position as Mother at least ensured that Gia wouldn't be treated as an outcast to be stared at during gatherings. A courtesy they seemed unable to extend to Luna, only reaffirming her understanding of Sua's choice of solitude. Being the odd one out was nothing new to her, though.

They stared at each other for a long moment before a slow smile spread across Gia's face that Luna could do nothing but reciprocate.

"What are you doing here all by yourself?" Gia asked.

"I'll slip in once the ceremony has started."

"Wait, it's not happening here?"

"No, it's in the Western Courtyard."

"Oh," Gia said, glanced at the gate entrance and then up at the statue of Sua Orro.

"It suits her."

"It does," Luna agreed, her stomach doing a flip when Gia slowly walked closer in a silver dress that perfectly complemented the black one Luna wore.

"You did a great job on the water fountain."

Luna dragged her gaze away from Gia toward the rock garden and water fountain feature she'd indeed put together.

"How did you know it was me?"

"It's your artistic style and you really do seem to like them."

"I find the sound of running water soothing."

Gia nodded as though she knew that. "How are you holding up?" she asked. "I can't imagine how difficult losing her was for you."

Gia's silver eyes shone with empathy and Luna shakily nodded. "I knew her all my life. She was this eccentric amalgamation of sister, friend, mentor, and mother. I'll feel her loss always."

Gia stepped closer, carefully, as though she was approaching a wild, injured animal. "I'm very sorry for your loss."

"Thank you," Luna murmured, unable to stop staring at the single long braid hidden beneath Gia's silver hair and the crescent moon trinket tied to its end that obsidian fingers lightly played with. The piercings were back too, a silver barbell through her eyebrow and a diamond stud glittered against an inky black nostril.

"I asked Torston to do it," Gia explained. "The piercings." She cleared her throat, shifted her weight and glanced at the gate again, then anxiously around the empty courtyard.

"They look very nice," Luna managed and was rewarded with some eye contact and a quick flash of a smile.

She'd thought that the instant she released Gia from the Soulbond she would embrace her freedom and leave. Leave Ederra. Leave her. Bind herself to Sean Williams. But Gia had continued to fight at her side. The sight of her in her armour made Luna's heart flutter each and every time. She was becoming a powerful Shield, and her commitment to guarding the Rift seemed unwavering no matter how often Luna brushed her off after each battle.

Gia had somehow managed to become even more attractive. She was brimming with excitement and hope, and while Luna wanted to be the cause of it, most of her had come to enjoy watching Gia grow into her own, perpetually in awe of the newfound confidence she had in her skin and the pride in her gait and stance. Seeing her take down that cyclops had been both petrifying and awe-inspiring, in spite of the sleepless nights that had followed because she'd nearly arrived at the Rift too late.

Politics and diplomacy with the races of Ederra hadn't been part of her anticipated duties as Mother. Sua had hardly seemed to care, though Sua had been around long enough to have earned unerring trust and respect without the need to constantly maintain it. Luna wasn't sure how to live up to her legacy when she could barely face Gia, despite so much time having passed since that night that had changed everything.

"I know I've been running off a lot," Luna said.

"That's okay."

"I—sometimes it feels like too much when I'm around you, if that makes sense?"

Gia searched her face and Luna had to tamp down on the magic surging in her chest, readying to take her away and escape the mix of emotions that threatened to smother her heart.

"I thought I was living my own life in Tristea," Gia softly said. "That I was making my own choices. Following my chosen path. I've come to realise that I was hiding and denying major parts of myself because I was afraid. But you knew that before I did…I don't regret the time I spent there, other than how wrong it was to do so while you were waiting for me, and I truly am sorry for that, Lu. I think part of me knew that when I met you, I wouldn't be able to leave again."

After she'd managed to calm enough to look past her own heartbreak, Luna was able to understand Gia's confusion with regard to their shared dreams. Brief questions—accusations—during fights at their Rift cleared up some things too. Then there was the fact that Gia had made it very clear what she didn't want from the moment they'd met. She hadn't been purposely deceitful. Gia had been as much of a casualty in their snowballing relationship as Luna had been.

Since the Arima bond had been severed, Gia had been infinitely patient, open and honest in a way Luna had thought she'd wanted, but now filled her with trepidation for some unfathomable reason. Sua's last words to her, though, had been a command not to be afraid to pursue her own happiness.

"I forgive you," Luna said, because she had, and because Gia seemed to need to hear it.

Gia winced as though slapped.

"Do you have any idea the gift you gave me by severing our tie?" she rasped. "I have the peace of mind now that if I died, you would go on living. I now have the freedom to decide what I want to do with my life. Where I want to live and who I want to build a future with. I now know beyond a doubt that all this love I feel for you, the way I long for you and crave your hugs and smiles, is simply because you're wonderful, and beautiful… and kind…and amazing."

Luna ducked her head. Her chest expanded and the tips of her ears grew hot when she saw the treacherous blue glow of her magic emanating from her body.

Gia loved her.

Did she, though? Or did she mean she loved her as a person?

Luna frowned. She felt Gia always. Sua's journal held instructions on how to mute the bonds she felt with all things magical and Luna had immediately muted her and Gia's magical connection as it had been far too reminiscent of the bond they'd once shared.

After the cyclops incident, though, she had reopened the connection. That day, she'd thought she had time to tactfully take her leave from Freya, but after teleporting into her own personal nightmare, she had vowed to never hesitate in journeying to the Rift when called upon again. Had she been able to feel Gia that day, she would have noticed her distress, and diplomacy and ancient alliances wouldn't have mattered.

Now she could feel Gia travelling across Ederra, exploring their world as much as she was exploring herself, as though Luna had truly given her that gift of freedom. She'd craved to join Gia on her adventures of discovery. Had wanted to share in them, but she'd been too scared to allow herself to take Gia up on her various offers to talk.

"You gave me back my life, Lu. I've never been more certain of who I am and what I want for my future. I'm still settling into myself, but I already know that guarding our Rift is something I do with honour and that gives me purpose. And whatever happens between us, I need you to know that meeting you has been the best thing to have ever happened to me. I will always be grateful that I was chosen to be your Arima. I hope that one day you'll be ready to allow me to try and make up for all the hurt I caused you."

Luna stared at the ground, unseeing, while her heart thudded against her ribs. Her brain seemed unwilling to aid in settling the distress in her stomach. She placed a hand on her abdomen, the need to run as strong as ever, but Gia's uncertain gaze trapped her there.

"Uhm," Gia croaked, backing away slowly. "I should go find the Western Courtyard before I'm late. Thank you for listening."

"What if I was ready?" Luna blurted. Gia stopped mid-turn and swung back to face her. "What do we do? Where do we start?"

The way Gia's face instantly brightened took Luna's breath away.

"I could make you dinner tomorrow? If you're free?"

Luna bit her lip, her insides jumping and twirling. She wasn't sure whether she was terrified or excited.

"Will you kiss me then?" she asked, without quite meaning to.

"If it feels right...and if you want me to."

"Do you want to kiss me?"

"Yes."

Gia's response was instant and succinct and nearly had Luna's heart tear through her chest. She licked her suddenly dry lips and tried not to stare at Gia's mouth. She'd almost kissed her that day of the cyclops. Might have given in to the urge had Gia not pulled away. "I'll be worried all day about it. It might influence the entire dinner." She flashed what she hoped was a cheeky grin, her cheeks quivering with the strain of her smile.

"It will be a very important kiss," Gia agreed and searched her face for a moment before she stepped closer. "Maybe if we get it out of the way now..."

Luna had wanted to seem brave with the flirting, but her fingers trembled when she placed them on Gia's hips, who softly gasped at the contact.

An obsidian hand gently cupped her cheek and Luna's eyes fell shut, leaning into the shaky touch and feeling drunk on the scent of Sweet Alyssum. Gia pressed in a little closer, until Luna could feel the heat of her body, her salient magic, but Gia waited until Luna opened her eyes again.

A thumb tenderly brushed her cheek. "I don't mind waiting, Lu. I'm already happy at the thought of spending time with you tomorrow. You don't have to do anything you don't—"

Gia's hum vibrated against Luna's lips. The kiss remained only a gentle press and a soft sigh, yet left Luna breathless and overawed. Or perhaps it was the addition of Gia's magic that swept through her body, seeming to tame the wild power that resided within her and soothingly settled back into the hollowness it had left in Luna's chest.

With a light squeeze to Gia's hips, Luna stepped away, needing to place some distance between her and that smile and those pretty silver eyes carefully studying her.

"That should relieve some of the pressure," Luna announced, her voice cracking. She cleared her throat and straightened her spine. "May I accompany you to the ceremony?"

She received shaky grin and a jerky nod, revealing Gia might possibly be as nervous as she was.

Folding her hands behind her back in an attempt to not touch Gia again, Luna fell in step beside her, practically floating on air while they walked down the pathway between the neatly trimmed hedges that led to the Western Courtyard.

The moon shone down on them through the dim path lights. Their shoulders occasionally brushed and Gia smiled each time she caught Luna dumbly staring at her.

Too soon they reached the courtyard that contained rows of wooden pews decorated with white flowers. The first half was filled with seated Guardians watching an Arima pair up on the dais. One had red hair, the other, green. Each wore a long, flowing white gown, the trains of which ran all the way down the steps and matched the blanket of apple blossoms that decorated the courtyard. On their heads were white flower crowns that glowed icy blue in the moonlight. They stared deeply into each other's eyes, seemingly unaware that there was a world outside the two of them.

Only Uda, in her golden robes and standing with the couple, noticed Gia and Luna's entrance and smiled widely over her words.

"Mother of Light, touch us with your grace and fill these warriors with your beauty and strength. Share with them your fertile nature from which all abundance flows."

Luna and Gia slid into the back row and Luna felt slightly lightheaded when Gia pressed against her side even though they had the entire pew to themselves.

"Holy Mother of Light and Life, guide these warriors through this divine transformation, which is the ultimate union of two souls."

Gia's hand rested on her own thigh, palm up, and Luna quickly glanced to the side of her face, wondering whether they were moving too fast and whether she was being reckless with her heart again.

Gia turned to face her and Luna froze, too slow to pretend she hadn't been staring.

"As you bind your magic," Uda said, "so your lives and souls are joined in a bond of love and trust. It's strengthened by the vows you have made. Like the moon, your love will be a constant source of light, and like the earth, a firm foundation from which to grow."

"Do you really love me?" Luna whispered into the thick air that had settled between them. Of everything Gia had confessed earlier, it had been the first time she'd told Luna that.

"May your bond have the strength to endure times of strain and disenchantment. May it remain tender and gentle. May it build a relationship founded in the richness of caring, the heat of passion, and the warmth of a loving home."

Gia seemed distraught at the question and Luna feared she would leave, that she'd misunderstood, but instead Gia took her hand and entwined their fingers, squeezing lightly.

"I do. So very much. And I promise that I'll show you that until you believe me, Lu. If you give me the chance to, all right?"

"All right." Luna nodded and released a shaky breath. "All right."

"Rise, Guardians of the Veil. Rise and bear witness to the bond shared between Sute Amorratua and Euri Leuna."

Grateful to move, Luna rose and tried to take her sweaty palm from Gia's hand, but Gia held on tightly, and brought her other hand over and stroked the inside of Luna's elbow, pressing their bodies close together. Luna dragged her gaze away from the silver eyes tenderly staring at her and swallowed thickly when she took in the various pairings in front of them, bodies glowing with magic, many also holding hands.

Up on the dais, Uda weaved her white magic around the wrists of the bonded pair, tying them together forever. "May you be for each other, sword, shield, and sanctuary."

Beside her, Gia softly glowed pink, her head ducked as though she was embarrassed by it. Luna's own magic surged in answer and she smiled at the soft gasp and furtive glance she received.

"I love you still," Luna murmured and pressed a light kiss to Gia's silver brow, watching as her pretty pink magic surged in response and her shoulders loosened as though a weight had been lifted from them.

They leaned into each other, their hands remaining clasped and their magic soothingly blending together.

"By the grace of the Mother of Light, you are now as your hearts have always known you to be."

Arima means Soul.

This book universe aims to explore the Arima bond spell and how it has morphed and extended beyond Guardians, manifesting in a variety of magical beings in different ways and drawing unsuspecting couples together throughout Lur Tristea and Lur Ederra.

The next book set in the Darke Universe:

FURY

Shayla Aja arrives in the small town of Nyx to visit her grandma Ellie who she hasn't seen in in a couple of years. She finds a lot has changed on the beekeeping farm, not only the house she had spent endless summers in, but also Ellie herself. The reason for these changes seems to centre entirely around Ellie's new apiary manager: August.

August is infuriatingly attractive, shamelessly flirts with Shay apparently only to get under her skin, and Shay's convinced that August is sponging off Ellie and taking advantage of her generous heart.

Needless to say, their relationship starts off shaky and is filled with suspicion and attraction. But when they attend the local farmers market and Shay experiences a magical incident, things between them change. Forced to trust August with this big secret, they grow closer and begin to open up to each other, revealing more about themselves, their pasts, and the life-altering events that had brought them both to Ellie's farm.

Bella Books, Inc.

Women. Books. Even Better Together.

P.O. Box 10543
Tallahassee, FL 32302

Phone: 800-729-4992
www.bellabooks.com

CPSIA information can be obtained
at www.ICGtesting.com
Printed in the USA
JSHW040213280721
17329JS00002B/4

9 781642 472356